She's in high heels; he w
Can these two opposites make romance in Metlin work?

HOOKED

Tayla McKinnon is not a small-town girl. The fashion blogger moved to Metlin with two goals in mind: help her friend start a bookstore and have a little fun. A year later, Tayla has made new friends, successfully launched INK, and is ready for a new challenge. Too bad she can't get a certain rock climbing comic book geek off her mind.

Jeremy Allen has been playing the long game with Tayla even though the avid outdoorsman was certain she was the one from the minute he set eyes on her. They might have different tastes, but their chemistry is undeniable.

When a job opportunity from a new fashion start-up lands in her inbox, Tayla takes it as a sign. She's not meant for a small town even though her best friend and her inconvenient crush are trying to convince her otherwise.

Jeremy can't believe Tayla would be willing to leave her new life behind, but maybe he's been playing it too cool. Summer in Metlin can sizzle, which gives Jeremy an excuse to turn up the heat.

Hooked is a stand-alone, opposites-attract romance in the Love Stories on 7th and Main series by Elizabeth Hunter, *USA Today Best Selling* author of *INK*.

PRAISE FOR ELIZABETH HUNTER

I simply adore this series. Elizabeth Hunter is able to create a world that you not only fall in love with, but want to jump inside and be a part of.

I have been obsessed with Elizabeth Hunter's Love Stories on 7th and Main series since Ink and seriously squealed when I saw that Tayla was going to get her very own story. I absolutely loved her and Jeremy. Their chemistry was sweet and sassy and the attraction and heat between them was amazing!!

Heartwarming, sexy, swoony and so adorable! I adored Elizabeth Hunter's first Love Stories on 7th and Main Series with Emmie and Ox, and this one with Tayla and Jeremy didn't disappoint.

This is the second book in the 7th and Main series set in Metlin, and things just keep getting better! Last time we fell in love with Ox, Emmie, Metlin and the bookstore. This round it's time for sassy, shapely, sexy and confident Tayla to fall for Jeremy...friendly, smart and smoldering nerd extraordinaire.

THIS LITERARY LIFE

HOOKED

A LOVE STORY ON 7TH AND MAIN

ELIZABETH HUNTER

Hooked
Copyright © 2019
Elizabeth Hunter
ISBN: 978-1-941674-41-3

Cover: Bailey Designs Books
Content Editor: Amy Cissell
Copy Editor: Anne Victory
Proofreader: Linda, Victory Editing

Recurve Press LLC
PO Box 4034
Visalia, California
USA
ElizabethHunterWrites.com

To everyone who climbs mountains
—whether they're the physical kind,
the mental kind,
or the kind that test your soul—
keep going.
Take breaks when you need to,
drink lots of water,
but don't stop.
And when you get to the top,
Pause.
Take a breath and enjoy the view.
Then reach your hand out
and help the person walking behind you.

CHAPTER ONE

TAYLA MCKINNON TOOK one step outside, glanced at the profusion of blossoms on the pear trees lining Main Street in Metlin, California, and reached for her handkerchief. She brought the delicately embroidered cotton square to her face.

Three... two... one...

"ACHOO!" She let out a massive sneeze that made her eyes water. Luckily, it would *not* smudge her makeup.

Waterproof mascara, T. Waterproof mascara is your friend in Allergy Town.

"Hey, Tayla." Ethan Vasquez stepped outside his hardware store and set up an angled chalkboard on the sidewalk, highlighting the classes he was offering that week. "How ya doing this morning?"

Tayla strolled toward him, keeping her handkerchief in her hand. "How much longer do these trees bloom?"

Ethan glanced up at the masses of white blooms. "The pear trees?"

Tayla blinked away the tears in her eyes. "No, the other trees making me sneeze."

He gave her a crooked grin. "Well, there are the almonds, the olives, the apricots, walnuts, the—"

"Ahhhh!" She threw her head back. "Why did I move to farm country?"

"I'm just saying it could be any of those." He shrugged. "But it's probably the pears. My mom's allergic too."

Tayla wasn't from Metlin. She was from San Francisco. A native of the cosmopolitan and cultured City on the Bay. The city that *didn't* have pear trees everywhere. How the hell had she ended up sneezing in Metlin?

"Tay!" A voice came from behind her.

Tayla turned and saw her best friend and roommate, Emmie Elliot, poking her head out of the bookshop and tattoo studio she ran with her boyfriend, Ox. Emmie sold books; Ox was a tattoo artist. Their shop, INK, had been a gamble that turned into a slowly growing success.

It was also the reason Tayla was in Metlin. She'd moved the year before to help Emmie fulfill her dream. She worked part time in the shop and lived rent free in the second-floor apartment with Emmie. Tayla had also started her own bookkeeping business that was taking off with the merchants in downtown Metlin. It was light-years away from the corporate accounting job she'd held in San Francisco, but corporate accounting wasn't something Tayla missed.

At all.

"Hey." Emmie walked out of the store with bare feet. She looked like she'd just stumbled out of bed, and her hair was twisted into a messy knot on her head.

Tayla surveyed the fashion disaster that was her best friend. "Did you just wake up?"

"Kinda?"

Tayla shook her head in wonder. She'd been up for over two hours. She'd curled and fixed her newly dark hair—she was experimenting with tones closer to her natural brown—expertly applied makeup, and chosen the perfect outfit to emphasize her voluptuous figure. The pink in the dress she wore complemented the undertones in her skin, and the orange stripe was a strong counterpoint that made her blue eyes more vivid.

She was a fashion blogger in addition to being a bookkeeper. Her hustle was strong, and she did *not* walk out the door without her face and outfit perfect.

"Why did I come out here?" Emmie looked half-asleep and definitely caffeine deprived. "Oh! Right. Did you want to meet at Daisy's for lunch?"

Tayla mentally scrolled through her calendar. "I have meetings at ten and eleven, but I'm supposed to do Daisy's books around two, so yes. I'll meet you there at... twelve thirty?"

"Ox should be able to watch the shop." Emmie walked toward her and pulled a small pack of tissues from her pocket. "Also, the handkerchief is cute, but this is spring in Metlin. You need the heavy-duty stuff."

"Fine." Tayla reluctantly took the small tissue package with the words NOW WITH MORE ALOE! on the side. "I bow to your rural-living experience."

"And this." Emmie handed over a bubbled strip of pills. "Antihistamines. Every day, Tayla. You have to take them every day."

Tayla took the pills. "Why do you want to live here again?"

"Because it's beautiful, close to the mountains, has great farmers' markets, and I'll be able to buy a house before I'm fifty."

She rolled her eyes. "Fine."

"I love you."

"Love you too." Tayla dropped the pills and the tissues into her bright pink shoulder bag. "But I don't love your trees." She put on her sunglasses and started walking toward the lot where she'd parked her car, then she turned and glanced back at the shop.

Light. Pretty white blossoms scattered on the sidewalk. Empty sidewalks.

"Stop!" She held up her hand. "Emmie, before you go back inside—"

"Morning outfit pic?"

"Yes." Tayla took the bag off her shoulder and adjusted the belt on the striped wrap dress to adjust the amount of cleavage it showed. "They just sent me this bag, and the light is perfect for spring photos with the flowers and everything."

She hurried back to Emmie and the line of blooming pear trees. "Can you prop the shop door open?" She glanced at the adorable new yellow bike Emmie had bought the month before that was chained to the rack in front of the shop. "That's good if we can get it in the background. I think if I stand here..." She looked up. "Ethan, can you shake this tree a little bit?"

Ethan, who'd been leaning in his doorway, looking bemused at the impromptu photo shoot, frowned. "You're already sneezing and you want me to shake *more* pollen on you?"

Noooooo, her nose yelled. She glanced at the bright vegan "leather" bag she'd been given and thought about handbag hashtags, follower counts, and her bank account. "Yeah. More flowers."

Emmie took Tayla's phone and opened the camera while Tayla gave her makeup a quick check. Her skin had a nice glow—that new highlighter was really working—and her gold-framed sunglasses and eyebrows were on point. She put the mirror away and held the bag in both hands, pushing her bust together as she positioned herself under the tree, looked up, and let out a fake laugh.

"It's so weird when you do that," Ethan said, reaching up with a rake and shaking one of the pear tree branches. White flower petals rained down on the sidewalk and onto Tayla.

"Fake laugh equals natural smile," Tayla said. She changed positions a few times. Put the bag over her shoulder. Looked at the camera. Then away from it. Turned and walked away. Turned back. "Emmie, how we doing?" She could feel her nose starting to twitch.

"Give me one more second..." Emmie stepped back, then stepped forward. "The light is tricky." She took a few more pictures and held out the phone. "Check 'em."

Tayla held her handkerchief to her nose and scrolled quickly through the photos. "I can use at least three of these, and the bag looks amazing. Thank— Achoo!"

"Achoo to you too," Emmie said. "Take your antihistamines." Tayla slipped her phone in the bag and gave up on her embroidered handkerchief to blow her nose with the paper tissues. "These *trees*." She leaned over and kissed Emmie's cheek quickly. "You're the best."

"It's kind of cold." Emmie looked down at her feet. "Have I been barefoot this whole time?"

"Yes. Go back inside before Ox comes and yells at me for making your precious little feet shiver." She turned Emmie by the shoulders and shoved her toward the door. "See you at lunch. Don't forget to post on the blog today. With pictures! Don't forget the pictures."

"Okay." Emmie waved over her shoulder. "See you."

Ethan walked back to his shop and propped the rake against the front of his display windows. "What about me? Do I get a kiss too?"

Tayla sashayed over to his doorway and crooked her finger at him. "Better believe it, handsome."

Tayla kissed Ethan's bearded cheek when he leaned down. Then she pulled away just as another sneeze exploded from her nose. "I think I'm allergic to you too."

"Nah." He grinned. "But I bet Jeremy would like it if you were."

"Hush." She shooed him away with a smile and a flip of her manicured hand. "Don't start trouble."

Ethan was an adorable bear of a man. Tall, broad shoulders, tan skin, and hazel-brown eyes with a belly that said he enjoyed a pint or two at the Ice House after work. He loved live music, trivia night at the pub, and bingeing the latest sci-fi or fantasy series on the weekend. He drove a big pickup truck and liked his women with more than a handful of ass.

In short, he was exactly Tayla's type.

And yet... no chemistry. None.

"Bye!" She walked down Main Street and turned right at the crosswalk. On the corner of Main and Ash were the dark windows of Top Shelf Comics and Games where the man who was definitely *not* Tayla's type would be opening his door in about an hour.

Jeremy Allen was sweet, geeky, and handsome as sin. His body told the story of a skinny kid who finally grew into his limbs and put on a nice amount of muscle. He had skin the color of mahogany, and his dark brown eyes glinted with humor. He wore his short hair twisted at the ends and a trim beard Tayla desperately wanted to run her fingers over. He had a near-obscene number of eyelashes. It was truly unfair.

That part of Jeremy was all Tayla's type. But in addition to loving comics and games, Jeremy loved *everything* about the outdoors. He climbed mountains in his spare time. He camped. He fished. He kayaked. He rode down giant hills on his bike.

Tayla was a yoga enthusiast and *loved* to dance. Hiking and fishing? Not her scene. So much dirt. So many bugs. She loved her bike, but she wasn't crazy enough to take it down mountains. She liked nature... through the pristine window of a well-furnished hotel.

Jeremy was also loyal, family-oriented, and had "long-term romantic partner" written all over his gorgeous face.

Tayla wasn't interested in long-term anything. She liked variety. In fashion, in work, and in men. Who could handle one person for the rest of their life? She'd be bored to tears.

And yet...

Even walking by his shop gave her goose bumps.

So. Inconvenient.

Tayla glanced at Jeremy's store and kept walking. She had a lot to do that day. The last thing she should be thinking about was a man who shouldn't move past the flirting stage. Tayla McKinnon had a life and a plan. Jeremy Allen wasn't part of it.

———

SHE WAS SNACKING ON A HANDFUL OF HONEY-ROASTED almonds from Frannie's Nut Shack when an email alert popped up in the corner of her screen. Seeing the name, she clicked on it. Tobin Carter was one of the few people at her old job she still kept in touch with because of their shared interest in side-eyeing celebrities on social media.

"Saw this," Tobin's email said. "Thought of you."

Tayla clicked on the link and was immediately taken to a blog post on SOKA, an emerging online marketplace for world fashion. She scrolled through the post announcing the launch of SOKA's new app, which would expand on their website, adding new social features and buy links for harder-to-find small designers around the world. Tayla's eyes locked on the bottom paragraph, which was underlined and highlighted in green.

Trendsetters, influencers, and fashion professionals interested in advancement opportunities on an exciting and diverse team are needed at all levels for SOKA's expansion.

Hmmmm.

Tayla clicked on the link and a form popped up asking for professional details. Education. Experience. Interests. Social media links. A few of the more unusual questions intrigued her. Dream travel destination. Favorite food. Most recent read. And the most intriguing: *Why is fashion important? Personally? Culturally? Globally?*

Glancing at Frannie, who was helping a customer while Tayla waited to go over year-to-date expenses, she started to fill out the form.

Why not? SOKA was gaining a ton of low-key attention, and they'd probably never read her entry anyway, so Tayla decided to go for it. She included all the professional details they asked for and opened up on the unusual asks.

Dream travel destination? *A beach resort in Zanzibar, preferably with many handsome men, a good DJ, and a limitless phone battery.*

Favorite food? *Tofu khao soi. It's a crispy curry noodle dish I can only get one place in the city, and it is amazing.*

Most recent read: The Wedding Date. *If you're judgy about romance novels, I have nothing to say to you. Get thee away and read some Nora.*

Why is fashion important?

Tayla minimized the window and decided to think about that one because it felt like too personal a question to answer between coffee and honey-roasted almonds at the Nut Shack.

Frannie walked back to the table just as Tayla brought her spreadsheet back up on the screen. "You ready?" She was carrying two cups of coffee. "I made a fresh pot."

Bless small-town manners. "You're awesome, Frannie."

The silver-haired woman settled next to Tayla and put on her reading glasses. "Okay. Let's try to make sense of all this."

"You can do it." Tayla highlighted the columns she needed to explain. "If you can run a successful business for thirty years, Miss Frannie, understanding all this stuff will be a snap."

TAYLA WAS STILL MULLING OVER THE QUESTIONS ON the SOKA form at the Ice House that night. Emmie and Ox were closing up the shop and planning to join her shortly. It was open mic night, which was surprisingly good instead of cringeworthy. So far some students from the music school had performed, two country-and-western acts, a jazz singer, and a folk harpist.

You couldn't say Metlin wasn't eclectic. A tad boring at times? Yes. But surprising too.

Why is fashion important?

Shallow.

Airhead.

Pig.

Perfectionist.

Dumb bitch.

Superficial.

Trashy.

Materialistic.

Ugly whale.

They were all labels that had been thrown her way more than once. Online and in person.

Tayla ignored the haters. People who didn't take the time to understand why fashion was important—especially to women over a size twelve—grated on her nerves. She'd minored in anthropology at college. To her, fashion and makeup were wearable art, just as complex and individual as any book, painting, or music.

Did the fact that major fashion houses often ignored big women bug her? Of course it did.

Did she wish the world hadn't become addicted to fast-and-cheap fashion that disregarded the negative consequences of the international garment industry? Yes!

Did that mean she had to look like a slob?

Not in a million years.

Fashion was expression. Fashion was armor. Fashion was art. It was a mask and a confessional. It was a mirror of popular culture and a challenge to it. Fashion made her feel amazing and powerful. Looking at fashion media made her nearly cry with joy at times, whether it was an exquisitely fitted gown on a Milan runway or street styles in Singapore.

Fashion *was* important.

Someone bumped her hip and nearly made her spill her cider.

"Sorry." Jeremy's dazzling smile flashed as he sat next to Tayla on the bench. "You looked mad at the world. Need another drink?"

She couldn't help but smile back. "I'm not finished with this one, but I'll never say no to a handsome man buying me a drink."

"What about an ugly one?"

Tayla looked around the room. "I don't see any ugly men here, only ugly attitudes." She grimaced when her eyes landed on the harpist. "Though I am questioning that one's comb-over."

"Earl hasn't been able to let go of his rock and roll past yet," Jeremy said. "The hair was his trademark."

"On the wild-and-crazy folk-harp scene?"

Jeremy stood, leaving his near-empty glass next to Tayla. "There were a lot of drugs in the sixties, Tayla. A *lot* of drugs. Even in Metlin."

She watched him walk to the bar. He was dressed in his usual uniform of broken-in jeans, a comic book shirt, and a worn flannel shirt. He wore nearly the same thing every day—unless he was dressing up—but it suited him. He nodded to grab Hugh's attention behind the bar. The bartender walked over and poured two pints, one dark lager and one cider, as he and Jeremy chatted.

They'd probably gone to school together. Hell, nearly everyone in this room had gone to school together at one point or another. Metlin only had two high schools. Hugh and his wife Carly ran Metlin Brewing Company, which sold beer to the Ice House where Hugh worked part time.

All the businesses in town were slightly incestuous when it came to it.

The Ice House was owned by Hugh's cousin George—also known as Junior—who had gone to school with Emmie. According to Emmie, Junior had been an asshole in high school, but he seemed to have improved over the years. Junior was Frannie's great-nephew, so she was a part owner of the Ice House even though Tayla had never seen her here.

Tayla looked around the bar where everyone chatted and drank, exchanging stories and listening to the music. Despite her expectations a year ago, Metlin had been welcoming to her. The friendliness had freaked Tayla out for the first few months she'd lived here. She was convinced it was an act. After all, Emmie hadn't shared the most flattering description of the small California town when she and Tayla had first met.

But it wasn't an act. People were just relentlessly outgoing. So weird.

Jeremy walked back to the long picnic table where Tayla had claimed some space next to a group playing Scrabble while they drank. He set down the drinks and swung his long legs over the bench. "Pear cider, right?"

"Yep. If the trees are going to make me sneeze, at least they make delicious cider I can drink."

"It's the least they can do," he said. "Want to play a game?"

She pursed her lips. "I'm not a game player, Jeremy. I've told you that many times."

His smile was slow and seductive. "I can think of a few games we could play. I bet you wouldn't say no."

She glanced at his hands. "I bet you— What did you do?" She grabbed his hand and turned it over. His palm was torn and scabbed. "Are you climbing rocks again?"

"Of course not." He closed his fingers around hers. "There's still too much snow in the mountains. I got this from being careless at the climbing gym. And if you wanted to hold hands, all you had to do is ask."

"I'll keep that in mind." Tayla gently tugged her hand away. Contact with Jeremy gave her goose bumps. She had to ration it out or she'd end up addicted. He was like liquor, dark chocolate, and a really good end-of-season shoe sale combined. "Where's the climbing gym? I didn't know you had one in Metlin."

"It's in Fresno. We don't have one here. But the one in Fresno gets lots of Yosemite tourists, so they stay busy. I go with Cary a few times a month during the winter."

Cary was Ox's silver-fox neighbor who farmed oranges outside town. He was well over forty, but Tayla wasn't blind. Now she had the happy mental picture of both Jeremy and Cary shirtless and climbing a rock wall.

She couldn't stop the smile. "Nice."

"Yeah? We can go if you want to try it."

"What?" She snapped out of her happy mental place. "Try what?"

"Climbing. I could take you to the climbing gym. It's fun, and they have beginner classes."

"You want to take this ass rock climbing?" She patted her hips.

Jeremy looked at them. "I would take that ass pretty much anywhere."

Tayla had never climbed. She loved yoga and was an avid biker, but she had her doubts as to how easy it would be to haul her backside up a cliff. Her curves were solid, but they were sizable. "Maybe another time. Upper-body strength is not my forte."

"I would spot you from the ground." His face was all seriousness, but his eyes told a different story. "I wouldn't take my eyes off you. Promise."

"I feel like this is mostly about you getting to stare at my butt. Am I getting that right?"

"Me?" He put a hand over his heart. "I'm only interested in expanding your athletic horizons, Miss McKinnon."

"I'm so glad I have friends like you looking out for me."

"It's the least I can do." He turned toward the stage when another jazz trio took over. "Want to dance?"

Tayla considered. She adored dancing, but dancing with Jeremy was treading a dangerous line. Depending on the song, it could be a lot of contact.

Danger! Smart Tayla warned. *Danger, Tayla McKinnon!*

Mmmmm. Evil Tayla purred at the prospect. *Do it. Live dangerously.*

"Sure." She set her cider down. "One dance."

"Only one?" He stood and held out his hand. "I might have to change your mind."

"You can try." Tayla took his hand, leaving her purse and their drinks to save their seats.

In a million years, she'd never leave her drink or her purse unattended in San Francisco. But she wasn't in the city. She was in Metlin. The girl who'd been sitting across from her would guard her drink and her purse with zeal, even though she and Tayla hadn't even exchanged names.

Jeremy pressed their folded hands to his middle as they worked their way through the crowd.

Was it wrong that she turned her palm into his abs to cop a feel? Jeremy's abdominal muscles were a thing of beauty. He worked hard. It would be wrong of her to ignore them. She wasn't usually into super-cut muscles, but she made an exception for Jeremy. He'd earned the muscles from doing outdoorsy things like kayaking and climbing mountains and... chopping wood? She had no idea. Mountain man stuff. They weren't just abs. They were *wholesome* abs.

Jeremy turned and pulled her into his chest. The song the band was playing was medium tempo, but the dance floor at the Ice House was crowded and they had to stand close. Tayla's eyes only came to Jeremy's chin. He linked their hands together, palm to palm, as his other hand rested at the small of her back.

He could dance too. It wasn't fair. Tayla felt herself zoning out, surrounded by the press of the crowd, the music, and the feel of Jeremy Allen's arms around her.

She felt his chest rumble and looked up. "Did you say something?"

His eyes crinkled with his smile. "Weren't you listening?"

"I was dancing."

"And I was telling you you're a good dancer."

"Thanks." She felt flustered. *Dammit.* "You too."

"I don't dance much."

"You should."

He wrinkled his nose. "Nah. I'm picky."

"About music?"

Jeremy leaned down and his breath tickled her ear. "About partners."

Tayla drew in the scent of his skin and a hint of his cologne. He smelled like sunshine and pine and a log cabin with a cozy fire. Jeremy Allen was the scent equivalent of a muscled action hero— pick your favorite Chris—in an ad for flannel shirts at Christmas. And judging from the length of time he lingered at her ear, she had no doubt he knew it.

Oh, he was good. He was very good.

And so very inconvenient.

CHAPTER TWO

"POP!" Jeremy stood in the doorway of the kitchen in the two-story Craftsman house on Ash Street and yelled down the hall. "We gotta get going."

His grandfather hated it when he yelled down the hall. He hated when Jeremy bugged him about the time. He also hated when they made it out to Lower Lake and the fish weren't biting anymore.

Jeremy had loaded the gear and tackle and pulled the truck out of the garage so his grandfather could make it down the ramp and directly into the old Chevy. Now he was just waiting. The sun wasn't quite up yet, but it would be breaking over the mountains by the time they made it to the lake.

"Pop!" He stood in the doorway and called again. He'd heard the old man moving around, so he knew he was awake. The door cracked open.

"I'm coming," Pop growled. "Hold your horses, young man."

"Holding them. The truck's loaded."

"Coffee?"

"In the thermos." The battered green thermos was the same one his grandfather had filled with hot chocolate for him when he was a kid. Now he filled it with black coffee for his pop. "Cary is bringing breakfast tacos."

"We ain't eating fish for breakfast, we ain't doing our job." Augustus Allen opened the bedroom door with his cane and walked slowly toward the kitchen door.

"Just in case," Jeremy said. "We can save the fish for lunch."

His pop muttered something unintelligible while he shuffled down the hall, straight through the kitchen, and toward the open door. The old man was wearing his usual uniform of overalls, a worn thermal shirt, and a quilted flannel shirt. His wrinkled brown face was shaved clean, just like it had been every day of his adult life, and his silver hair was clipped short against his skull.

"Morning, Pop." Jeremy leaned over and kissed his pop's head. "How'd you sleep?"

"Like an old man," Pop said. "Don't get old, son. It's damn annoying."

Jeremy smiled. "I don't much like the other option."

A gruff laugh. "Well, you got a point there."

Jeremy had moved back to Metlin from Los Angeles three years before. His grandfather had broken his hip and needed help. Augustus was refusing help from his son and daughter-in-law, but Jeremy and Pop had always had something special, and Jeremy's mother had appealed to her son to help.

Once Jeremy convinced Pop he was doing Jeremy a favor by allowing him to live upstairs at the house on Ash, his grandfather acceded to letting Jeremy live with him. Augustus got company during his recovery, and Jeremy got a rent-free place to live while he started Top Shelf Comics with the boxes and boxes of old comic books his pop had kept in the attic.

Over the years, the uneasy dance between grandfather and grandson turned roommates had matured into one Jeremy cherished. His pop was such a huge part of his life; he couldn't imagine living without him.

When he'd first moved back to Metlin, he'd been reluctant to return to a town that had seemed stifling to his teenage self. He'd escaped immediately after graduation to attend business school in Los Angeles. Jeremy had attained a degree in finance that he still put to occasional use, but he had missed his family. He'd missed community. And he'd really missed the mountains. He'd been thinking about moving out of LA, but not back to Metlin. Maybe Fresno.

Life had other plans.

He glanced out the door over his grandfather's grey head and watched the sky turn pink over the Sierra Nevada mountain range. Snow still covered the peaks of the mountains, but it was spring and the melt would be starting soon. In a few months, the heat would bake the valley floor and he'd escape every chance he got to the cool meadows and heights of the mountains, sometimes joining his mom and dad at their cabin on Upper Lake and other times camping in the grassy valleys between his favorite climbing spots.

"Gonna be warm today," Pop said.

"I think so too."

"Might get some rain tomorrow though."

"The farmers won't like that with all the trees in bloom."

Pop grunted as he climbed into the truck. "The weather cares less about farmers than the government does."

Jeremy smiled as he closed the door and walked around to the driver's side. It was an old complaint. His pop had run a small herd of cattle in the old days, along with tending some orange groves in the foothills.

They backed out of the driveway as the sky turned purplish blue and puttered through town until they came to the highway. Jeremy turned left and drove through town and out to the country, headed to the reservoir where they'd cast their lines and hope the bass were hungry.

Pop stared out the window, watching the spreading land and rolling orange groves, the trees heavy with fruit. He'd sold his land to a big ranch years ago after Jeremy's grandmother had passed and was more than happy to turn his farming know-how into consulting work for the local citrus co-op. Moving into town had allowed him to take part in his grandchildren's lives in a way he hadn't been able to for his own children.

Farming and ranching was time-consuming work, and Jeremy had never been tempted to follow in his grandfather's footsteps. His own father had been a high school shop teacher and coach. His mother was a pediatrician originally from Chicago who'd fallen in love with Metlin and his father when she'd been sent to the valley to run a rural clinic.

And Jeremy had a comic book shop. He liked it, but his true passion was anything in the mountains. Fishing, camping, and rock climbing didn't pay any bills, but his shop was making it. He hosted game nights and was more than happy to have a safe place to let his geek flag fly. He and Ethan hosted *Game of Thrones* watch parties and Magic tournaments people paid to attend. The same activities that would have gotten them beat up in high school.

"What you got going on at the shop this month?" Pop asked.

"I'm doing a cross promotion with Emmie next week."

"How's the old bookshop doing?"

"Good. We're doing games at my place that feature books or manga or comics. Stuff like that. Emmie's got a bunch of kids from the middle school book club signed up for it. They've all bought the Harry Potter series from her, so we'll see if they want to buy any of the Harry Potter games too."

"Computer games or real games?" Pop asked.

Jeremy smiled. "Computer games are real games, Pop."

His grandfather grumbled. "I don't know 'bout that."

"We're doing both, but focusing on tabletop games. We're starting a chess club too."

Pop nodded approvingly. "Every child should know how to play chess. That's a thinking man's game."

"Only we're calling it wizard chess and dressing up in costumes."

"Lord." Pop shook his head. "Whatever makes you happy, J."

Jeremy couldn't stop the smile. His pop had taught him how to fish, how to camp, and how to paddle a canoe, but he'd never understood Jeremy's love of comics. He'd only kept the comic books in the attic because they were books. And one did not throw away books in the Allen family.

His parents had thought he was insane to start a comic and game shop in Metlin, but they went with it. Pop had been even more skeptical, but it had always come back to that.

Whatever makes you happy, J.

Surprising everyone, including Jeremy, the shop had kind of taken off. He'd hit the market at the right time. Geek stuff was cool now, thank goodness, and Jeremy managed to pay his bills with enough hard work and imagination.

More than once he'd had to stifle a laugh when one of the older jocks from school brought an eager son or daughter into the shop. The kids' eyes would light up with wonder at the walls of comics, games, and fandom T-shirts while the parents looked lost.

But credit where credit was due, most of them were also supportive even if they didn't get it. People changed. Towns changed.

"We gonna be late," Pop muttered. "Fish won't even be biting anymore."

Jeremy sighed and rubbed his temple. Old men, on the other hand, did not change. "We'll make it."

"You stayed out too late last night."

"I was home before ten, Pop."

"Humph." Pop opened the thermos and poured some coffee in the mug Jeremy kept in the center console. "You spend any time with that sweet girl?"

"We danced." Jeremy smiled at the memory. "It was nice."

It was more than nice. Holding Tayla that close had been intoxicating. He hoped it was a fraction as good for her as it had been for him. Dancing with Tayla gave him all sorts of ideas about foreplay. They moved well together. It was instinct. Chemistry. Just the memory of it heated his blood.

Jeremy was making progress. He knew Tayla didn't think she was the settling-down type, but he thought otherwise. She thought they were too different, but he thought that made things fun.

He was hooked on Tayla McKinnon. Like a fish on the line. Completely and utterly hooked. But she was playing with him. Reeling him in for a little while, then letting out the line. It only made him crazier about her.

She was smart and sexy and hot as sin. He loved her attitude. Loved that she was particular about her looks and her image. He loved the games she played—even though she said she didn't—and the fierce loyalty she showed her friends.

An idiot might look at her and see the superficial. Jeremy wasn't an idiot. There was nothing false about Tayla. She was true to herself and to her friends. But she was cautious about who she let in and what she allowed the world to see. He respected that.

A man wanted to please a woman like that, because pleasing her would be damn hard. She was a challenge. Like climbing a mountain or navigating a new trail. He was still studying her and mapping his route. When conditions were right, he'd make his move.

His pop thought he was nuts.

Pop had met Tayla McKinnon six months ago and hadn't stopped giving Jeremy shit about her since then. Tayla was "that sweet girl" and Jeremy was a "damn fool" for not moving faster with her.

Sweet thing like that is gonna get snatched up by some smooth talker if you don't hurry up. Fine women like that don't last long in Metlin.

Progressive, Pop wasn't.

"Dancing ain't enough," Pop said. "You gotta woo that woman, J."

"Woo? I don't even know what that means."

"Woo, dammit. Give her flowers. Take her to dinner. Open doors. Buy her... candies." He tossed back his coffee. "I don't know what young women like these days. Just make an effort."

"I am making an effort. But I'm taking my time. Didn't you tell me anything worth doing is worth doing well?"

"Measure twice, cut once applies to building a shed, Jeremy, not to wooing a woman."

Jeremy grinned. "I'm still getting to know what she likes. She's cagey. It's fun. She's fun. The whole thing is like a dance, okay? I know what I'm doing."

Pop shook his head. "You're a damn fool."

"Thanks, Pop."

"Don't look to me for sympathy when she runs off with some other fella. You've been sitting on the fence with this one for too damn long."

"That's really not the way it works anymore, but I'll keep your advice in mind."

———

"WHAT ARE YOU WEARING?"

Tayla stopped at the sound of Emmie's horrified voice as she walked into the living room. She looked down at her outfit. "What?"

"Is that a sexy witch costume?"

Tayla shrugged. "You told me game night was wizard-themed this month and I should dress up." She held up her wand with a flourish. "I dressed up."

"It's middle school book club night." Emmie marched toward Tayla and pulled her open robe across her midriff and cleavage-baring top. "You can't wear this."

"So judgy. You know I look amazing."

"Yes, but you also look over-the-top sexy. Which if we were going to the Ice House on Halloween would be awesome. But we're going to family game night at Top Shelf. I'm sure Jeremy will love it, but I'm guessing all the parents won't."

"I love your outfit." Tayla tried to distract her. "It's got kind of the crazy fortune-teller thing going on. I like it. The glasses are a nice touch."

"I'm supposed to be Professor Trelawney."

"Nailed it."

"Can you please go put on slightly more clothes?" Emmie gave her the puppy dog eyes she used on Ox when she needed him to lift something heavy. "Please?"

Tayla rolled her eyes. "Fine. But I want it on the record that I look hot as hell."

"You totally do. In fact…" Emmie handed her the broom from the kitchen. "Hold this in a provocative manner."

"You know I will." Tayla posed as Emmie snapped a picture. "You sending that to Jeremy?"

"Mmm-hmm." Emmie gave her a wicked grin. "I do love tormenting him."

"Funny thing—so do I." Tayla turned and walked back into her room, stripping off the cleavage-baring top and reaching for a less revealing one. She'd known she couldn't get away with the first top, but she also knew Emmie would send a pic to Jeremy. She had to get back at him for that indecent dance the other night.

Oh, he'd been playing the sweet and courteous dance partner. His fingers hadn't even strayed below her waist. But he knew what he was doing. Chivalry like Jeremy's was nearly as indecent as her cleavage. So much restraint. So much left unsaid. It drove her absolutely crazy.

If he was that hot when they were in public, what kind of reaction could he provoke when they were alone?

This was not okay. She had to regain control.

Tayla left her robe open and put on a white button-down shirt with a loose school tie hanging between her breasts. Then she put on fake wire-rimmed glasses and pulled her hair into a messy bun. When she walked out to the living room, Emmie frowned.

"That is somehow even more indecent, but I can't put my finger on why."

"Then I have accomplished exactly what I intended."

They walked downstairs and across the street, joining the small stream of foot traffic headed toward Top Shelf Comics and Games. Mostly it was one or two parents with a couple of kids between the ages of eight and thirteen. Almost all the kids were dressed up. The adults were not.

Tayla didn't care. She knew she looked fabulous.

She looked forward to game night most months. It was where she'd met Jeremy's grandfather, who was a complete riot and managed to make overalls a fashion statement. And she'd seen his parents once, though they hadn't been introduced.

It was small-town nostalgia at its best. Families getting together to play games. Shops open late. Checkers tournaments at the diner. Bingo in the park. Hamburgers and hot dogs. Beer and popcorn.

It was brilliant marketing on Jeremy's part. He usually had a theme related to something going on in town—a new movie opening, high school homecoming, the book club—and he donated the games for all the businesses who agreed to stay open. Any activity that would attract more than the usual gaming crowd. He put a lot of work into it, but he sold a ton of games and usually attracted quite a few people who hadn't known a gaming and comics shop had opened in town.

Tayla could admire Jeremy's hustle even if she was annoyed with his game.

And it was a game. She knew it was a game. He thought he was luring her into his world. He thought if he played everything right, she'd fall for him.

Ha!

She fell for no one. She was in charge of her life and her hormones. His tempting, small-town-hunk charm was not irresistible.

This wasn't a Hallmark movie, dammit.

She was in Metlin as long as she wanted to be there, but it wasn't going to be forever. She wasn't a forever kind of girl.

Tayla and Emmie walked into Top Shelf, following a family with two small rainbow-colored unicorns holding hooves. Jeremy's eyes caught Tayla's outfit and bugged out for a second before he turned his attention toward the kids.

"Welcome, unicorn maidens!" he said. "You will be relieved to know that we have put a protective ward around the shop tonight so you don't have to worry about any evil wizards drinking your blood."

The girls giggled. "Thanks, Mr. Jeremy."

"But I'm guessing you have magic that would probably turn them into glitter dust or something if they tried being evil, right?"

No! It should not be legal for anyone to be that cute with children!

"Yep," the littlest unicorn said very seriously. "There would be glitter everywhere. And guts." She giggled. "It would be really gross."

"I understand." Jeremy put his hand on his chest. "Please try to control your unicorn magic so we don't have a horrible mess we have to explain to the store elves later."

"Okay!" The two unicorns skipped back to the short table where a game of Candy Land was going while Jeremy said hi to the parents.

Tayla finally got a chance to take in his costume. It was almost as if they'd planned it. He was wearing a sweeping black robe with silver threads in it over a pair of dark grey pants and a white shirt. With a bow tie.

How did he make bow ties hot?

Now she was imagining doing dirty things to Jeremy while he wore a bow tie.

Dammit.

"Hey." His smile was just a little crooked. "Is there a delinquent student witch on the premises?"

"I beg your pardon, Professor." Tayla pulled her wand from the messy bun on her head and put it to her pursed lips. "I'm a naughty librarian witch."

Emmie shook her head. "Is the book club here? You know, the *middle school students* who are the guests of honor tonight?"

Jeremy nodded toward the back room, never taking his eyes off Tayla. "They're in the back tournament room. My pop is teaching them chess, and he even agreed to call it wizard chess for the night."

Tayla grinned. "Is Gus wearing his overalls?"

"Yes, but he put on a black shirt and a bowler hat for the occasion."

"I love him so much."

"You're trying to kill me with that outfit, aren't you?"

"Is it working?"

"So very much."

CHAPTER THREE

TAYLA SURVEYED THE CROWDED SHOP. "So this looks really fun. The book club tie-in was brilliant."

Jeremy put his arm around Emmie's shoulders. "My coconspirator is kind of known for being brilliant."

"Thank you, Professor," Emmie said.

Jeremy was wearing a wide smile. "Everyone really got into it. It's been awesome, and I've already sold a dozen games."

"Nice!" Emmie turned and high-fived him.

Geeks. They were such geeks, and they were both adorable.

Tayla just shook her head. "So what are you two nerds planning for next month? I think people are pretty game for anything in this town—no pun intended. As long as you're not reading *The Hunger Games*, you should have a good turnout."

Jeremy and Emmie took a step apart and exchanged a furtive look.

"Why not *The Hunger Games*?" Jeremy asked.

Tayla closed her eyes. "You're reading *The Hunger Games*, aren't you?"

"What's wrong with *The Hunger Games*?" Emmie asked. "That's what the kids voted on."

"I'm more concerned for the game tie-ins that you two would try to cook up."

"An archery tournament would be fun! We were going to coordinate with the local Boy Scout troop so it'd be safe and everything."

Tayla turned to Jeremy. "And this relates to your shop how?"

"It doesn't. I just wanted to shoot stuff with bows and arrows." He turned to Emmie. "But you could probably get Greg at Metlin Outfitters to cohost that, now that I think of it."

"Oh, that's a great idea."

Leave it to Jeremy and Emmie to turn what should have been a moneymaker for their own shops into a promotion for someone else.

"Hey!" Tayla waved her hand. "Voice of capitalistic self-interest here. Greg is doing just fine. Summer is coming and his shop is crowded. Emmie, you and Jeremy need to be focused on keeping people's heads in books and games now that everything is warming up. Pick a different book and find a cross promo, because this night brings in too much traffic for both of you to just give it away." She pointed at Jeremy's register. "You've had a line all night."

"And Kim said we've already gotten four new sign-ups for the romance book club from the moms here." Emmie sighed. "I think we'll have to shoot bows and arrows on our own time, Jer."

"I can live with that. But don't change the book. I can think of plenty of combat and survival games for the next club read." He offered Emmie his knuckles to bump. "Chill, Em. Tayla's right."

Tayla smiled. "You're so sexy when you say that."

"What? That you're right?"

She heaved a dramatic sigh and fanned her face. "You said it again. And it was just as good as the first time."

Jeremy gave her a wicked laugh and leaned down to her ear. "You're right," he murmured. "I'm *very* sexy."

Emmie rolled her eyes. "Leaving now. Carry on. Don't scar the children please."

Tayla pursed her lips and managed to swallow the embarrassing *hhngh* sound that wanted to leave her throat when she smelled Jeremy's cologne and felt the tickle of his beard against her jaw.

Play it cool. This is Jeremy. The man needs no encouragement.

"Don't you love how it was good for both of us?" she whispered back. "I'm right and you're sexy."

"Oh, it would definitely be good for both of us," he said. "Just tell me when and where."

"And be that obvious?" She leaned back to meet his eyes. "What's the fun in that?"

"It'd be fun." The corner of his mouth turned up. "You know it would be."

Tayla had no doubt. Jeremy would be one of those lovers she laughed with. He'd tease her in the best way. He'd make her laugh as much as he'd make her moan. Everything about the electricity between them told her she would not regret pursuing a relationship with this man.

Except...

His eyes narrowed. "What are you afraid of, Miss McKinnon?"

"Nothing." She leaned over, kissed his cheek quickly, and cleared her throat. "I better go help Emmie with those book club sign-ups."

She escaped before she started seeing forever in his eyes.

What was she afraid of?

Oh, just everything.

She walked to the back room where Jeremy's grandfather was teaching a group of kids how to play chess. His bowler hat was adorable and yet completely dashing. If Jeremy aged as well as his grandfather, whatever lucky girl he eventually married would be very happy.

"Miss Tayla." He gave her a nod. "Young people, this is one

very smart lady. How much you wanna bet she knows how to play chess?"

"You're not supposed to bet us, Mr. Allen," one kid piped up. "Jeremy said you can't take any money off us tonight."

"No bets," Tayla said. "And of course I play chess, but backgammon is my game." She offered Gus a wink. "I'm a numbers girl."

Gus turned to the kids around him. "You all got the basics?" When they murmured agreement, he said, "Set up games and I'll come around and check what you got going after I get a drink." He grabbed his cane, walked over, and offered Tayla his arm. "How you doing tonight, young lady?"

"Better now that I have dashing male company." She walked with him toward the table where lemonade and iced tea were set up. "Gus, when are you going to ask me to dinner?"

He chuckled. "I told you it's not fair of me to lead you on when I'm still in love with another woman."

"I had to try."

"How about that grandson of mine?" Gus asked. "You gonna give him a chance?"

"A chance at what?" She poured two cups of lemonade and handed one to Gus.

"To take you out. I see you two making eyes at each other."

She put a hand on her chest. "Have I said no?"

"That fool boy hasn't even asked you out, has he?"

She smiled. "We're friends, Gus. We hang out all the time."

"That's not what I'm talking about, and you know it."

Tayla sighed. "You know it's complicated."

"What's complicated?" Gus frowned. "You like a girl. You like a boy. You ask them out for dinner. Or to the movies. Or—"

"Netflix and chill?" Tayla interjected.

Gus gave her a suspicious look. "I have a feeling I don't really know what that is, judging by that innocent look on your face. You young people make it more complicated than it needs to be with your phones with little pictures. How you supposed to have a conversation with a woman like that?"

"You're old school," Tayla said. "I like it."

"Do you?" Gus looked at her from the corner of his eye.

"Don't give me that look." She couldn't stop the laugh. "And don't start messing with his head, Gus. We're doing just fine." *And I don't really know if I'm staying in this town, so don't get attached.* "Besides, we're really different. I'm not into all the outdoors stuff. He and Emmie were talking about archery earlier." She shook her head. "I don't even know."

"Nothing wrong with having different interests. That's what keeps things interesting."

"I'm taking you back to the wizard chess room now." She steered him through the growing crowd, mindful of the uneven floor in the old building where Jeremy had his shop. "Teach those kids something."

"I'm not dropping this," he said. "No matter what either of you say."

Either of us? Had Jeremy talked to his grandfather about her? Shit. That wasn't good. She flirted with Jeremy. He couldn't get attached. Tayla wasn't made for long-term relationships. If Jeremy got attached to her, that would ruin everything.

She left Gus in the back room with the chess kids and drank her lemonade in the corner of the room, watching the crowd that filled the comic book shop.

Emmie with Ox at her back—he'd finally finished work—laughed with a couple who held a baby in their arms while their younger kid played with the train table in the corner. Daisy, Spider, and Ethan were watching a table where Jeremy was supervising a large tabletop game with a wizard theme. It was the same game set up in an attractive display by the door, the one people had been walking out the door with all night.

He was good at this. Jeremy had the ability to create passion in other people. If he was excited about something, he could infect others. He was a natural salesman without being obnoxious about it.

"Just tell me when and where."

Never and nowhere.

Sadly, Jeremy Allen was a keeper, and that was the one kind of man that Tayla strictly avoided. She'd been drawn in, and she needed to be better at keeping her distance.

Tayla felt her phone buzz in her pocket. She opened it, then nearly deleted the message, thinking it was from the SOKA mailing list. Her thumb had nearly swiped all the way to the left before she caught the subject line: *We're interested if you are.*

She slid her thumb back and tapped on the message.

Dear Ms. McKinnon,

We enjoyed your interest form, and we'd like to hear more from you. Could you please fill out the extended interest form and attach a current résumé when replying to this email?

Sincerely,

Kabisa Nandi

SOKA Team Building

PS: No one here would dream of insulting romance novels. We pass too many around the office.

Well. This was an interesting twist.

———

Tayla sat down at Café Maya the next afternoon with thoughts tumbling through her head. She'd filled out the extended interest form for SOKA and quickly updated her résumé to send this morning. She'd spent most of her morning messaging back and forth with various online friends, trying to find out just who else had been getting interest from the company and what the buzz was around social media.

31

She was more confused than ever.

While multiple blogging friends had filled out the interest form, only a few had been approached for more information. She'd been fielding messages every time she checked her phone.

OMG!

Ur perfect. Brilliant.

Btch, id hate u but i like u 2 much.

Wait, what form? SOKA is expanding? How?

I havent heard but OMG coolness!

If you work there do you get a discount?

They emailed you back? K.

Tayla raised her eyebrow at that *K. Whatever, Lyssa. Be a bitch.* The rest of her blogging friends were excited. A few were being cagey enough that she guessed they'd also gotten interest and viewed her as competition. That was fine.

Tayla never minded healthy competition. She wasn't a back-stabber and she knew her worth. She'd play the game until it wasn't fun anymore. She had a business of her own, and she was growing her social media presence. She didn't need SOKA, and she wasn't going to jump through any hoops she didn't feel like jumping.

She regularly brought in a small side income with product placements and scored plenty of freebies from growing brands. It wasn't a lot, but it was enough to feed her shopping habit, and it was getting a little bigger every month.

"Hey!" Emmie set her purse on the extra chair and sat down. "Why do you look mad?"

"I'm not." She put down her phone. "I'm not. I'm just..."

"Online drama?"

"Always." She slid her phone in her handbag and looked around the café. "It's slow enough Daisy should be able to join us."

"Cool." Emmie stretched her neck and rubbed her eyes. "I was shelving used stuff today. My eyes are killing me."

"You should have worn your glasses."

"I know." Emmie sniffed and wiped her tears with a napkin. "I should know better by now, but I've been taking antihistamines because of the trees, so I didn't think that much about the extra dust, and I just—"

"There's a company in the city that asked for my résumé." The knot in her stomach loosened as soon as she said the words, but a lump settled in her throat.

Emmie blinked. "The city? What city?"

"San Francisco of course."

Emmie kept blinking. It was like she'd been caught in a loop.

Daisy sat down while Emmie was blinking. "What's wrong with your eyes? Did you forget to take your antihist—"

"Tayla's moving back to San Francisco," Emmie blurted. "She's leaving us."

Daisy turned to Tayla. "What?"

"I'm not moving," Tayla said. "Or... I don't know. They just asked me for a résumé. They didn't offer me a job or anything."

Emmie's eyes were pleading. "But they will because you're awesome. And then you'll leave us."

Daisy's voice was quiet. "What's the job?"

"It's for a fashion start-up. They're expanding—"

"Shit. You're leaving." Daisy sighed. "Have you told Jeremy yet?"

"I'm not leaving! You're not listening. They *just* emailed me back to ask for a résumé. They haven't even asked for an interview yet. I have no tech experience, you guys. I'm probably the last person—"

"Do they have a website?" Daisy broke in. "This start-up?"

"Yeah. It's called SOKA. It's kind of like Etsy, but curated international fashion only. Kind of midsized companies and individuals. Fair trade stuff. Handmade things. But from all over the world."

"Do they have an app yet?" Emmie asked.

"That's what they're developing right now. That's why I may be completely out of this. I'm not a tech person."

"They already have tech people," Emmie said. "That would be the first thing they lined up. If they're advertising for new team members, they want sales. They want marketing. They want word of mouth. You're brilliant at all that. They're going to love you, Tayla."

Daisy gave her a sad smile. "You'll be perfect for them. You're smart and fashionable and business-minded. You connect with people. You're amazing at reading trends."

Tayla put her head in her hands. "You guys are acting like they've already offered me a job. They haven't. There are a million people out there who are going to want to work with them. Literally people all over the world. There is no guarantee they're going to be interested in a chubby Instagram model currently living in the middle of nowhere."

"Metlin is hardly the middle of nowhere. And plus-sized fashion is one of the least-served segments of the marketplace." Emmie was still wiping her eyes. "If they're smart, they're going to snap you up."

"Are you crying about this?" Tayla said. "I'm not dying, Em. I have a job prospect. That's it."

"I know." She sniffed. "And you're going to be amazing. And I know you miss the city. We'll just miss you here. I'd gotten so used to you being here, I just assumed you wanted to stay, and I guess I shouldn't have."

"Will you stop? I haven't decided anything yet."

"Have you told Jeremy?" Daisy asked.

"Why do you keep asking about Jeremy? I just told *you*," Tayla said. "Why do you think I would have told him yet?"

Daisy and Emmie exchanged a look.

"What is that look?"

"Just..." Emmie shrugged. "You two are close."

"No, we're not. We're friends." Tayla took a sip of iced tea, trying to rid herself of the lump in her throat. "Just like you and Daisy and I are friends. We're friends. That's all."

"You're so full of shit," Daisy said.

"Yeah," Emmie said. "I'm trying to think of the last time we exchanged sexual innuendos the way you and Jeremy do, and I'm coming up blank."

"You're imagining things. Just because you all are happily married and..." She looked at Emmie. "...whatever you and Ox are, doesn't mean I want a boyfriend. I don't do boyfriends."

"You and Jeremy are perfect for each other," Daisy said. "And it's obvious the chemistry is there. Why wouldn't you—?"

"'Cause we're not perfect for each other, okay? And I don't want a boyfriend." Tayla's cheeks flushed. "Some people aren't made for monogamy. Some of us don't want to be tied down. Don't want to come home to the same person every day and every night. Don't want to get bored always knowing exactly how the day is going to go and what the other person is going to do and what the other person is going to say and..." She looked up at Daisy and Emmie. "No offense. Relationships are nice. For other people."

Daisy leaned her chin on her hand. "No offense taken. I just think it's amusing that you think being married to Spider is either boring or predictable."

"I wasn't thinking of Spider."

Emmie was smiling. "She was thinking of Ox. She thinks Ox is boring."

"I'm not thinking of either of your partners, okay?"

"Who were you thinking about?"

"I don't know."

Daisy said, "She's imagining a fictional person she'd never fall in love with in the first place. She's imagining being married to an accountant or something."

"Hey! I'm an accountant."

"See? Most people think accountants are boring, and aren't they wrong?"

"Yeah?" Tayla said. "Most people in relationships start complaining about them after about three years. And then they get married, and it's one long stream of complaints for the next twenty-five or thirty years. They're miserable, but they do nothing to change it. Why on earth would I want that?"

Emmie looked at Daisy. "This is about her parents."

"Will you shut up?" Tayla said. "I'm going to miss you so much when I move back to the city. Sarcasm font."

Emmie narrowed her eyes. "You know, you don't have to say 'sarcasm font' when you're actually speaking. We get it."

Daisy reached for her hand. "We love you, and we don't want you to leave us. Who on earth is going to know all the French history answers for trivia if you leave? Spider will never forgive you if you abandon the team and we have to start paying for beer on trivia night."

Tayla groaned. "You guyssssss. Why are you making me feel guilty for a job I don't even have? A job that you both said I'd be perfect for?"

"Because we love you, you pain in the ass. And Metlin would suck without you." Emmie stood. "I have to get back to the shop. I'll talk to you later."

"I thought we were having lunch," Tayla said.

"Yeah? I thought you wanted to live here. Guess we were both wrong."

Tayla narrowed her eyes as Emmie walked out of the café. She nearly followed her to keep arguing, but Daisy put a hand on her arm.

"Don't," she said. "She's upset. You're pissed off. Both of you need to cool down. You've been thinking about leaving for a while, haven't you?"

Tayla took a deep breath. "I've been here over a year. I never intended to stay. I moved to help Emmie open the shop. She's open. It's running. She's doing really well. She doesn't need me anymore."

"It's not about needing you. It's about loving you. She loves you. Did you tell her you were thinking about moving back to the city?"

"No."

"So you've been thinking about it for a while, but she's just now hearing about it."

"She's not my mother, Daisy. Trust me, she doesn't have the functional alcoholism for it. And this is all ridiculous because I don't even have a job offer yet. And if I got one, there's no guarantee I'd take it."

"You'd totally take it."

"Okay yes, I would." Tayla leaned closer. "Working for a company like that is my dream job. I'd be an idiot not to take it. They probably have health insurance. Vacation days. And... retirement contributions. Do you know how behind I am in retirement planning? *401k me, baby.*"

"I know." Daisy's smile was sad. "If you get this, I will be so completely thrilled for you. You'd be amazing and fabulous and perfect. And that's part of the reason Emmie's kind of bitchy. She knows you have a really great chance of moving out of here and leaving us for a great new job. She will be happy for you eventually because she loves you. But give her time."

Like always, Daisy's calm voice of reason settled her down. She was like the big sister Tayla never had. Or wanted, for that matter. She preferred being an only child.

"I do think you need to tell Jeremy," Daisy said.

"If I get the job, I will. If they never call me back..." She looked at the menu. "Then it's no big deal. Jeremy's a flirt. You guys are reading way too much into our relationship."

"Uh-huh."

CHAPTER FOUR

IT WAS Thursday night and Jeremy hadn't seen Tayla in days. He kept missing her at the bookshop and the Ice House. She and Emmie sounded like they were fighting about something, but Jeremy was determined to stay out of that. It was never a good idea to get in the middle of friends or sisters who were fighting. He'd learned that the hard way.

But the third Thursday of every month was trivia night at the Ice House, and he knew Tayla would be there. Daisy, Spider, Ethan, and Tayla had a regular team.

He stepped into the building just in time to hear the next question.

"Question fifteen!" Hugh shouted. "We're halfway through, people. In what 1979 movie was a spaceship named *Nostromo* featured?"

Jeremy rolled his eyes. They could at least make it a little difficult. There was low muttering around the room as teams wrote their answers down on their papers.

Spider shouted from the corner. "Gabe, you better put your phone away. If you don't know that one, you're a bigger idiot than I thought."

"I'm texting my mom, asshole."

"I'm watching you."

Spider took trivia seriously. But then, Spider took everything seriously. When Jeremy had been in high school, Spider had terrified him. At least until Spider figured out that Jeremy didn't have any romantic interest in Emmie; then they were fine.

He grabbed a pint at the bar and nearly ran into Tayla.

"Hey." He couldn't stop his smile. It was automatic every time he saw her. "Wow. You look amazing tonight." She was wearing some kind of wraparound dress with pink and yellow stripes.

Tayla cocked her hip to the side and posed. "Thanks. You're not looking bad yourself. I like the vest."

"Thanks." The tweed vest over a clean shirt was his one nod to dressing up that night. "Can I get you a drink?"

Her blue eyes went wide. "That would be awesome. Spider gets cranky if I leave the table too long."

"I'll grab you a cider."

Her dimple peeked out. "You always know what I want."

He looked her up and down, from the pink earrings to the tips of her pointed flats. "I'd love to show you just how much."

"Shameless." She winked at him.

"You like me that way."

Tayla laughed as she walked away. Jeremy went to the bar and ordered a cider from Junior, who was behind the bar. He made his way to the table in the corner where Spider, Daisy, Ethan, and Tayla were huddled over a paper.

Spider looked up with narrowed eyes. "Oh. It's you."

"Yes, and I'm not working with any other teams." Jeremy pulled a spare chair from a table nearby. "Why do you take this so seriously, man?"

"I don't compete in anything unless I plan on winning."

"I agree with that philosophy." Tayla reached for the glass of cider. "Thanks, Jeremy."

Ethan caught Jeremy's eye over Tayla's head. "She tell you yet?"

"Did who tell me what?" Jeremy sipped a new stout Hugh and Carly had just put out.

Daisy and Tayla exchanged a look.

"What?" Tayla hissed. "I told you—"

"Did you actually think you could keep news private in Metlin?" Daisy asked her. "It's like I said. You have to tell him now."

Jeremy felt his heart pick up. "Tell me what?"

Everyone looked at Tayla, and Jeremy could tell she was annoyed, but he was too worried to have any sympathy.

"Question seventeen! Which American state is known as the Garden State?"

Spider grabbed the paper and started muttering under his breath.

"What's going on?" Jeremy said. "Is everything okay?"

"Everything is fine. Everything is great." Tayla's voice was clipped. "I happen to be exchanging emails with a company in the Bay Area who *may* want to interview me for a job. It's not a big deal."

Job.

Bay Area.

Job.

Interview.

He felt his face freeze. "You're moving?"

She set her glass down. "I'm not moving. Not yet. But probably someday, yes. I mean, I'm not from here. All my family is in the Bay Area, so—"

"Emmie says you hate your family." Spider finished his beer and set the empty glass down hard. "Why the fuck would you want to move closer to them? You have family here. We're family."

"It's not all about my family," Tayla said. "This job would be my dream job. Literally my dream job, okay? And maybe it'll come to nothing, but I applied because it's my dream job, and I wish you all would stop freaking out."

Jeremy forced his face into a smile. "That's exciting." His heart was racing. He felt like he wanted to puke. "So they emailed you back?"

"Yes." Her cheeks were flushed. "I filled out an interest form, and they emailed me back. They've emailed me a couple of times now. I think they may want me to come up for an interview."

"In San Francisco?"

"Yeah." Her chin lifted. "In San Francisco."

Was it healthy for your heart to be this irregular? Jeremy felt it going a million miles an hour, then it felt like it stopped completely. That couldn't be healthy.

"That's... fantastic." He swallowed hard. "So exciting. What's the job?"

"They're filling a number of positions, but this would be blogging and influencer outreach. I'd be evaluating their social media network and pairing the right influencers with companies that fit their style and budget audience."

Oh shit. "You'd be an amazing fit for that." She was perfect for that. She was fantastic. They were going to hire her as soon as they set eyes on her.

Tayla finally met his eyes. "Thanks. You're like the first person who's been happy for me."

"Of course." He glanced around the table. All eyes were laser focused on him. He kept his smile plastered on. "I mean, how could we not be happy for you?"

You're a schmuck, Jeremy Allen. And the woman you're half in love with has been looking for a way out of town while you've been playing some stupid long game.

"Everyone knows Tayla is fucking amazing," Spider said. "And she could do whatever she wants. But no one wants her to move back to that shithole city."

"San Francisco is not a shithole." Tayla glared. "It's a beautiful city."

"Whatever," he muttered.

Daisy said, "Spider doesn't like any city, Tayla. It's nothing about San Francisco in particular."

"Not true. I like Milwaukee."

"Really?" Jeremy snapped out of his frozen state. "Milwaukee?"

Ethan took a drink. "That's random, dude."

Spider shrugged. "I like what I like."

"Question eighteen is next. Which famous lead singer was born Farrokh Bulsara?"

"I know that one," Ethan said. "Give me the paper."

"Everyone knows that one," Daisy whispered. She wrote Freddie Mercury on the answer form.

Ethan, Daisy, and Spider started bickering over the answer sheet as Jeremy and Tayla fell silent. Jeremy forced the smile to remain on his face the rest of the night, and Tayla avoided his eyes.

Jeremy finished his beer and made his excuses while Tayla was in the bathroom. He had to get out of the pub. He couldn't bear the pressure in his chest another minute. He walked out the door and into the cool night air, taking a deep breath as soon as he was alone.

Tayla was leaving. If it wasn't for this job, it would be for another one. She wasn't settled in Metlin like he thought she was. She was looking for a way out.

So where the hell did that leave him?

———

JEREMY TRIED TO CLEAR HIS MIND AS HE GRABBED THE green jug halfway up the bouldering wall. He glanced up to see Cary to his right, already nearing the top of the wall. They'd come to the climbing gym at the last minute to find the top-roping area full with a beginner class, so they decided to spend their time practicing on the bouldering wall.

The large plastic hold he'd grabbed with his left hand was called a jug. He could fit nearly his entire hand around it. He stretched his right leg out and pressed his toe to the wall, shifting his weight so he'd be able to boost his body up to the small hold —or crimp—he needed to grab with his right.

"You all right?" Cary had reached the top and was watching him.

"Fine." Jeremy grunted and used his left leg and torso to reach up. His fingers curled around the crimp for a sweet second before his knuckles gave out.

"Shit." He felt himself slip. He fell backward, bracing himself as he landed on the thick mats at the base of the bouldering wall.

Cary was already climbing down. "You okay?"

Jeremy shook his hands. "I'll be fine. I shouldn't have tried a V3 before I started conditioning more."

"Legs?"

"Yeah." His legs were weak from the winter. He hadn't been biking or lifting as much because he hated working out at the gym. It left him unbalanced on the wall. "I should have stuck with the twos this early in the year."

Cary hopped off the wall and dusted his hands off. "I wondered where your head was when you hopped on that three." He grabbed a bandana from his pocket, wiped his forehead, and shook his silver hair out before he tied it back to keep it out of his eyes. "Hell, that route I took was a hard V1. We just got here, man. Still warming up. What's bugging you?"

Leave it to Mr. Nakamura to know something was bothering him.

Cary Nakamura was older than Jeremy by at least fifteen years, and he'd been Jeremy's shop teacher for a couple of years in high school. Jeremy had reconnected with him on a mountain bike trail after Jeremy had moved back to Metlin. Cary had been the one to suggest Jeremy try rock climbing, and they'd been climbing together ever since.

They were still beginning climbers, but they pushed themselves every summer. Rock climbing had become Jeremy's driving passion when he wasn't at work.

"Tayla's interviewing for a job up in the Bay Area," he said. "I just found out last night."

Cary's eyebrows went up. "Just interviewing?"

"Yeah." He walked to the bench on the far wall to grab his water bottle.

Cary shrugged. "So she's interviewing. She might not get it."

He took a long drink. "Whether she gets this job or not, it's a problem."

"Because that means she's looking to leave."

"Yeah." He sat on the bench and watched a group of college-aged girls approach the wall on the right side. They were smarter than him and started up a V2 route. "I thought she liked Metlin. I thought she wanted to stay. She's been picking up work, building a business, living with Emmie. Why would she move back to San Francisco?"

Cary sat next to him and opened his water. "I think she likes it here, but she's not *from* here. She doesn't have any roots, you know. No family. She might have just wanted a new scene for a couple years. Now she's ready to go back."

Jeremy turned to him. "That leaves me shit out of luck, man."

"Yeah, it does." Cary took a long drink. "Should have asked her out a year ago."

"I'm not twenty-two. I'm not interested in just hooking up anymore. And Tayla was pretty vocal about not wanting a boyfriend."

The corner of Cary's mouth turned up. "And you thought you'd be the one man who could change her mind?"

"Don't make me sound like an asshole. It wasn't like that." It was kinda like that.

"That girl..." Cary grinned. "She's a riot. Cracks me up every time I see her. But she's like the walking definition of a free spirit, man. If you had wedding bells in your head, I don't know if you ever stood a chance there."

"You know what? People are full of shit. They say they don't want a commitment or to be tied down, and then they fall in love and get married. So call me a hopeless romantic—"

"You're a hopeless romantic."

"I'm not the one hung up on the same woman for five years when she won't even give me the time of day, so shut the hell up."

Cary grimaced. "Fair."

Jeremy stared at the bouldering wall, watching the group of girls shouting encouragement as each one carefully chose holds and followed their route.

When he'd first started climbing, he'd been so enthusiastic he fell constantly. He wanted to try everything and do everything at once. Bruises and a fractured tibia had forced him to take a step back and reevaluate his strategy.

Jeremy decided to tackle rock climbing the same way he had school or getting his degree or building a business. Make a plan. Stick to the plan. Don't rush. Don't get overenthusiastic.

That approach in climbing had led to success. He was a far better climber than the crazy kid who'd thrown himself up rock walls and hoped he might stick.

He'd met Tayla and decided the same systematic approach would work. But maybe what he needed was less of his careful plan and more blind enthusiasm.

Cary said, "You know, if you're really into this woman, you need to forget about her moving away. Don't think about it and just go for it."

"And resign myself to getting my heart smashed when she leaves?"

"Will it be any less smashed if you don't even try?" Cary leaned forward and looked into Jeremy's face. "At this point you don't have anything to lose. The worst that could happen is she moves away. And right now that's what she's planning anyway."

Jeremy considered it. The idea had merit.

Cary continued. "She *does* like it here, but like I said, she doesn't have any roots. There's nothing holding her in Metlin."

"I know. That's the problem."

"So... maybe try giving her a reason to stay." Cary shrugged. "Like I said, you've got nothing to lose."

———

JEREMY WRAPPED A TOWEL AROUND HIS WAIST AS HE left the upstairs bathroom and heard his grandfather shouting from below.

"Dinner's ready!"

"I'll be down in a minute, Pop."

His grandfather never came upstairs anymore; he lived his life in the kitchen, the small front room, and the first-floor bedroom that overlooked the back garden. The upstairs bedrooms and bathroom were all Jeremy's.

The only downside to this was that his pop spent a lot of time yelling up the stairs. Jeremy would have known dinner was ready from the smell of tri-tip. He didn't need his grandfather hollering at him.

Of course, he didn't tell his grandfather that. Especially not when the man cooked dinner at least three times a week.

Jeremy pulled on a pair of jeans and a comfortably worn T-shirt. His hands were still sore from the climbing gym, and his back ached. His legs would hurt tomorrow, but the soreness was welcome. His body was waking up, stretching like the trees, getting ready for the summer.

He walked downstairs and found a sliced tri-tip on the kitchen table along with a pot of beans simmering on the stove.

Once a cowboy, always a cowboy.

"Want me to make a salad?"

"Not for me." Pop stood at the stove and spooned pinquito beans over his steak.

Jeremy threw a steamer pack of vegetables in the microwave. "You know, fiber is a good thing."

"That's what the beans are for."

"I'm glad I don't have to share a room with you, old man."

Pop chuckled as he sat at the table. "I'll eat your carrots or whatever you're making. Just don't expect me to make them."

"Fair enough." He leaned over and kissed the top of his pop's head. "Thanks for dinner, Pop."

"How's Cary?"

"Good. His oranges are all in."

"Tangerines?"

"Just starting."

Pop grunted. "Water's looking good this year."

"Yeah, he's not sorry to see the rain go though. Or the cold."

"It was a cold winter." Pop dug into his steak. "He plant anything?"

"I don't think so. Just pruning the oranges this year. He did mention putting in new acreage, but I think he was talking about the Oxford ranch."

Pop shook his head. "That girl gonna ruin that ranch."

"She's not ruining it; she's planting trees."

His pop grunted. In Gus's opinion, anything that displaced cows for crops was a crying shame. He'd had to do it himself and always regretted it. According to him, Melissa Rhodes was ruining the Oxford ranch by cutting back on cattle and turning the most fertile parts of their land into orange and tangerine groves.

Jeremy served himself beans, grabbed the veggies out of the

microwave, and poured them in a cereal bowl. He put the lot on the kitchen table and sat across from Pop. "You say grace?"

"Waiting on you."

Jeremy lowered his head as his grandfather blessed the meal. "Amen." He put a scoop of vegetables on Pop's plate.

His grandfather raised an eyebrow.

"Don't." Jeremy took two. "They're good for you."

"I don't remember you being my mama."

"Do you want a lecture from your daughter-in-law? Eat some vegetables. You can pick out the lima beans if you want. I won't tell anyone."

"I'll eat the green stuff if you get me a beer."

Jeremy rose. "Done." He grabbed two cans of Metlin Brew from the fridge and set them on the table.

His pop looked at the can with suspicion. "What's this?"

"Local beer, Pop. We're supporting Metlin businesses."

"Do I want to know how much this cost?"

"Not when I'm the one buying it." Jeremy cut his steak and devoured it. He was hungry. "You meet with your chess club today?"

"No. Frank had a gout flare-up."

"I'm sorry I asked."

"We fishing this weekend?"

"I don't know. You want to fish?" His brain kept circling back to Tayla. "Pop, when you were talking about wooing the other day, what did you mean?"

Pop opened his beer. "Why you asking me now?"

"Because Tayla…" He took a deep breath. Let it out. "She's probably interviewing for a job up in the city."

"San Francisco?"

"Yeah."

Gus shook his head. "What's that girl thinking? That's no place to live. Can't see the damn sky in the city."

"She likes it, Pop. Now talk to me about wooing."

Pop leaned his elbows on the table. "What are you thinking? You finally gonna get off the fence? Now that she's getting ready to move? Don't you think you're a little late?"

"Are you willing to help me or not? I need to get down to wooing quickly if I'm going to convince Tayla to stay in Metlin."

"You think you can woo that woman into staying in this town instead of moving to San Francisco?"

"I can try."

Gus nodded slowly, a smile curving the corner of his mouth. "You get your confidence from me. It's good you asked."

Jeremy felt a kernel of dread. "You know what? I can do this. I'm just going to ask her out and see what happens. I mean, what's the worst—?"

"You gonna leave this to chance? Not for this girl, Jeremy Allen. We're gonna make you a plan."

Plans were good but... "Why do I feel like I'm going to regret this?"

"Probably the same reason I feel you're gonna mess it all up," Pop muttered. "Now finish your dinner and I'll teach you how to woo."

CHAPTER FIVE

THE BUZZ of Ox's tattoo needle hummed in the background, Emmie was helping an older customer find a new mystery series, and Tayla sipped a latte while she sat on a barstool and messed with the accounts.

She and Emmie had made up because of course they had. They'd been best friends for years. Emmie apologized for not taking the news about Tayla moving well and promised not to sabotage her interviews.

But Tayla could tell her best friend was still displeased about the idea of Tayla moving.

She was totaling end-of-month merchandise sales in the computer when Jeremy walked through the door.

She looked up and gave him a smile. "Hey!"

"Hi." The corner of his mouth was curled up and his beard was freshly trimmed. He wore a pair of dark jeans, purple canvas Vans, and a black CITIZEN OF WAKANDA T-shirt under a grey vest.

Damn, the man was hot. Just... hot. Mouthwateringly, infuriatingly attractive on every level.

He leaned over the counter and grabbed her cup of coffee. "Latte?"

"Yes." She narrowed her eyes when he took a drink.

"Mmm." He licked his lips and set her cup down. "Nice."

"Did you come over here just to steal my coffee?" It was presumptuous and... also kind of hot. "Or did you need to talk to Em?"

"What are you doing this weekend?"

"Farmers' market on Saturday and movie marathon on Sunday with Ethan, Emmie, and Ox. Want to join us?"

"I have Sunday dinner in the mountains with my parents, but how about we go out Saturday afternoon after the market?"

"Yeah, that sounds fun." The email notice binged on her computer, and Tayla looked at the screen. "Who all's coming?"

"Just you and me." He grabbed a hard candy from the bowl by the register. "Pick you up at four?"

Tayla looked away from her computer. "Wait, what?"

"Four works for me." He popped a yellow hard candy in his mouth. "Does four work for you?"

"When?"

"On Saturday?"

"Um..." What was happening? "Yes?"

"Cool." He waved at Ox. "I'll text you details tomorrow. Hey Ox, Cary said he wanted to talk to you about a new piece for his leg or something. You super busy right now?"

"I have time next week." Ox was changing needles and looking over the back of his customer with a smile teasing the corner of his mouth. "Tell him to call me."

"Will do." Jeremy backed out of the shop, opening the door as an older woman walked in with two small children. "See you, Tayla." He winked. Then he was gone.

Tayla's eyes went wide. "What just happened?"

Emmie walked from between the shelves with a stack of books in her arms. "Did Jeremy just ask you out on a date?"

Ox was laughing from his side of the shop. "That awesome."

"No, it wasn't!" Tayla turned to Emmie. "He ambushed me."

"He did." Ox bent over his customer's back. "And it was awesome. Ted, I'm starting on the fill. Don't move."

The man sucked in a breath. "Okay."

Emmie cocked her head at Tayla. "I thought you'd decided you weren't going to date anyone in Metlin to avoid the—quote —'small-town busybodies and their stupid wedding-bell assumptions.'"

"He outmaneuvered me." She was pissed and yet simultaneously impressed. "Fine. He got me this time. I am going for a date with Jeremy Allen on Saturday." She'd go out with Jeremy once. Then she would make it clear that she was not dating anyone in Metlin, particularly when her future was up in the air.

"I'm just saying it's about time," Emmie said. "You guys have been flirting shamelessly for months now."

"But at four? Who plans a date for four?" Tayla closed her computer. "It's too late for lunch and too early for dinner. Maybe there's a movie he wants to see before dinner."

A movie with Jeremy would be fun enough, especially if it was something he could geek out over. "Is there a new superhero movie opening this weekend?" Tayla was a fan of dinner *after* movies and not before. After all, it gave you something to talk about instead of staring at soup. "I don't remember hearing about one opening."

"Dinner and a movie?" Ox said. "Are you kidding?"

"This is Jeremy." Emmie started ringing up her customer. "You think he's going to do an indoor date?"

"Shit." What did that mean? "What kind of date isn't indoors?"

"Oh!" Emmie smiled. "Maybe you guys are going rock climbing or something cool like that."

"Rock climbing?" She felt the color drain from her face. "No. I don't rock climb. I don't have a single date outfit that fits with climbing rocks."

This was not okay.

Ox was still smiling in the corner, the smug bastard. Maybe she didn't like Emmie's boyfriend. He'd seemed awfully cooperative with Jeremy when he'd been taking advantage of her distraction. Tayla narrowed her eyes as she watched the front of Top Shelf Comics through the windows of the bookshop.

Jeremy Allen thought he could outmaneuver her?

The man had no idea what was going to hit him.

———

"ARE YOU REALLY PISSED AT JEREMY?" EMMIE LOUNGED on Tayla's bed, staring at the closet. "I thought you liked him."

"Do you actually think he's going to want to go rock climbing?" Tayla stood in front of the small closet in her room at Emmie's, staring at her clothing options for outdoor fun. "Because that would have a definite influence on my answer to that question."

"Uh... probably not rock climbing?" Emmie said. "But also probably something outside."

"I do like him." Tayla pulled out various combinations of clothing, discarding one outfit, rearranging another. "But I told you we have very different lives."

"So did Ox and I."

"We like different stuff."

"But you also like learning and experiencing new things. You both like to travel. You know tons of interesting people. You—"

"Jeremy Allen has forever eyes. He's not a fling; he's a keeper. And that's not me. You know that's not me. How many 'very nice guys' have I dated—guys you liked—and I ended up breaking up with them because I got bored?"

"Okay yes, but you only have this hang-up because your parents are miserable and should have gotten divorced years ago."

"Yes. That is absolutely why I have this so-called hang-up."

She took a sundress off a hanger and held it up in front of the full-length mirror on the back of the wall. "But that doesn't mean I'm wrong. Name one guy that I've wanted to spend more than six months with."

"Mark Santis. You were together for nearly six months and you liked him just fine until he wanted to introduce you to his parents, and then you bolted."

Tayla hung the sundress back in the closet. "You know, evolutionary biologists propose that humans evolved to live in serial monogamy, not with a single partner their entire life. I would be fine with serial monogamy, but most men who want monogamy are ridiculously conventional and want it for the rest of their life instead of just for a few years."

"Imagine that, someone not wanting to put an expiration date on a relationship. How outrageous." Emmie rolled her eyes.

"It's contrary to human biology, Emmie. Don't argue with science."

"Humans evolve, Tayla. We live to be ninety-six. We stay in relationships longer than our prime reproductive years. We eat *cheese*. Call me crazy, but maybe we're more than our biology. In fact, if you don't believe humans have evolved enough to be successful monogamists, I don't think you should be allowed to eat cheese."

"Nice try, *you monster,* but you don't get to make the rules about cheese." She took a jumper off a hanger and turned to Emmie. "Jumper, yea or nay for outdoor fun?"

"Good in theory, but what if you have to pee in the woods? You'd have to get completely undressed."

"I am not going anywhere that I have to pee in the woods!" She tossed the jumper on the bed. "Who wants to go anywhere on a first date that doesn't have a *bathroom*?"

"Didn't he text you? What did he say?"

"He said: 'Wear flat shoes and something casual. Bring a sweater. It might be cool later.' He did not specify what later meant. Or what kind of casual I should wear." Tayla growled. "Men are the worst. I should wear a business-casual suit just to show him."

"I don't think Jeremy knows what business casual is."

"But honestly, does anyone? It's way too broad—"

"Wait." Emmie held up a finger. "I have an idea." She got her phone out and scrolled through the contacts, tapping on a name while Tayla glared at her. "Hey, Valerie! How you doing?" Emmie paused, sitting up on Tayla's bed. "Uh-huh. No, that sucks." Another pause. "So do you think you're moving back? What do your parents say?" Longer pause. "That sucks." Emmie glanced at Tayla, who was standing at the foot of the bed with both hands on her hips.

Oh right. Remember me? Standing here?

Emmie nodded. "H-hey, Valerie? When you went out with Jeremy Allen back in high school, what was a typical date like?"

Tayla whispered, "You're asking his high school girlfriend?"

"Uh-huh." She listened. "But nothing too... Really?" Emmie's eyebrows went up. "Huh. That's unexpected." Emmie smiled. "Me? No, I've got a boyfriend. My best friend is going out with him on Saturday and she's not exactly the outdoorsy kind. I thought I'd ask you."

"This is ridiculous," Tayla said. "Leave that poor woman alone."

"Call me the next time you're back, okay? I reopened my grandma's bookshop. It's really cool now. There's a tattoo parlor on the other side. See you! And say hi to Kevin." Emmie tapped on the phone to end the call. "Not rock climbing."

"I don't even want to ask, but I feel compelled—"

"They went out driving a lot, up to the mountains. Over to the coast. Did lots of stuff with friends, which I can second. Bonfire parties. When they were alone, they went to secluded places for obvious hormonal teenage reasons. You know, I assumed he was a late bloomer because he's so quiet, but you know what they say about the quiet ones—"

"What was the surprising thing?" Tayla waited, still irritated that Emmie had called the woman. Would this Valerie person call Jeremy? Would Jeremy think she was nervous about this date? *Did she somehow time-warp back to high school?* Because this whole conversation was ridiculous.

"The surprising thing?" Emmie grinned. "I'm not going to tell you."

Tayla shook her head. "See, this is why I prefer dating in the city. No one knows anything and you don't have the ghosts of girlfriends past available for predate phone consultations."

"Yes." Emmie tossed her phone to the bed. "Much better to date a possible serial killer instead."

"I don't assume anyone I haven't known since birth is probably a serial killer. That would be the difference between us. Also, the people I went to school with are *more* likely to be serial killers, not less."

"Fancy private schools are weird."

"You have no idea." Tayla turned back to her closet. "I refuse to spend more time on this until he gives me more information."

Emmie was lying back again, staring at the ceiling fan. "Are you really going to leave me?"

Tayla went to lie next to her. "Eventually it was going to happen. You knew this."

"But I thought we'd just move houses, not towns."

"I never promised I'd stay here."

"I know." Emmie reached for Tayla's hand. "I just assumed that the low cost of living and stable real-estate-market values would seduce you."

"I do love a low cost of living."

"Economic prospects are better here."

"That would be true unless I have the chance to do something amazing professionally in San Francisco." She rolled toward

Emmie. "I wouldn't leave for another accounting job. I don't like it that much, and honestly, I prefer making my own schedule like I can here with the bookkeeping business."

"See, I knew you liked it—"

"But this isn't an accounting job." Tayla propped herself up on her elbows. "This is possibly getting in on the ground of something very big. This is new trends in the industry. This is a company with tons of buzz and the financial resources to back it up. This is possible stock options. Serious money. Financial freedom from my parents forever if it actually takes off."

And rubbing success in their faces. She didn't say that part.

"I know." Emmie sat up straight. "Wait! This is an online company! What about telecommuting? You could telecommute!"

"The company website said they encourage person-to-person collaboration and keeping in touch with their local markets. Doesn't sound like telecommuting is their jam. Besides, if I'm going to be pursuing a career in fashion, do you really think Metlin is the place I need to be? Street fashion here is..."

"Eclectic?" Emmie fell back on the bed.

"That's one thing you could call it." Actually that was a pretty accurate description of Metlin. There were as many students as there were farmers and mechanics. "Emmie, this is also about me moving back to the city. I moved to Metlin to help you—"

"Because you are thoughtful and awesome."

"—but I never intended it to be permanent. And beyond all the cool business opportunities, this job could make a real difference in how the world sees and consumes fashion. SOKA promotes fair trade and thoughtful consumption. They're like that fancy outdoor-clothing company that Jeremy probably owns stock in, except they sell purses and dresses and gorgeous fabrics instead of... I don't know, windbreakers. They're an ethical curator. How rare is that?"

"I hate it when you're right, and it happens so often."

"You love me."

"I do." Emmie rolled over and stared at Tayla. "So you should take this job if they want you. For all the important reasons, and also it would be hella fun, and also you could totally rub this in your parents' faces."

"I knew I picked you as a best friend for a reason. You understand my pettiness."

"Your parents deserve it."

"The only shitty thing about moving back to San Francisco would be I'd be leaving you here. And that will truly suck."

"And leaving Daisy. And Spider. And Ox and Ethan. And Jeremy."

Tayla felt a clutch of panic in her chest. Now that she was actually thinking about pursuing this job, she realized how much she had become invested in this town. Did she even have three friends in San Francisco that she liked as much as her friends here? Her closest friend in the city had been Emmie. And Emmie was in Metlin now.

She'd be leaving friends here. She'd also be leaving a job she enjoyed. No more coffee at Frannie's Nut Shack while she tried to explain accounting software. No more free pie at Café Maya. No more joking about pink hair with the old dudes at Metlin Farm Supply when she went in to do the books. No more good-natured flirting with the hot barbers at Main Street Clip and Cut. Yeah, a couple were old enough to be her dad, but that didn't mean they weren't hot. She'd even miss Ginger's biting humor at Bombshell Tattoos when she stopped in to do the books. That place was hilarious, even if it did mostly smell like stale beer.

She'd be leaving all that if SOKA offered her a job.

"I'm getting ahead of myself," she said, playing with Emmie's long hair. "They haven't even called me for an interview yet. Until I'm on my second interview at least, we can't talk about this anymore. Until the second interview, it's pure speculation."

Emmie nodded. "Okay. So until they call you for a second

interview, we pretend like SOKA doesn't exist and you're here forever."

"I'm not sure that's what I said."

Emmie sat up with a smile on her face. "Which means you totally need a fantastic outfit for your date with Jeremy."

CHAPTER SIX

ON SATURDAY JEREMY stood in front of a mirror, checking his outfit. Favorite jeans that Ginger told him made his butt look good. Leather belt with his favorite Avengers buckle. Fitted T-shirt and vest. It was outdoorsy but hopefully stylish enough to impress Tayla. He checked his hair and combed through his beard with a pick, patting it and wondering if he should have gotten a fresh trim on Friday.

No, too formal.

But would Tayla appreciate formal?

Maybe, but he wanted to surprise her, not fall into expectations.

The whole point of this date was to shake things up. For her. For him. They'd been dancing around each other for months. He needed to know if he could really get to her, and that meant taking her out of her comfort zone and forcing himself to make a move.

Jeremy realized that he'd been playing the long game, but he'd also been too cautious. He'd been afraid of pushing for more because she might have given him a decisive no. As long as they were just flirting, the possibility was always there.

But that left them in a holding pattern. And Tayla was looking to leave.

Forget about her moving away. Give her a reason to stay.

Cary's advice kept circling his mind. Of course, Cary had also been in love with his neighbor for years and had done nothing about it, so maybe he gave shit advice. But his pop's advice had also been good.

You can do this, Jeremy. Be yourself. Be charming, but put yourself out there. Be willing to take a risk.

He grabbed his keys and walked out to the packed truck. The ice chest and all the supplies were in the back. Daisy and Ethan had texted to say the campsite was ready.

Here we go.

Jeremy walked down the stairs. "Bye, Pop!"

"Have a good time. Be respectful. Listen more than you talk."

"Got it." *Listen more than you talk* was the overarching theme of Pop's wooing lessons. That and a lot about flowers. Pop really put a lot of stock in fresh flowers.

Jeremy drove a few short blocks to Main Street and turned left. He parked in front of INK and walked in, enjoying the cheerful chime of the old-fashioned bell over the door.

"Hey, man." Ox was between clients, washing equipment in the corner. "She's upstairs."

"Should I wait or go up?"

"Em just ran up there a second ago, so I think they'll be back soon."

Jeremy perched on one of Ox's barstools and watched the hum of activity in the store. No one was behind the counter—probably because Emmie was upstairs—but the new clerk, Kim, was reading to a group of kids in the corner while a bunch of parents with farmers' market canvas bags rested their feet in the sitting area with the refurbished couch and colorful cushions.

"You guys staying busy?" Jeremy asked quietly.

Ox nodded. "It's steady. Saturdays are good. You?"

"Jules is watching the shop this afternoon. Saturdays can be kind of quiet for us unless we're hosting an event. We're busier Friday nights."

"We're a little closer to the market."

"Yeah, that definitely helps with Saturday traffic."

Ox smiled. "So what do you have planned for the big date?"

"Not saying a word."

"Fair enough." He glanced up from the sink. "You know she's a girly-girl, right?"

"Since I've spent more than five minutes with her, yeah. I know. As long as she's not wearing heels, she'll be fine."

"Okay." Ox offered Jeremy his knuckles. "Good luck, man. I've gotten attached to the girl. She's hilarious. And on a pure self-interest level, Emmie'll be a mess if she leaves."

Jeremy took a deep breath. "I'm not thinking about that right now."

"Probably a good idea."

Jeremy turned when he heard the door to the back hall open. The hall that led to the upstairs apartment Emmie and Tayla shared. Emmie walked out and over to Ox.

"Hey, Jeremy. She'll be down in a sec."

"Hi." A wide smile crossed Ox's face. "Missed you."

"I was upstairs half an hour at most."

"Yeah. And I missed you." He kissed her quickly. "I got another client coming in ten."

"Want a coffee?"

"Sounds good."

I want that. Jeremy watched Ox and Emmie with no small amount of envy. He wasn't made for playing the field. He'd tried dating around in Los Angeles, and it had left him feeling empty. He wanted a relationship. A partner. If that made him uncool, he was fine with that.

The door closed and Jeremy turned.

Tayla walked out, wearing dark ripped jeans, a bright yellow top, and a green canvas jacket that showed off her waist. The jeans hugged the curves of her ass and legs—she had great legs—and a pair of checked canvas flats completed the look. Her brown hair was pulled into two braided buns, and she carried a flowered backpack.

The girl would look adorable in a paper bag, but Jeremy had never even caught a hair out of place.

"Damn, Miss McKinnon." He walked over to her. "How do you always look perfect?"

Tayla's cheeks pinked just a little. She turned her cheek and Jeremy planted a kiss. "Since my date was being so mysterious, I figured I better be prepared for anything. There's even a first aid kit in my backpack."

He looked her up and down again, just to appreciate. "Does your first aid kit have anything for the heart attack you're giving me with this look?"

"You gonna tell me where we're going?"

"It's a surprise."

"Sorry. You don't get into my first aid kit until I know where we're going."

Ox muttered, "A first aid kit? Is that what the kids are calling it now?"

Emmie punched his arm and walked toward the door. "I'm going down to Café Maya. Have fun, you guys."

Jeremy held out his hand and reached for the backpack, which Tayla handed over. He slung it over his shoulder and wove their fingers together as he led her toward the door, thrilling at the feeling of her hand in his. "See you, guys."

"Bye, Ox!" Tayla looked happy, but there was an evil glint in her eye.

Perfect.

When she fell for him, he wanted her to fight it. Just a little. It would make the surrender all the more satisfying.

HOT. MOUNTAIN MAN HOT. BEARDED, CHISELED, mountain man hot. Tayla eyed Jeremy from across the cab of his truck, which was as clean as she'd ever seen it. Jeremy looked like he could be in an outdoor-gear catalogue. She might not have wanted to climb boulders, but she definitely appreciated the definition rock climbing gave Jeremy's shoulders.

I'd climb him.

He glanced at her and the corner of his mouth turned up. He'd caught her staring.

"You should look outside," he said. "Enjoy the scenery. The wildflowers are incredible this year."

"I'm enjoying the scenery." Her eyes didn't move from his profile.

Jeremy chuckled. "I love it."

"You like when I stare at you?"

"You play the best games without playing any games."

Tayla burst into laughter. "You're right. I make no secret of my purely superficial appreciation. You're an incredibly handsome man."

"Thank you. And you are a very beautiful woman."

"Thank you. We definitely need to take pictures together."

"Don't you worry." He glanced at her before his eyes turned back to the twisting road. "You'll have plenty of Instagram-worthy moments."

"It doesn't bother you?"

"Your Instagram habit?" He shook his head. "Nope."

"A lot of it is business."

"I know. It's smart." He glanced at her backpack. "You pay for that?"

"Nope." She picked it up with a smile. "Freebie from a company looking for placement."

He nodded. "See? Smart. I know a perfect spot to take a picture of you with it."

Tayla felt her dimple popping. "You're kind of awesome."

"Miss McKinnon"—he cut his eyes to the side—"I'm just straight awesome. No kind of."

"So why did you wait so long to ask me out?"

"Good question." He kept his eyes on the road and took a long time to answer. "Why didn't you ask *me* out?"

Tayla nodded. "Fair."

"But you asked first?"

"No, I'm not gonna cop out." She cocked her head and thought about all the reasons she'd been keeping her distance from Jeremy Allen. "Because I've always known that I probably wasn't staying in this town. And you're not the flinging kind."

"The flinging kind?" He looked over. "I'm not flingable?"

Tayla laughed. "Do you want to be flingable?"

Jeremy's laugh was deep and full. "I don't even know how to answer that." He pulled the car over into a curve of the road and leaned toward her. "I don't want to think about tomorrow. Or next month. I want to be with you right here and now." His mouth was so close she could feel his breath on her cheek. "You with me?"

She looked him straight in his big brown eyes. "Yes."

His smile nearly took her breath away. "Good." Jeremy reached across and popped her door open. "First stop, let's get you that pretty picture."

He led her toward a gate in the barbed wire fence, and she followed him over a dirt trail across a pasture teeming with wildflowers.

"Are those cows?"

Jeremy smiled. "Yes. The friendly kind."

"Is there an unfriendly kind?"

"Any cow with a calf," he said. "Bulls sometimes. If you end up in a pasture with either of them, stay away. Even if the babies are cute."

"Or just stay away from any animal larger than you?" She held his hand as they walked. The path was fairly even, in a mild rising slope. She could see oak trees in the distance and wildflowers were everywhere. "How about here?"

"Let's see." He let go of her hand. "Give me your phone."

"Okay." Tayla handed it over and slung the backpack over both shoulders, adjusting the straps. "How does it look?"

"Cute," he said. "Not as cute as you."

"You got all the lines, Mr. Allen." She was wearing her sunglasses and took them off to check her appearance in the lenses. "Is my makeup okay?"

"I'm probably the wrong person to ask about that, 'cause I always think you look great." He narrowed his eyes. "But for now unlock your phone and walk ahead of me."

"Oh, gotcha." She grabbed her phone back and opened the camera. Then she hooked her fingers in the straps of the backpack and started walking up the slope, surrounded by flowers.

She could hear Jeremy moving around behind her. "Walk back a little and do that part again."

"Okay." She turned and saw him sitting on the ground.

"I'm trying to get the tree in the distance."

Tayla glanced at the tree. It was a good idea; the sky was bright blue and fluffy clouds rose over the mountains on the horizon. "Cool."

She continued walking up the hill, keeping her eyes on the tree and ignoring the sound of Jeremy taking pictures. She stopped when she heard him running to catch up with her.

"Check these out." He handed her the phone. "I think they're good."

They were good. He'd captured several pictures of Tayla walking up the verdant hill with swaying red and yellow flowers surrounding her. The flowers in the field echoed the flowered pattern on the backpack. The twisted oak tree created a focal point in the distance.

"These are great."

His smile lit up his face. "Excellent. Let's keep going." He grabbed her hand and kept walking. "So what's this I hear about you not liking the outdoors?"

"I have no idea. I love dining alfresco. Visiting beach clubs. Enjoying an irish coffee at a ski resort. I'm practically a Girl Scout."

"Were you really?"

Tayla laughed. "Not a chance. Far too pedestrian for my parents. I was in all the kids' classes at the yacht club though."

"Ah, so you come from snobbery. I didn't know that about you."

"Yes, we had only the finest snobbery at the Bay City Yacht Club."

He shook his head. "I'm trying to imagine you at a yacht club and failing miserably. When you said you grew up in San Francisco, I was thinking Haight-Ashbury."

"Sadly, closer to the Marina. The Haight is my people though."

"So how did the yacht club like the pink hair? Or were you dying it blue then? To fit in?"

Tayla burst into laughter. "I can't decide if you're making a joke about old ladies or not."

He smiled. "I wasn't. My pop would smack me upside the head if I made jokes about any woman's hair." He stepped over a creek that cut through the meadow. "I was thinking about blue hair and... I don't know. Boats? You might be shocked to know that I was not raised near any kind of yacht club."

"You didn't miss anything." She shook her head. "No blue hair. I just kept my head down and left as soon as I could. I played the obedient daughter, got them to pay for school, and got my own place as soon as I got a job. Then I started dying my hair. Getting the tattoos. Generally driving them even crazier than I did before. We don't speak much anymore, but no one is surprised or shocked by that."

Jeremy paused at the top of the hill. "That's sad."

She shrugged. "It's my normal. It's not a big deal. Most of the people I grew up with hate their parents. It's practically a tradition among the country-club set. They hate them until they turn into them."

"Maybe it's tradition, but it's still sad. Your family should be your biggest fans."

"Is yours?"

"Embarrassingly so." He closed his eyes. "Do you know my mom started reading comics after I bought my shop? She said if I was going to sell something, she had to know what it was so she could recommend it. She's addicted to *Saga* and *Lumberjanes* now. And yes, she tells all her patients her son has a comic book shop."

"Your mom sounds adorable."

"She is. Now, come this way. Let's see if the light works."

Jeremy led her across the top of the hill and toward the oak she'd seen in the distance. Beneath it was a tumble of moss-covered granite rocks and what remained of the twisted roots of another oak. Tayla looked at the waning light and the shadows the tree cast on the rocks and roots below it.

"This is perfect!"

"Good! So find a spot sitting in there and… pose. Or whatever you do with your product-placement stuff."

She unlocked her phone for Jeremy and walked over, climbing up the roots before she turned. "Do I look okay? I didn't even check my hair."

"You look great." His smile was infectious. "Just climb around like that for a little bit and I'll take pics."

She explored the mangled roots and rocks beneath the tree, then she found a broad boulder and took off her backpack, sitting and propping the backpack beside her. "How's this?"

"Fantastic."

She changed positions a few more times, showing the bag at different angles. "Okay, I need my phone for some close-ups."

Jeremy jumped up the rocks like a mountain goat and handed her phone to her. While she positioned the backpack for a few close shots, she watched him from the corner of her eye.

Mountain man hot. Thoughtful. Cute, cute, cute. Good sense of humor.

If Tayla was the keeping kind, she'd totally want to keep him.

But she wasn't. So she focused on what Jeremy had said.

I want to be with you right here and now.

Here and now? That she could do.

———

TAYLA LEANED HER HEAD INTO THE SUNBEAM ON THE far side of the truck. She'd taken off her jacket to enjoy the sun on her fair skin. Her eyes were closed, and she was more relaxed than he could ever remember seeing her. Jeremy smiled and sped toward the surprise he'd planned on the edge of Lower Lake. They'd been on their date for a little over an hour, and so far, so good.

She'd taken the walk through the meadow in stride. He thought she'd even had fun climbing around on the roots and rocks of the old oak. That land used to belong to his grandfather, and he'd grown up playing in the fields and trees. He'd learned how to ride a horse in that meadow. He'd gone there to cry privately when his grandmother passed. Seeing Tayla there made him happy.

"You hum under your breath," she said, her eyes still closed.

"Does it bug you?"

"No." She opened her blue eyes and watched him. "I just realized you don't have music on."

"Sometimes you don't need music."

"I always have music on. Or a podcast. Or... something."

"Noise." Jeremy shrugged. "I love music, but sometimes I like quiet. It's good for the soul."

"You have mentioned the soul unironically, and this is officially the weirdest first date I've ever been on."

Jeremy smiled. "I think I'm going to take that as a compliment."

"It's not an insult."

"Good."

"Are we almost there? Wherever there is?"

"Yep. In fact..." He made one last turn through the gates of the recreation area. "We're here."

"The lake?"

"Have you been?"

She squinted. "Once. Late last summer. It was very hot."

"Then you haven't seen it in springtime. Which is the only time to see it." He stopped at the pay station to grab a permit for the rest of the day. Then he jumped back in the truck and continued the winding drive to the lakeside. They passed families starting barbecues and fishermen heading out for the dusk catch.

"Are we swimming?" She was smiling. "I didn't bring a suit."

"The water's still a little cold for that." He left the main recreation area and headed to the group site he'd called and reserved the day after she said yes. It was a little bit away from the other picnic tables and usually only available for groups, but the ranger was an old friend of his dad's and he let Jeremy reserve it.

They drove around the last bend, and he watched her face as she spied what Daisy and Ethan had set up.

Tayla's mouth dropped open. "What is... Are we *camping?*"

"You call this camping?" Jeremy stopped the car and hopped out, waving at Ethan and Daisy as they drove away. "This is, at the very least, *glamping.*"

"How did you even...?" She spotted Ethan's truck. "Ethan and Daisy helped with all this?"

The group barbecue site sat directly on the edge of the lake, secluded by a stand of sycamore trees. A series of logs had been laid in a circle to create a firepit. There was a pavilion and a large

tent facing the shore and laid out colorful blankets and a low table
with cushions around it. Daisy and Ethan had come later to put
up the finishing touches.

There were mosquito coils wafting around the site and
citronella candles burning in mason jars to keep the bugs at bay.
Fresh flowers and dishes—real dishes, not paper—were already
laid out on the small table. A string of solar lights hung from the
trees to the tent.

Jeremy unloaded the ice chests from the back of the pickup and
set them in the shade beside the tent. "What do you think?"

Tayla was turning in circles, taking it all in. "This is *stunning*.
You had all this stuff?"

"The tent is Daisy and Spider's. They use it for a guest house
since their place is so tiny. The blankets are mine and my mom's.
Uh... the little table is mine actually. Long story." He rubbed the
back of his neck. Was it too over the top? "I just wanted to do
something fun and surprise you."

"I'll admit I suspected we'd be going on a picnic. But this is
like..." She turned to face him. "This is like a luxury picnic from a
period movie or something. Only cooler because"—she pointed to
the bathrooms in the corner of the group site—"there's
plumbing!"

Jeremy grinned. "I thought you didn't like the outdoors."

"I like this." Tayla stepped closer and tugged on the edges of
his vest. "I like you."

Well, shit.

There went his heart.

Jeremy bent down, took her chin between his fingers, and
kissed her.

71

CHAPTER SEVEN

THE KISS SPUN out like one long, sweet sigh. Jeremy's lips were soft and warm. His beard tickled her mouth, and she felt a shiver race down her back. She stepped closer and slid her arms around his waist between his vest and his shirt, running her hands along the warm ridges of muscle at the small of his back as their bodies pressed together.

He was hard and lean. She was soft and curvy. His hand fell at the rise of her hip and he squeezed. Tayla sighed in the back of her throat. His other hand came to rest on her shoulder blade, long fingers running up and down in a line between her shoulders.

It was perfect. Slow and luxurious. He wasn't pushing for anything. He was savoring, like she was a treat he'd been waiting to enjoy. Jeremy took her lower lip between his teeth and tugged just a little before he released her.

"Hmmm."

Tayla blinked her eyes open. "Hi."

"Don't tell my pop, okay?" His voice was rough.

"That you kissed me?"

"That I enjoyed my dessert before dinner." Jeremy squeezed

her hip one more time before he stepped back, rubbing his thumb along his lower lip. "Let me get this set up and we'll eat."

Tayla felt flustered. Confused. Dates were charming get-togethers in glittering places where everyone tried to impress each other. This date was all that... but it was also something she couldn't quite put her finger on. It was going to drive her crazy. *He* was going to drive her crazy. That wasn't in the plan.

"Can I help with anything?"

Jeremy cocked his head at her. "Are you joking? This is for you. Sit down and enjoy the scenery. Watch the lake. Relax. I know you had a long week. It's tax season."

It was tax season, but she was a bookkeeper this year, not in an accounting firm. "Still, I want to help. You've done all this—"

"You can plan the next date," he said. "And pick some music. There's a speaker in the truck."

"Okay." The next date? How was she going to top this? "And don't think I don't see what you're doing, getting me to commit to date two before date one is over."

"I'm just saying you're going to have to work to impress me." He spread his hands out. "There are candles. And scenery." He popped open a Tupperware. "And a lot of cheese."

She scowled at him. "You fight dirty, Mr. Allen."

"The gauntlet has been thrown, Miss McKinnon." He tossed a cloth napkin on the table. "Okay, that was a napkin and not a gauntlet, but the challenge stands." He set a bottle of wine on the table. "I await your response."

"You are such a geek." She couldn't stop the laugh. "Fine. I'll plan the next one."

Wait, wasn't she going to tell him she didn't date? Especially in Metlin?

She could tell him next time. It would be rude to give him the big "I don't date" speech in the middle of what was—by any objective standard—a truly awesome date.

Plus hanging out with Jeremy was fun. And relaxing. He was

an excellent kisser. He made her laugh. And she wanted to see what he was like when he was being slightly less proper.

She wandered down by the lakeside, snapping pictures and posting them to social media. She'd already posted pictures with the backpack and added links. She took a few pictures of the tent, leaving Jeremy out of the frame, teasing her followers with captions like...

He didn't have to go to all this trouble—jk he totally did.

What do u know? Country boys speak romance. Lucky me.

Big girls. Hot dates. She included a few appropriate—or inappropriate—emojis on that one.

The likes on the backpack pic were insane. The likes on the tent pic were even better. Who knew dating could be good for traffic?

"I'm putting pics of the tent and stuff on Instagram, but not you, okay?"

"Okay."

"I won't post any pics of you without your permission. It's a hard and fast for me. But I will totally insinuate shit without tagging you. Just so you know."

He chuckled. "That's fine, Tayla. I don't mind."

"Are you on Insta? Facebook?"

"Nope."

"Snapchat? YouTube?" She took a few ninja pics of Jeremy bending over the table. She was only human, and he had a great ass. "Do you post any rock climbing videos or stuff like that?"

"No videos. No snaps. No faces or books." He straightened from setting the table. "I have an Instagram feed for the shop and a website for the shop. That's it though. Nothing personal."

Tayla blinked. "Wait, what?"

Jeremy laughed. "I'm a dinosaur, but it's by design."

"Nothing? Not even a weird LinkedIn profile you don't remember activating but somehow it's still there?"

He narrowed his eyes. "Okay, I might have one of those."

"I think everyone does." She climbed on top of a log and walked the length of it, feeling like she was back on her elementary school playground. "Logs are fun."

"I'm gonna leave that joke alone and tell you rocks are more fun."

She wrinkled her nose. "You're going to try to get me rock climbing, aren't you?"

"You know, people at all different fitness levels can start—"

"Whoa there." She held up a hand. "I'm plenty fit, my friend."

Tayla had been wanting to try a few yoga poses on the log, but she wasn't exactly in the right clothes. She toed off her shoes and moved to mountain pose. She closed her eyes, centering herself and feeling her energy from the soles of her feet on the curve of the smooth wood and up her spine. Her breath expanded her lungs and flowed out, opening her senses.

She stretched her toes and shifted her weight to her right foot. Were her jeans stretchy enough? She'd try a dancer pose and see.

Tayla lifted her left foot and stretched her arms, her left moving back to hook her thumb around her big toe and the right stretching forward. She lifted her heart and released her breath as she opened her eyes. The lake spread out before her, a smooth mirror reflecting the green hills and darkening sky. *Wow.* She hadn't been expecting the wonder.

"Beautiful."

She turned her head to the side and caught Jeremy with his phone up. "Are you taking my picture?"

"Trust me when I say you're going to want a copy of this one. You look incredible."

She released her foot and stretched her arms out and up, re-centering her feet and aligning her spine, her hands coming to rest in front of her heart. "It's beautiful here."

"You know, the gates open at dawn all summer. If you ever wanted to come up here to practice, no one would bother you."

She jumped down off the log and immediately felt the dirt coat her toes. Shit. She'd forgotten she was in the natural world and not the friendly yoga studio on 7th Avenue. "I'll keep that in mind."

She dusted off as best she could and walked over to the blankets with her shoes in her hand. "Told you. Plenty fit, thank you very much. I just have no need to climb rocks."

He threw his head back and groaned. "With your sense of balance, you'd probably be amazing on a bouldering wall."

"So you want to give yoga a try?"

Jeremy spread his hands out. "Sure. I could stand to be more flexible."

Dammit. He'd called her bluff. She'd been sure a Metlin boy would consider yoga too girly for his big manly body. "Okay, I'll keep that in mind."

He bent down and lit the candles on the small table. "Sensing a possible theme for our second date."

"Would I be that predictable?" She sat on a wide blue cushion by the table. "So, this is supercute and everything looks delicious."

"I'm glad you like it. Do you like salmon?"

"I do. I love salmon."

"I might have known that because I bribed Emmie to tell me secrets."

Tayla smiled. "What did you bribe her with?"

"I promised to start carrying more romance manga at the store."

"That sounds like a uniquely Emmie bribe." Tayla reached for a glass of white wine and eyed the chilled salmon on her plate. Jeremy had complemented it with a green salad and half an artichoke. "Okay, this all looks amazing. Sauvignon blanc?"

Jeremy reached for his fork. "No. A Spanish wine. Albariño. Try it. Since the salmon is cold, it should taste great with it."

And he knew wine too. The man was ridiculous. She gave up. She lifted her glass. "Cheers. To the best picnic I've ever been on."

"Cheers." He clinked his wineglass with hers. Then he took a bite of salmon and licked his lips after he swallowed. "This is delicious. Eat. The light show starts when the sun goes down."

"Light show?"

———

HOURS LATER, AFTER WATCHING A METEOR SHOWER and drinking hot chocolate by an actual campfire, Jeremy drove Tayla home. She'd pitched in to break down the tent and helped him throw everything in the back of the pickup. Now she was wrapped in one of the blankets and looked like she was falling asleep.

They rolled over the hills and back into town. Quiet music on the radio. Silence between the two of them.

He didn't question whether she'd had a good time. Tayla hadn't hidden her enjoyment. She was completely open about her feelings, both her irritation with the dirt and bugs and her delight at the meteor shower, the lakeside, and the picnic.

Her head fell forward and jerked up. Her eyes flickered open. "Are we back?"

"Almost."

"Hmmm." She unbuckled her seat belt and scooted closer to him, laying her head on his shoulder. "Don't crash."

"Don't do anything crazy and I'll do my best."

"Was that a veiled reference to road head?"

He shook his head and tried unsuccessfully to smother a smile. "Woman, you have a dirty mind."

"I read a lot of romance novels. They're good for the imagination."

"I'll remember that."

She turned to him, her face glowing in the streetlamps as she leaned her chin on his shoulder. "Good idea."

Damn. If he wasn't driving, he'd kiss her. He exited the

highway and turned north on 6th Avenue before he turned right again on Main. "And you're home."

"Am I?" She was staring at the storefront. "I don't know if I am, Jeremy." Her voice was stripped of artifice. She sounded lost.

You don't know where home is.

He put his arm around her and kissed the top of her head. "Home for now."

"Yeah." She scooted over and opened the door before he could hop out of the truck and open it for her.

Jeremy walked around and grabbed her backpack from the toolbox in the back of his truck, making sure there was no dust or dirt on it. He turned to hand it to Tayla and found her standing right in front of him.

"Hey," she said.

"Hey." He put the backpack on the ground, cupped her cheeks with both hands, and kissed her. He wasn't polite this time. He'd been hungry for her all night.

Tayla's mouth tasted like chocolate and strawberries. His tongue stroked hers, teasing the inside of her mouth until she opened more. His palm ran down her neck, his thumb brushed over her pulse, and he stroked her shoulder. Her arm. Her waist. He slid his thumb into the back pocket of her jeans and cupped her ass.

Fine, fine ass.

Tayla pressed her body closer. She couldn't have missed his body's reaction to her; she didn't seem to mind. Her hand dug into the small of his back, giving him all sorts of ideas.

He swallowed the groan that wanted to leave his throat and ran his teeth along her full lower lip, licking the edge with the tip of his tongue.

Her nails dug into his skin.

"Mmmm." He savored one more taste of her tongue before he let her go. "You should go in."

Her eyes were closed. Her lips were flushed and swollen. "I'm thinking about so many other things than going inside right now."

Jeremy smiled and bent down to her ear as he gave her ass one more squeeze. "To be continued."

"You're evil," she whispered.

"I'll take that as a compliment."

"It's not an insult." She bent down and picked up her backpack, reaching for the keys in the front pocket. "I'll see you later. Send me a dirty text when you get home."

He pointed toward Ash. "When I get home in like three minutes because I live around the corner?"

"Yes. Then." She unlocked the door and waved at him. "Dirty texts. I'll be expecting them."

As you wish. He almost said it, but she'd seen *The Princess Bride* too. He wasn't putting himself out there like that. Not yet. "I'll text you."

She blew him a kiss and closed the door, locking it behind her, and Jeremy got back in the truck. He drove up 8th Avenue, crossed Central, and turned left on Oak. When he got to Ash, he turned right and pulled into the driveway. Hopping out, he opened the gate and pulled the truck into the backyard. He'd unload everything in the morning before he headed to the mountains.

He closed the gate and got out his phone, then he found a picture Cary had taken of him during a particularly muddy hike last spring in Yosemite when they were going up to some falls.

He texted the picture of him covered in mud to Tayla.

There you go. Hope that's dirty enough for you.

I requested textS. Plural. I'm going to need more than this.

Just how dirty are you looking for?

The series of emojis she sent back was enough to make him blush even if he didn't understand what half of them meant.

———

TAYLA SMILED EVERY TIME HER PHONE BUZZED, TRYING to ignore the multiple pictures of Jeremy covered in varying levels of dirt. In many of them he was in a climbing harness that gave her too many ideas. In others, he was shirtless and sweaty. She responded to each with increasingly dirty innuendo.

Yes, almost dirty enough.

Now without the harness.

Tell me more about ur knot-tying skillz. She added a raised eyebrow emoji to that one.

Between responding to texts, she reread the open email on her laptop. She'd been checking her mail when Jeremy's first text came in. It was an inescapable habit. She couldn't sleep without checking her email.

HEY, TAYLA,

We love your résumé, your writing voice on your blog, and your social media feeds. Everyone in the office is impressed with what you might bring to the team.

I know you're not in the Bay Area anymore, but would you be willing to come up for an interview? Our team is built on person-to-person contact and community, so we prefer in-person meets to video conferences. Let me know what your schedule is like.

All the best,

Kabisa Nandi

SOKA, Inc.

CHAPTER EIGHT

LUNCH AT CAFÉ MAYA meant Daisy was always working, which meant once a month, Tayla insisted they have lunch someplace other than downtown. She'd driven them to a sushi place in the strip mall off the highway, hoping it lived up to its online reviews. "Have you been here before?" Daisy asked. "I'm so excited. We never go for sushi. Spider isn't a fan."

"I've been here a couple of times," Emmie said. "It's really good. As good as anything you can get in San Francisco. People just don't come because of the location."

"You're just saying that because SOKA wants me to come in for an interview." Tayla put her bag on the extra chair of the table the waitress waved them toward. "And you know I miss sushi."

"I'm telling you that because it's really good. It's the only sushi place Cary's mom will go to in Metlin."

Cary's mom had grown up in Japan, so Tayla gave the strip mall sushi place the benefit of the doubt. The exterior didn't look like much, but the interior was cute with adorable pictures of cats eating sushi on the walls and a truly impressive display of origami in a corner of the bar.

"I'm telling you it's good." Emmie sat across from Tayla. "It has nothing to do with you wanting to move back to the hellhole of urban congestion and tech bros."

Tayla just rolled her eyes. Emmie had mostly come around about her moving away, but she still liked to get snarky. Then again, if she didn't get snarky, would she be Tayla's best friend?

"What should we order?" Daisy opened the menu. "What's good?"

"Everything I've ordered has been good, so what do you like?"

The waitress walked up. She was a short Asian woman with a curvy figure and her hair twisted up in a knot. The edges of her bangs were spiked and tipped with gold dye. "Hey." She pointed at Emmie. "You've been here before. You can't handle your sake."

"You are correct." Emmie raised her hand. "And I promise not to order any today. Also, I'm working, so I definitely shouldn't order it."

Tayla said, "That makes me think you should." She opened the menu. "Why else do we work for ourselves? I'll have a bottle of nigori and a water please."

"I like it." The waitress looked at Daisy. "How about you? Want a glass to share?"

"Sure. Emmie, you're driving."

"I guess I am," Emmie said. "And I'll just have a green tea. Thanks."

The waitress wrote on her order pad. "The chef got some fatty tuna in this morning that's pretty amazing. So that's the special. And spicy cucumber salad with octopus. You guys have any questions?"

They conferred a few minutes before they ordered a mixed nigiri platter with the fatty tuna and a large salad to share.

Tayla watched the server walk away. She was probably nineteen or twenty with a really cool and funky style. Student at the local college? Aspiring sushi chef? Something about her style reminded Tayla of the restaurant. Fun. Cool. Unexpected. Especially for Metlin.

When the server came back with their drinks, Tayla asked her, "Did you help design the restaurant's interior?"

A smile lit her face. "Yeah, I did! It's my brother and sister-in-law's place, but I'm going to school for art, so they asked me to help." She pointed to the cat paintings. "Those are mine."

Emmie said, "You painted them? That's so cool. They're really funny."

The server shrugged. "This place is kind of quirky, you know? So I wanted to do something fun that would make my sister-in-law laugh. My brother is super serious and traditional, but she's not."

"I love it." Tayla got out her phone. "Are you on Insta? What's your name?"

"I'm Mika. Yeah, I'm on Insta, but I actually set up a website after a bunch of customers asked about my work." She glanced at the counter. "I'll bring you my card because I really need to get my other table."

She left, and Tayla perused the walls of the sushi place again. "Emmie, you should ask about hanging some of her work at INK. Ox might go for some of her stuff too."

"I was just thinking that. I already had that guy from the music studio asking if I ever exhibited local artists. He was fishing, but it's a cool idea."

Daisy said, "You could ask for some of Cary's photographs too if you wanted."

Tayla frowned. "I didn't know Cary was a photographer."

"Oh yeah. He's amazing. It's part of the reason he started climbing." Daisy smiled. "You should ask Jeremy about it."

"I might." Tayla looked around the restaurant. "You know, SOKA could sell this kind of stuff too. Art. Lifestyle stuff. Right now they're focused on clothes, but that could translate into more of a lifestyle curator, you know? Art. Home goods. Interesting accessories."

"You should bring it up if they ask you about it at your interview," Daisy said. "I think companies are looking for that kind of initiative these days. Shows you have a creative mind."

Tayla sipped her sake. "Fashion is innately creative."

Emmie added, "And if you want a reference about all the cross promotion you've done at INK, I could totally give you one. You're awesome at all that kind of stuff."

"I'll keep that in mind."

"So when's the interview?"

"I sent them a couple of dates next week that would work for me. I'm waiting to hear back."

"And while you're waiting, we can grill you about your date." Emmie rubbed her hands together. "I've been waiting for this."

"What are you talking about?" Tayla asked. "You were waiting up for me on Saturday night."

"And you told me nothing!"

"I told you it was nice." It was so much more than nice. "What else do you want to know? Daisy helped him set it up. Don't tell me you haven't already talked about it."

"Actually, I kept my mouth shut," Daisy said. "I was sworn to secrecy, and I take that seriously."

"I need to hear it from you," Emmie said. "I'll start slow. Is he a good cook? I've never seen him cook."

"Yes. We went on a picnic and the food was great. He may have bought some things though. Not sure. Don't care."

"A picnic by the lake? That could be romantic or loud."

"It was romantic. Very. He did an excellent job setting it all up."

"That was all him, by the way," Daisy said. "I just helped bring stuff."

"The tent was amazing."

"Tent?" Emmie's eyebrows went up. "My, my. Is the city girl going wild? You were in a tent?"

"It was one of those luxury safari tents like they have at music festivals. There were flush toilets very nearby."

"That explains it." Emmie waited for Mika to set the sushi down, thanked her, then refocused on Tayla. "So you had dinner by the lake. I saw the pics on Instagram. You went hiking before?"

"We went for a walk. Not a hike." Tayla chose a piece of tuna with her chopsticks. Yum.

"It looked like you went on a hike."

"It wasn't." Or… was it? There hadn't been a path. They'd been walking in dirt and there were lots of trees and flowers. Damn it, Jeremy had tricked her into a hike. He was getting way too good at this.

"Now the real question." Emmie leaned forward. "Is he a good kisser?" She narrowed her eyes. "Wait, do I want to know if Jeremy's a good kisser? Is that weird?"

"It's a little weird," Daisy said. "So I'll ask. Is he a good kisser? Is the beard scratchy?"

"No." Tayla smiled and shook her head. "And yes. He is. That's all I'm going to say. We had a beautiful dinner in the outdoors. Lots of fresh air and sunshine. And I'm planning the next date."

Daisy and Emmie were both speechless.

"What?" Tayla shrugged. "What was I supposed to do? Tell the man sorry, this is the most amazing date I've ever been on, but we definitely can't repeat it?"

"The most amazing date you've ever been on?"

"You're planning a date?" Emmie blinked repeatedly. "You don't plan dates."

"Well…" That was true. She usually insisted on men planning dates for her. Which generally led to a series of forgettable dates unless the conversation was really stellar. "He went to a lot of trouble to plan this, and I thought I'd take him out of his comfort zone a little and see how he does."

Daisy cocked her head. "So you're planning an interview with a fashion company in San Francisco and also an elaborate date with a mountain man in Metlin."

Tayla spread her hands. "What can I say? I'm a woman who multitasks."

———

Initially Tayla had been hesitant to take the bookkeeping job at Bombshell Tattoos. The business was run by Ginger, Ox's ex-girlfriend, who'd been more than antagonistic to Ox and Emmie on occasion. That said, sometimes people brought out the worst in each other, and Tayla had a feeling that was the case with Ox and Ginger.

A conversation with Spider had reassured her, and Tayla took the job and hadn't regretted it.

Yes, Bombshell smelled a lot like stale beer much of the time.

Yes, the clientele ran a lot rougher than INK.

Yes, Ginger yelled. A lot.

But she didn't yell at Tayla. She just had a short fuse when it came to a couple of the artists who worked for her. Generally the ones who fucked up. She told them so regularly.

"Your area looks like a damn pigsty, Cash. Clean it up."

"I have a client coming in five minutes."

"All your clients are late because you're constantly running behind!" Ginger put her hands on her hips. "This isn't a debate. Don't be a fucking slob."

Cash muttered under his breath as Ginger shot daggers with her eyes. Then she turned back to Tayla and asked, "So, what were you saying about my net income?"

Tayla ignored the blaring music Cash turned on in the back of the shop. Ginger had hired her to do the books, but she'd also asked Tayla for help balancing her budget. Tayla was happy to do it. For a little extra fee. "You're doing fine, but I've been tracking for a few months now, and I think there are ways you could trim your expenses. The cable, for example. I don't ever see anyone watching that TV when I'm here."

"Yeah, maybe once or twice a month for a game. Mostly I just wanted Wi-Fi. The cable package kind of came with it."

"Check with them again. You should be able to get internet without cable." Tayla slid over a sheet of paper. "Here's a list of suggestions for things I think you could cut without missing them much, or certain things that seem high. These are just suggestions, by the way. It's your business, so you may have different priorities than me."

The corner of Ginger's mouth turned up. She was a hard woman, but she was beautiful. She was petite and had an hourglass figure. She leaned into the rockabilly style in her hair and her wardrobe. It really worked for her.

Tayla noticed her dabbing her eyes with a tissue. "Allergies?"

"This fucking town. Ever since I moved here, I'm flat-out miserable for two weeks every spring. At least it's only two weeks. Better than it used to be."

"Really? For some reason, I thought you were born here."

"Me?" She laughed. "Hell no, I'm from LA. Born and raised in Long Beach."

"So how did you end up in Metlin?"

Ginger rolled her eyes. "Oldest story in the book. Followed a guy. Started a business. Guy took off, but so did the business." She took out her vape pen and stood. "I had better credit, so the building was in my name. And I bought it when it needed a ton of work, so it was cheap. To get a place this size in LA?" She shook her head. "No way. I'd be working for someone else. I don't always love it here, but I hate taking orders. So I stay."

"Cool." Tayla opened her laptop.

"You thinking about leaving?"

"Yeah. I may have a job in San Francisco. But don't worry—if I do go, I'll give you at least a month's notice to find someone else."

"Cool." Ginger walked toward the door, paused, and turned around. "It's not a bad place. You know I have my issues with Ox, but most of the people around this neighborhood are good. And honest, which you can't say for every place. And they give a shit, which is pretty rare these days. Just putting that out there."

"Thanks, Ginger." She pointed at her laptop. "I'll have this done in about half an hour."

"Cool." She stepped aside to let a tattoo artist with a red Mohawk through the door. "Nice of you to show up, Lee. What the fuck? You had someone here half an hour ago, and I had to make excuses for you."

"You didn't make excuses, you gave them my cell phone number."

"Because I'm not your damn mother, you little shit!"

Tayla put her headphones on and let the sounds of Halsey take her away.

———

CARY OPENED HIS LAPTOP AND SPREAD A MAP OUT ON Jeremy's gaming table. The shop had just closed, and they were taking advantage of the quiet.

"I don't know, man. I've never been up to this spot, but there are two or three well-mapped routes." Cary tapped his fingers on the map. "We'd probably both need to bring a few extra anchors, but if we got another couple of people, I think it'd be challenging but doable. And the views of Grand Sentinel are supposed to be amazing."

Jeremy nodded. "Morning climb?"

"From what other people have posted, you want to start early so you reach the crux before it gets hot. And if you make good time, there's a second, shorter climb just across the ridge."

"That sounds cool, but if we start too early, the visibility is going to suck. The cliff is west-facing. It'll be completely shaded."

"The trail starts here." Cary pointed to the map. "And it's a couple of miles to hike in. Not bad. We could start early or we could camp the night before and start in the morning."

"I like the camping idea. You have any other climbers in mind?"

"Couple I met earlier this year. Husband and wife about our level. No hotheads." Cary rolled up the map. "I'm too damn old for hotheads."

Jeremy's phone buzzed in his pocket. He took it out and read Tayla's message.

"You're sure smiling a lot these days." Cary closed his laptop. "I take it that means good things are happening with your girl."

"We've only been out the one time. Met for drinks the other night with a bunch of people at the Ice House. She told me to reserve Friday night for her."

And Jeremy was excited. More than excited. He was having trouble keeping a stupid grin off his face anytime he thought about it. The girl who didn't date, the girl who always played it cool... was planning a date for him.

Cary nodded. "Good deal. You talk to her much on the phone or anything? How's the conversation? Does she talk to you without arguing?" Cary looked off into the distance. "That would be so nice."

"You're showing your age." Jeremy dodged to avoid Cary's punch hitting his shoulder. "Texting, man. The girls love texting."

Funny texting. Dirty texting. By the time Jeremy finally got his hands on Tayla, she was going to be in for a very long night.

"Bullshit. Women like to talk." Cary slid his laptop into a messenger bag. "Who wants to communicate in little pictures?"

Tayla. Tayla fucking loved to text, and Jeremy wasn't complaining.

"Listen, old man, I'll start taking your romantic advice when you aren't spending every night alone at your mom's house. How's Melissa, by the way?"

The corner of Cary's mouth turned up. "Pissed off at me because I'm not taking her calls right now."

"Why aren't you taking her calls?"

"'Cause I need a break from frustration." Cary growled, pushing his silver-black hair from his eyes. "That woman drives me insane. She doesn't have enough to do; she wants to micromanage my orchards too. And she wants to share a booth at the farmers' market this summer which... I don't even know where to start with that one."

"That sounds like something I don't need to know about."

"Hell, I don't want to know about it." Cary walked to the door. "And you can give me shit about living with my mom, but just remember, if your mom cooked like my mom, you'd be living at home too."

"Pop is hanging out with his buddies, so it's frozen pizza for me tonight. In short, you may have a point."

"Man, don't eat frozen pizza. That's just sad." Cary paused at the door, fiddling with his messenger bag. "So let's start putting it together. Say... next month? What weekend works for you?"

"Let me check with my mom, 'cause I know we've got a family thing next month. I'll text you."

"Cool. I'm doing a surf weekend with some friends on the twentieth. Any other date I can do."

"Got it." Jeremy walked over to open the door. "See ya."

"Later."

Jeremy locked up and thought about going home, but his pop was at the senior center for bingo, so Jeremy knew he was on his own for dinner. Cary was right. Frozen pizza was just sad. Then he glanced at Tayla's text.

I hope ur ready to be wowed this weekend.

She'd inserted the wow-face emoji along with the martini glass, the dancing couple, and an inexplicable dinosaur.

We're going dancing at Jurassic Park?

You have amazing powers of perception. So what do you think? Heels or flats?

You can only wear heels when you dance with dinosaurs. I saw that in a movie once.

She sent back a laughing face emoji.

Jeremy hesitated, then went with it. He tapped her picture and called. Tayla picked up after two rings.

"So forward, Mr. Allen. You just call a girl with no warning?"

"Only you." He glanced at the clock. "Have you eaten?"

"No, I just finished work." Her muffled voice spoke to someone in the background. "Sorry, Emmie and Ox are going out. I'm tired, honestly. Kind of a long day. I'll probably just grab—"

"Let's walk to Tacos Marcianos." Jeremy winced. She was going to say no. "It's just a few blocks and I'm starving. Have you been?"

"Wait... what?" She cleared her throat. "I'm not really dressed to go out. I just kicked off my shoes and—other than for dinosaurs —I'm not sure I have it in me to put heels back on. Much less go for a walk. My feet are killing me."

"Borrow Emmie's bike then. I'll meet you at the shop and we can ride over. The tacos really are great."

"I mean... I hear people talking about it, but—"

"Come on. It doesn't matter what you're wearing. I don't care."

"All men say that and none of them realize what they're saying."

"Tayla, you could make jeans and a ratty T-shirt look amazing. Have dinner with me. Be spontaneous. You can't leave Metlin without going to Tacos Marcianos."

Tayla huffed out a breath. "Fifteen minutes."

"I'll put on a clean shirt, but I'm warning you, I'm not fancy either."

"Whatever. Men actually *can* look good in jeans and a ratty T-shirt. I refuse. Give me fifteen minutes and I'll meet you in the front of the shop."

"Done." Jeremy grinned. "See you in a few."

CHAPTER NINE

SHE MET him on the corner of 7th and Main, wearing a pair of flowered Bermuda shorts, a comfortable and breezy orange top, and a bright blue hoodie. Pink canvas flats rounded out the look.

"Look at you." Jeremy braked on the street. "You're like a really cute ice-cream cone."

Tayla checked him out. He was wearing—as promised—a pair of nicely worn jeans, a Captain America T-shirt, and black Chuck Taylors.

She walked to the curb, eye to eye with him. "Hey."

"Hey yourself." He hooked a finger through her belt loop and tugged. "And by ice-cream cone, I mean you look edible."

"I know what you mean." She allowed herself to be pulled and met his lips in a playful kiss. "You look nice too. Long day?"

"Not too bad. You?"

She put her wallet and phone in Emmie's basket and hopped on the bike. "Long. Very long. And then my mother called, and that always becomes a thing."

"Oh yeah?"

She had to smile. He was being so very casual even though she knew he was dying to ask. Jeremy had one of those families that reminded Tayla of the Waltons. Or the Bradys. Only not blended. He spoke of his parents lovingly. His sisters were actually his friends.

So weird.

"Yes, it becomes a thing because she wants to talk for an hour because she's miserable and has no friends. You know where we're going, right?"

They cruised east on Main. The sun was setting behind them, and the lampposts started to flicker on in the late-afternoon shadows. They rode past the familiar storefronts and into a more industrial section of Metlin Tayla hadn't explored.

"Yep. Just follow me." Jeremy frowned. "Why doesn't your mom have any friends?"

"Because she's a miserable person who needs to make everyone else miserable so she doesn't feel bad about her life." Tayla stopped at 9th Avenue and waited for the traffic light. "And she's a functional alcoholic and has been for years. That doesn't help."

Jeremy pulled up beside her. "That's sad."

"Yeah. It is. But her problems aren't mine and I have to set boundaries." She started peddling when the light turned green. "According to my therapist."

"Well then, you should do what the doctor ordered. It still makes me sad that you have to."

"I stopped being sad a long time ago. So tell me about this legendary taco place. I think Emmie avoids it."

"No idea why. Maybe she hasn't been recently. Turn left up here." Jeremy peddled forward and looked both ways before he turned left on 10th. "So the Marciano family are the owners. And when I was growing up, it was just a regular taco place, you know? Family restaurant. Kind of a hole-in-the-wall. Grandma and son cooking." He turned right and Tayla followed him. "And then Raquel came back from college and took over. And Raquel? She has a sense of humor."

Tayla spotted it from a block away. It was unmissable.

"It's amazing!" She couldn't keep the laugh inside. "How have I missed this?"

The exterior was a cinder block building typical of midcentury diners and drive-ins. The flat roof extended over a shaded area with metal-and-fiberglass picnic tables and a wide bar in front of a walk-up window. That's where the typical stopped.

The entire place had been painted in purple and green. A cartoon mural featuring a mariachi band of little green men decorated the side of the restaurant facing the parking lot.

"There's not much more than warehouses this far past 7th, so unless you know it's here, it's easy to miss."

"Marcianos!" Tayla said. "Martian tacos. Holy shit, that's awesome."

"It's a Metlin treasure." Jeremy grinned. "Wait until you go inside."

"Is that a crashed flying saucer on the other side?" She craned her neck. "This is the best."

The place might have been in the middle of warehouses and auto shops, but it was obviously popular. Teenagers filled the picnic tables, and little kids ran around the grassy area by the flying saucer. Men and women speaking a mixture of Spanish and English glanced at them as they parked their bikes. Most were holding white paper boxes or bags.

"So the portions are big?" Tayla noticed the take-out containers.

"Depends on what you get. Some people just order extra to take home. I always get tacos, which are small. That way you can try a bunch of her weirder recipes."

"I am genuinely excited about this." Tayla took Jeremy's hand when he reached for it. "I have to come back for lunch and take pictures."

"Raquel would probably love that. She does all that kind of online stuff."

They walked in the restaurant, and it didn't disappoint. The interior was a brilliant play on traditional Mexican art—the Aztec warrior, the Mexican caballero, the folkloric dancer in colorful dress—only all the faces had been replaced by little green men. Funky-colored booths, colorful traditional tiles, and vintage lights rounded out the feel of a really cool and modern twist on a traditional restaurant.

"This is amazing. Who painted those pictures? She could sell posters. And T-shirts."

"I have no idea. I think her parents probably thought she was insane when she started, but it's so great, right? And her menu is even better."

They walked up to the counter and stood behind two other couples, giving Tayla time to look at the menu.

Lots of meat options, but lots of vegan too.

Fried squash tacos with *cotija* and red sauce. Avocado, fresh corn, and roasted poblano. Brisket with mushrooms. Along with some traditional. Carne asada, chicken mole, and tacos *al pastor*.

"What should I get?" Tayla asked.

"Honestly, anything. I've never had a bad meal here. Tacos are little. Taco-truck size. It's my treat, since I was the pushy one. You can get next time."

"Fair enough." Tayla ordered four tacos and an *agua fresca* with watermelon and mint. She and Jeremy grabbed a table in the corner, and she reached for her phone only to come up empty. "Oh shit!"

"What?"

"My phone and wallet! I was so distracted I left them in the bike basket." She stood and nearly tripped over her feet. "Shit."

"Relax." Jeremy slid out of the booth. "Calm down. I'm sure they're still there. Hold the table and I'll go look."

She bit her lip until he walked back into the restaurant, holding her wallet and phone.

"See? No problem."

"I can't believe they were still there."

He gave her a rueful smile. "This is Metlin, Tayla. Not San Francisco."

"Crime happens everywhere."

"True." He slid across from her. "But it happens less in Metlin."

She didn't have a comeback because there wasn't one. Jeremy was probably right; crime was lower in Metlin. So were cultural attractions, plays, concerts, and job opportunities.

Tayla couldn't fault the tacos though. "These are amazing." She took a second bite of the avocado, corn, and poblano taco. "I can't believe I'm eating tacos on a date."

"Too messy?"

"So messy." She wiped a smear of salsa from her chin. "You're hard to say no to, Jeremy Allen."

"Good." He smiled a little. "Keep that attitude and we'll be just fine."

There is no we.

She should have said it—it wasn't good for him to get his hopes up—but she didn't. She finished her first taco and ignored the little tug of doubt in her heart that threatened her equilibrium. "This is a great place. Thanks for suggesting it."

"No problem. Cary made me feel guilty about eating frozen pizza. I decided to drag you along." He was eating vegetarian for the night. "We're planning a new climb next month, and I'm still feeling a little slow from the winter, so I should definitely be eating better."

"You don't climb at all during the winter?"

He shook his head. "Not really. Indoor stuff. We did one trip down to the desert last year, but I can't travel too much with the shop, and my favorite spots are up in the mountains here."

"You love the mountains."

His smile turned dreamy. "I feel... centered there. I can

breathe. When Cary and I are climbing, all I'm thinking about is the next hold. The rest of the world kind of falls away."

"All joking aside, you guys are safe, right? I watched that movie with the free solo guy—"

"Amazing film." He took a drink of his soda. "Not at all like what we do. I'm too much of a chicken to free solo. And my mother would kill me if she ever found out I did that."

"The regular climbing doesn't bother her?"

"She doesn't love it, but she knows how much I do." He wiped his mouth. "And she knows I don't climb alone and I'm really careful." He put his elbows on the table and leaned toward her. "What's the most dangerous thing you've ever done?"

"Date in San Francisco."

He chuckled.

"I'm only kind of joking." She smiled. "Uh... I don't get off on adrenaline, so it's kind of limited. I ate blowfish in New York once?"

"The poison fish?" His eyes went wide.

"Do I look dead?" Tayla laughed. "I mean, yes, it's poisonous if it's not cooked right. You have it at a special restaurant where the chef knows how to prepare it. Then it's safe."

"Unless the chef is having a bad day. Then you *die*."

"You have to think positive."

"Was it worth it?"

Tayla wrinkled her nose. "Honestly? No. I don't recommend. I didn't think it tasted good at all. It's just the thrill. I went with a guy I was dating who thought trying weird foods would impress me."

"In New York?"

"I moved there for a year once. Just wanted to try it out. But I didn't like it as much as San Francisco, so I moved back."

"Hmm." He leaned away from the table. "So did it? Impress you, I mean. Should I start looking for scorpions or snails or something?"

"Please don't." Tayla started to laugh. "That was all about him, not me. He had a very boring job and ended up doing all sorts of weird stuff to prove how manly he was. Not a good look."

"Ah, I get it. You get some of those guys at the climbing gym sometimes."

"Yeah? Do they have *tactical* gym bags?"

Jeremy laughed. "Yeah. And beefed-up trucks. They don't usually make it very far. Climbing's not really a show-off sport." He stretched his arms across the back of the booth. "Or it isn't around here. I don't know. I tend to stick with my friends, and none of them are assholes."

Tayla watched the lean muscles flex in his arms and chest. The easy comfort with his own strength and his self-confidence.

What was it about him that was so damn attractive? He was handsome, but he wasn't the *most* handsome guy she'd ever dated. He wasn't the most successful. He was into her, but he wasn't fawning.

Jeremy said, "Those kinds of guys are the ones that usually beat me up in high school, so I tend to avoid them. They always seem like they have shit to prove, you know? And that's not me."

There it was. That was it. He had nothing to prove. Jeremy Allen was a man who knew exactly who he was and what he wanted. He didn't need to show off, because he knew his worth.

A slow smile grew on his face. "You enjoying the view?"

"Yep." She pushed her empty plate to the side and leaned her elbows on the table, staring at him. "It's very scenic."

He made his pectoral muscles jump. One side, then the other. "Better?"

Tayla nearly had to grab her napkin to cover her snort. "You didn't just do that." She laughed into her napkin.

Jeremy started laughing too, his deep chuckle filling the booth. "You were the one staring."

"You are... impossibly cute." She curled her finger at him to come closer, and he did. Slowly she ran her fingers along his jaw until he leaned far enough forward that his lips touched hers. She kissed him, enjoying his lips like dessert.

Jeremy Allen was very fun to kiss. If she wasn't careful, she could get addicted.

He licked the edge of her mouth before he sat back. "Spicy."

"Me? I'm sweet as sugar."

"You're sweet and spicy." His smile reappeared. "I bet you're even a little sour sometimes."

"Maybe." She sipped her drink. "Do you like sour candy?"

"It's my favorite. Makes my mouth water." He licked his lips.

"Oooh." She narrowed her eyes. "You know exactly what you're doing, don't you?"

His smile slipped just a little. "Most of the time. With you, Tayla, I'm never sure."

"I'm going up to interview at SOKA next week." She didn't know why she blurted it out. "They asked me to come up and meet their team."

Jeremy nodded. "Cool. That's exciting." His warm brown eyes didn't waver from her face. "You'll kill it. I'm sure of it."

Tayla couldn't speak. Her heart was racing. Why was she nervous? What was it about this man that made her break her own rules? She was out with him on a night she'd planned to stay home, riding a bicycle, for God's sake, eating messy food and kissing him in the middle of a restaurant.

"Come on." Jeremy rose and held out a hand. "I love hanging out with you, but I can't lie—I'm beat and Pop's going to be home soon. He'll start calling me if I stay out too late."

"Is it totally weird living with your grandpa?"

"Uh… Yeah. Sometimes. But he's a pretty good roommate and a decent cook. Plus if I didn't live with him, he'd have to move up to the mountains with my parents and leave his house and all his buddies. My sisters are both married, so my living with him is the best solution."

She couldn't make a joke about that. Not even a little bit. "You're a good guy."

"I'm lucky." He twisted their hands until they were knit together, palm to palm. "I have a really great family. You gotta take care of that."

Tayla and Jeremy unlocked and hopped on their bikes, waving at the people outside who lifted a hand to wave goodbye.

Farewell, unknown people. I don't know who you are, but you seem friendly. Everyone smiled in Metlin. It had creeped Tayla out when she first moved here, but she was starting to get used to it.

People smiled in San Francisco too. Maybe not as much, but they smiled.

Kind of.

They rode back to Main and turned right, going against traffic as they biked single file. Tayla stayed behind Jeremy. Not only did he know the town better, but if she stayed behind him, she got to enjoy the view of his tight little butt.

It was an excellent view.

The streetlamps were on and the sun was down when they got back to the bookstore. Jeremy leaned across his bike and gave her a quick kiss. "I can already feel my phone buzzing. Apparently it's past my curfew." He grinned. "See you on Friday."

"See you!" Tayla was smiling as she waved.

You have become one of the waving people. What is wrong with you?

She sighed when she locked Emmie's bike on the street and unlocked the door to INK. It was late and she wanted to sleep. Too bad all she could think about was Jeremy Allen.

TAYLA SPENT THURSDAY AFTERNOON DOUBLE-CHECKING her plans for Friday night. It was the first time she'd ever planned a date, and she was surprised how much fun it was. Everything was set and would be amazing. She was positive.

Friday morning was spent scouring the SOKA website. She'd set an interview date with them for the following Thursday. She could take the train up Wednesday night, stay at her parents' house on the edge of Russian Hill, and grab a car the next day before her interview. After that, she'd try to crash at Tobin's apartment for the rest of the weekend. Since she had an interview at SOKA, maybe Tobin would be curious enough to put her up.

She had a key to her parents' house and access to her room there, but Tayla avoided the Mansion of Guilt whenever possible. If Emmie was still living in the city, she would stay with her, but Emmie was in Metlin of course.

Tayla scanned the household accessories section and found a few items. A small footstool made in Northern Thailand and some baskets from Peru. Very few choices.

She browsed through some of the new dresses from a Nigerian dressmaker she'd ordered from before and seriously considered grabbing a handbag from a designer in Yunnan Province in China.

All the merchandise on the SOKA site was made either by individuals or small fair trade businesses. Unlike other sites, everything was curated and leaned toward the higher end of the market. You weren't going to find a thirty-dollar pashmina, but if you wanted to spend real money for the handwoven Kashmir original, you could find the genuine article at SOKA.

You could also find bargains if you happened to find a new designer who was trying to promote their shop, but those items were rare. Usually, by the time SOKA picked up a shop or artist, they already had a decent market. SOKA was closer to a really great online international department store. They carried menswear, women's clothing, of course, and a decent selection of kids' stuff—if you wanted to spend hundreds of dollars on a handmade baby wrap, that is—but they were lacking in housewares and accessories.

Interesting. That was definitely an area they could expand.

It made Tayla even more excited about the interview. Working for a company like SOKA would be a dream come true. It would be a challenge to find new products and the right promoters for them. It would also be amazing to work for a company with such clearly stated social goals.

She'd have health insurance. She'd have a retirement fund. She'd have workmates.

She'd also have a boss. Tayla wasn't too sure how she felt about that part, but bosses didn't have to be jerks. It just so happened her last two had been. That wasn't a rule though. Maybe she'd just had bad luck.

There was a link to a *Chronicle* article in the media section, talking about the founders of SOKA, Azim Asani and Kabisa Nandi, a husband-and-wife team from Kenya who had taken the idea of a tech start-up into the fashion world, seeding money from their own successful womens wear line to smaller companies who then gave them exclusive rights to sell their products. Their business had only expanded from there.

It was an innovative approach to world fashion that created a lively site with positive user interaction, inclusive fashion, and ethical manufacturers.

SOKA was ready to take off, and Tayla could be a part of it. She could make her mark on something meaningful and big, along with something she was passionate about.

All she had to do was leave a town she'd started to love.

CHAPTER TEN

JEREMY STOOD in front of the mirror and straightened the knot on his bow tie. He might have gone for casual on his date with Tayla, but with her date—even though she hadn't clued him in— he erred on the side of formal.

He'd inherited one of his grandfather's suits from the 1960s and had it tailored to fit him—he was a bit slimmer than Pop when he was in his prime. He didn't think a full suit was the right look, but he'd taken the blue-and-green tweed vest and teamed it with a tailored shirt, slacks, and a green bow tie. The look was sharp but also a little playful. He thought Tayla would appreciate it.

While he dressed casually day to day, Jeremy had inherited a love of dressing up from his grandfather. Jeremy still remembered his grandparents putting on their best and going out dancing when he was little. His grandfather's suits and his grandmother's fancy dresses had made an impression. He liked feeling fancy, and he loved that Tayla did too.

"Pop!"

His grandfather's voice boomed up to the second floor. "What?"

"You remember I'm going out with Tayla tonight, right?"

"And I'm having dinner with the queen. What are you bragging about?"

Jeremy couldn't stop the smile. "I just wanted to remind you." He sprayed on a few shots of cologne, patted his beard with a little oil, and combed through it before he looked at his face from the right. From the left.

Ready.

He looked good, and so would she.

Jeremy walked through the kitchen on his way out the door, pausing for his pop to give him the once-over. A raised eyebrow and a long nod was all Gus had to say, but that was enough.

"You show that young lady a nice time," he said. "See you tomorrow."

"See you."

He walked down Ash and around the corner to Main. Tayla had told him to meet her in front of the bookshop, and he was there in the space of a few minutes. He pushed the door open and smiled when he saw Emmie.

"Hey, girl. How you doing?"

Emmie grinned when she saw him. "You look perfect."

"I take it you know what we're doing?"

"I have been sworn to secrecy, so don't even try."

Jeremy looked over at Ox. "You?"

The man was looking through equipment catalogues or something and barely registered Jeremy being in the room. "Huh?" He looked up. "Oh hey. Looking sharp, man."

"He has no idea what you're doing." Emmie clapped her hands. "But I do! Tayla will be down a minute."

He heard her steps moments later. She had to be wearing heels. That was the only thing that made a sound like that. When she walked through the door, his heart nearly stopped.

She leaned against the doorjamb and appraised him. "Heya, handsome."

"You're gonna kill this man before he reaches thirty." Jeremy put a hand over his heart. "You look sexy as hell."

She was wearing some kind of tight blue dress that hugged her curves and made her eyes even bluer. It looked like it wrapped around her body and tied at the waist, but there were drapes and hems and a pair of chunky heels with a strap. Jeremy didn't understand women's fashion, he just appreciated it when it was done right.

And Tayla was doing it so very right.

He wanted to get her alone and unwrap her down to her skin. If he was a betting man, he'd bet on garters and lacy something or other holding everything in place.

He whistled. "Damn."

She stepped into the shop, and Jeremy walked slowly around her. They looked each other up and down.

"Doesn't he look perfect?" Emmie couldn't contain her excitement.

"Don't *you* look perfect?" Jeremy muttered.

"You look pretty good yourself, Mr. Allen. Love the tie."

"You look like the femme fatale in a film noir. But hotter, 'cause you're in color."

The cool fell away and her eyes lit up. "That's exactly what I was going for. We're going to have so much fun."

"And no joke, I bet you can dance in those heels, can't you?"

She turned and cocked her hip at him. "You bet I can. And they make my legs look great."

They make your ass look even better.

Jeremy cocked his elbow out. "Miss McKinnon, shall we?"

She sauntered over—it was a definite saunter—and took his arm, clutching her bag in her other hand. "We shall."

Just as they walked toward the door, a black Cadillac from the 1950s pulled up to the curb and a gawky teenager got out. "Hey, Tayla!"

Jeremy started laughing. "What is this?"

"I couldn't find a Caddy from the forties, so 1957 will have to do."

He took a step back. "Are you for real?"

The young man walked around and opened the door, holding it as they climbed inside. He was red-faced and still bore signs of acne, but he'd made an effort to dress up. "Hey. I'm Jeff. I'm your personal driver for tonight. Please don't smoke in the car—my grandpa will kill me."

Tayla and Jeremy slid inside.

"I do the books for Jeff's grandpa's garage. He has this amaaaaazing collection of classic cars he shows, and he was sweet enough to let me borrow this one if I paid Jeff to drive."

"I'm trying to earn money for my class trip this year," Jeff said as he started the Caddy. "And I help my grandpa when he shows the cars, so he trusts me to drive them."

"Better you than me." Jeremy would be paranoid about scratching an automobile this pristine. He should take a picture of it for Pop. He turned to Tayla. "I'm gonna need a picture of you in this dress, leaning up against this car. That's nonnegotiable."

"Only if you send a copy to me."

"Done." He stretched his arm across her shoulders and felt a frisson of heat when their skin touched. "I am really struggling to imagine what in Metlin we're going to do that warrants this kind of car, but I'm just going with it."

"Good." She snuggled into his side. "Fasten your seat belt, Mr. Allen, it's going to be a bumpy date."

NOT EVERYONE COULD LOOK SEXY IN A BOW TIE, BUT Jeremy Allen could. The man looked as delicious in formal wear as he did in hiking clothes.

There ought to be a law...

Just kidding. Tayla loved that he'd taken the time to look so good. She was excited. Everything was going perfectly.

"So do I find out what we're doing yet?"

She shook her head. "It's a surprise."

They pulled up to the warehouse-like building on the south end of 7th Avenue only a few minutes later. The old industrial area was a mix of garages and body shops, interspersed with gyms, a few coffee shops, and a few new antique and secondhand stores. As Main Street had grown more expensive, some businesses had moved to more affordable areas like this one.

Including one of Tayla's newest accounts.

Jeremy read the newly painted sign hanging in the front. "No way." He turned to her with a grin on his face. "I heard about this!"

Plan Your Escape was a travel agency that had made a severe U-turn when the internet was born. The couple who ran it, the Baylors, had struggled for years after the internet travel boom, until one of their kids was inspired by the name of the travel agency and a YouTube addiction.

Jeremy couldn't wait for their driver to let him out. He opened the door and held his hand out for Tayla. "Metlin's first escape room. I can't believe it's open."

"Well, it's not. Technically." She took his hand and stepped out of the car. "They're planning three rooms, and only one of them is finished. Luckily..." She did a little curtsy. "Yours truly is the Baylors' new bookkeeper. Frannie recommended me to them because Mrs. Baylor is her goddaughter or something."

A friendly middle-aged woman opened the door. "Hey, Tayla! Right on time. We're ready when you are. Just the two of you?"

"Yep."

She pursed her lips. "The rooms are set up to have at least four people solving the puzzles, but yours should be okay. You won't *need* four people. I'll just give you a little more time on the clock. That fair?"

Jeremy said, "Sounds good to me." He turned to Tayla. "You have no idea how excited I am. Have you done one of these before? I've seen them online, but I haven't actually done one."

"Only once. And our group didn't make it out in time. Too much fighting combined with margaritas." She winked at him. "We'll do our drinking after the room."

Mrs. Baylor waved them in. "You two look perfect. Do you mind if I take some pictures before you leave?"

Jeremy looked at Tayla and shrugged. "Fine by me."

"Sure. Thanks for letting us in early."

Mrs. Baylor walked through a small reception area with benches and a counter. It was clearly where parties would wait their turn. There was a photo area with different backgrounds set up. One looked like a jungle. Another looked like a spaceship. And the last one...

"The only room that's ready to go is the detective room." Mrs. Baylor looked over her shoulder. "And you two look perfect. Tayla, you're just the cutest thing."

Jeremy put his arm around her waist. "Agreed."

She turned left and led them down a corridor that moved from industrial grey to wood paneling. At the end of the hallway was a frosted-glass door with the words FRANK CARTWRIGHT, PRIVATE DETECTIVE etched into the glass.

"Okay, I'm going to start the clock. You usually get twenty minutes, so I'll set it to forty since it's just the two of you." She gave them a little smile. "You get three hints, so press the intercom on the desk if you run into trouble. After the three hints are gone, you have to wait until the time runs out for the door to open or solve the puzzle on your own."

"Got it." Tayla felt a rush of excitement. She loved puzzles, and this promised to be a good one.

"You're the first people to actually try this other than my kids."

Jeremy said, "I'm really excited. Thanks so much for letting us preview."

"I don't think there will be any problems—there weren't when Austin and Devon did it with their friends—but I'll be on the other end of the intercom."

"Thanks, May." Tayla gripped Jeremy's hand. "You ready?"

He held up a finger. "Should we go to the bathroom first?"

"Oooh, good thinking. You go first."

"Thanks."

When Jeremy had walked down the hall, Mrs. Baylor cleared her throat.

"I should let you know—because you're on a date—that the rooms are video monitored. Just... to let you know."

Tayla let out a sharp laugh. "Thanks. We'll try not to shock anyone."

"Oh, I used to work in a library." She started down the hall toward reception. "I'm pretty much impossible to shock. Just open the door and close it when you're ready to start. The room sets when you close the door."

Tayla waited for Jeremy, then took her turn in the bathroom. When she walked back, he was leaning against the doorframe of the detective room, legs crossed casually at the ankles.

"Heya, doll."

She smiled. "I see you've gotten into the spirit of things."

His grin looked like a little kid's. "I am so ready for this. You?"

"Yep." She opened the door. "Let's do it."

The interior of the escape room looked exactly like a detective's dim office from the 1940s. A cluttered desk with a green glass lamp. Papers scattered over messy filing cabinets and a low sofa with cushions tossed around. The taped outline of a body was stuck to the industrial carpet between the desk and a coat closet.

"This is so cool." Jeremy shut the door, and the lights flickered.

A record player began a scratchy tune, and Billie Holiday's voice started singing "I'll Be Seeing You." Tayla walked over to the oversized desk and picked up a piece of paper.

"'Welcome to the office of the late detective Frank Cartwright.

Unfortunately, Frank met his end working on a case, and no one has been able to solve it or his murder. Find the clues, solve Frank's murder, and escape the room.'" Tayla looked up. "That's it."

"That's all we get to start?" Jeremy walked over. "What's all this?"

Tayla leaned over the desk and started spreading papers. "Files and... there's some photo— Hi!" Jeremy had walked behind her and grabbed her hips. "Hey. Hi there." She couldn't stop the smile.

"Hey." He bent over her back and ran his lips against her ear. "Before we get too busy with this mystery—"

"I should let you know there is video surveillance of these rooms." She felt a laugh start to work its way up.

"With a desk this big"—he snugged his hips against her ass —"and a dress like this, that's probably a good idea."

He fully covered her, bracing his arms on the desk and kissing the sensitive spot below her ear. Tayla's instinct was to press her ass back and into his hips, tease him like he was teasing her, but she didn't want an audience.

"I think we better..." She let out a breath. "Wow, you are really good at that."

Jeremy stood straight, gripped her waist, and spun her around. "Mm-hmm." With his hands still on her waist, he urged her up to sit on the edge of the desk, then he stepped between her legs.

"We really shouldn't—"

His kiss stopped her words. Jeremy played his tongue along the seam of her mouth until her lips opened and she tasted him. His strong hands gripped her hips, digging into the soft curves. Tayla was about to throw caution and all professional prospects with the Baylors out the window when Jeremy stepped back, licked his lips, and gave her a little smile.

"I couldn't pass up the chance. You in this dress. The music." He looked around. "The atmosphere..."

"Agreed." She was breathless when she hopped off the desk. "But we now only have thirty-five minutes to solve this case, Mr. Allen."

"Then we better get to work."

———

TAYLA'S STOMACH HURT FROM LAUGHING. "NO, YOU'RE the one who spent like five minutes telling me the tissue box was a clue!"

"I'm just saying..." He shook his head and took another sip of his manhattan. "The pattern on the box was deceptive. It definitely looked like it meant something. Besides, you're the one who insisted we had to look for a manual to tie a half-Windsor knot. You kept interrupting me. I had to just tie it and dangle it in front of your face."

"Not every man would know how to do that."

"Well, this one does."

She sipped her martini. "I think you let me look in the file cabinet longer than I needed to."

"You were bent over in that dress." He leaned to the side to sneak a peek at her backside. "The view was too good for me to spoil it."

She set her glass down. "We'll get it next time."

"It won't be as fun though because we know most of the puzzles. We only missed it by a few minutes."

"And if you hadn't kept trying to convince me to join you on the sofa, we would have solved it."

He shrugged. "I have no regrets."

The words hit her with unexpected force.

No regrets.

No regrets for the time they were spending together. No regrets for the kisses they shared. Or the laughter. Or the chemistry.

No regrets.

She swallowed hard and played with her dessert spoon. "Did you get enough to eat?"

Jeremy stretched back and spread his arms. It truly was an impressive sight. "Plenty. PJ's was the perfect end to the night."

They'd left the escape room laughing, having not solved the murder of Detective Frank Cartwright but having had a blast solving the myriad puzzles and codes the escape room presented.

Jeff, their teenage chauffeur, drove them to PJ's, a restaurant in the basement of the old courthouse on Main. It had an art deco theme and mixed great cocktails that it paired with small plates. Marinated short ribs with mushrooms, gourmet mac and cheese, wedge salads with green goddess dressing. The whole restaurant had a vintage feel with a beautifully restored bar.

They sipped cocktails, ate delicious food, and shared stories. Jeremy told her tales about living in LA for college, fresh from a small town, and Tayla horrified him with the worst of her prep school antics.

"The only positive aspect I can see for going to a Catholic prep school is the uniforms on the girls," he said. "My teenage self would have had more than a few dreams about that."

"But not your adult self, right?"

Jeremy nearly spit out his drink. He swallowed while shaking his head. "So over it. Very, very over it." He narrowed his eyes. "Are there guys…?"

"Oh yeah. When I was living in San Francisco, if I told guys I'd gone to Saint Francis Prep, so many of them asked if I still had my uniform." She shook her head. "As if. So weird."

"I have many thoughts." Jeremy finished his cocktail. "That I'll vent when I'm out with my buddies and not on a date." He tried to protest when the server came by and Tayla grabbed the leather envelope with the check. "Are you sure?"

"Don't even try." She opened her wallet. "This date was mine to plan."

"Yeah, and it was a lot fancier than mine."

She shrugged. "But not as labor intensive. Seriously, this one is on me."

He reached across the table, took Tayla's hand, and kissed her knuckles one by one. "Thank you for dinner."

Mmmmm. If paying for dinner got her that response more often, she'd be more inclined to offer. Jeremy had been the epitome of a gentleman all night—save for his slipup on the desk at the escape room. She wanted to get him alone and see if he'd slip up more.

"Are you ready?" She left cash for the server. "Should we have our driver take us back to my place?"

He nodded, his eyes lighting up. "That sounds like a great idea."

CHAPTER ELEVEN

THEY DROVE BACK to Tayla and Emmie's apartment, and it was everything Jeremy could to do keep his hands to himself.

Teenage boy watching through rearview mirror. Must. Not. Grope. Tayla.

He held her hand and played with the smooth curves of her fingernails as they drove the few blocks back to her place. Tayla slid her ankle along his when she crossed her legs.

Keep. Hands. To. Yourself.

Jeff stopped at the curb and quickly exited the driver's door to let them out. Jeremy got out first, then waited for Tayla to exit, extending a hand to help her out of the low sedan.

"Jeff, thank you so much! I already paid your grandpa, but I want to—"

"Let me." Jeremy stopped her before she reached into her purse. "Let me get it."

She paused a second before she nodded.

Jeremy handed the young man a very generous tip. "Thanks, man. You're a great driver."

The boy's eyes bugged out before a grin lit up his face. "Thanks, man. Have a good night. Bye, Tayla!"

"Bye, Jeff. Tell your grandpa I said hi."

"I will."

The Cadillac sped off into the night, leaving Tayla and Jeremy on the sidewalk.

"That was a pretty nice tip," she said.

"I remember being that age." He put his hand on the small of her back. "Can I walk you upstairs?"

"I was just about to invite you in for a drink."

Jeremy hesitated. "Are Emmie and Ox—"

"Staying out at the ranch this weekend. It's his mom's birthday."

"Nice." Privacy. It was a novel concept for Jeremy these days. "Then I would love a drink. Thank you."

She unlocked the front door, and they made their way through the darkened bookshop, up the stairs that led to Tayla's apartment.

Jeremy had been in their apartment before. He'd spent time there starting back in high school when he and Emmie had hung out. Since Emmie had moved back, he'd come over for movie nights and dinners.

But he'd never been up there alone with Tayla. "I feel like a teenager sneaking around," he whispered. "This still feels like Betsy's house."

Tayla smiled "Emmie's grandma?"

"Yeah."

"Well." She opened the door, and the smell of feminine life surrounded him. It smelled of coffee, beauty products, and something fruity. "It's not Betsy's house anymore."

As soon as she closed the door, Jeremy swung Tayla around and pressed her against it. He gave in to the urge to kiss her. And then some. His lips took hers in a greedy kiss, and his hands ran from the curve of her shoulder, following the smooth line of her back, over the swell of her ass. He pressed and gripped, reveling in the soft, firm flesh. He took two full handfuls and squeezed.

Jeremy released her mouth and pressed his lips to the delicate, fragrant skin of her neck. He didn't know what perfume she wore and he didn't care.

"So I guess you're an ass man." Tayla's voice was breathless, and her hands steadied themselves on his shoulders, kneading the muscle.

He smiled against her skin. He left one hand on her ass and ran the other up her hip and side to cup her breast. "Nah, I like it all."

She shivered when he skimmed his thumb over her nipple. "Jeremy—"

His mouth returned to hers, swallowing her words.

She nudged him back. "My room."

"You sure?"

"Emmie and I have a firm no-fooling-around-in-common-spaces rule."

He shrugged and released her. "Fair."

Tayla took his hand and led him to her room. Jeremy couldn't keep his hands off her. Her skin was so smooth. She was delicious. Soft flesh and ample curves. He wanted to strip her to the skin and put his mouth on every inch of her.

When the door to her room was closed, it was Tayla's turn. She pushed him against the door and ran her hands down his chest. "You're all muscle."

"I was a skinny kid," he said. "And the opposite of athletic. Weight lifting was the only thing that kept me from getting picked on."

"It worked." She unbuttoned his shirt across his abdomen and slid her hand inside. "Mmm."

He smiled. "You like?"

Her mischievous smile returned. "Well, I don't know. I might have to explore more."

"I love the outdoors, so"—he let out a hard breath when her hand glanced over his erect cock—"I'm a fan of exploration."

"A big fan?"

"Fairly big."

Her clever fingers finished unbuttoning his shirt and spread it open only to find his undershirt. "You have way too many clothes." She began to pull his undershirt up.

"I can always— Ahhh." He sucked in a breath when her fingers played in the soft hair below his belly button. "I can always take the shirt off, but that does seem a little unfair since you're still dressed."

"I don't want the shirt off." She inched the undershirt up and pressed a kiss on his chest. "Ever since game night, I've had dreams about doing dirty things to you while you're wearing a bow tie."

He slapped a hand hard against the door when her teeth scraped over his nipple. "I'm fully in support of all your dreams. Fuck."

Her fingers went to his belt and she slowly slid them under his waistband.

"Tayla—"

"You said you felt like a teenager sneaking around." Tayla smiled when she unbuckled his belt. "Why don't we do sneaky teenager things?"

He looked down at her, her red fingernails scraping along his belly, scarlet lips curled into a wicked smile. Jeremy laughed. "I didn't have a good enough imagination to dream you up in high school."

He leaned down and took her mouth as she slipped her hands into his boxers and pushed them down his hips. Her warm hand enveloped his cock and squeezed.

Jeremy groaned. Tayla released his mouth and knelt down, kissing his belly once before she took his erection in her mouth.

Fuck. Yes. Please. Good. So good.

She hummed with his cock in her mouth, purring like she was enjoying the most delicious treat in the world, and all rational thought left his mind. All he could think was how good her mouth felt. He closed his eyes until he realized what he was doing.

You idiot. You could be watching Tayla give you a blow job.

He opened his eyes and watched her, hands holding his hips, her mouth around him.

Fuck me, that's the hottest thing I've ever seen.

He came embarrassingly fast. Well, he would have been embarrassed if he'd been able to think about anything. His entire body felt the release and he sagged against the door.

Tayla rose, running her hands along his thighs. "Mmmm. That was even better than I expected. And I have high expectations." She walked to the bedside table and wiped her mouth before she took a drink from a water bottle. "Water?" She held the bottle out to him.

"Later." Jeremy followed her, hitching his boxers up so he could walk. He bent over behind her, laving his tongue along her neck and cupping her breasts in both hands. "I have something to do before I get a water break."

Her hips arched back, pressing her ass into his groin. "Is that so?"

Jeremy squeezed her breasts, thumbing the erect nipples as he kissed behind her ear. "Does it turn you on?"

"You playing with my breasts?"

"No, giving me a blow job." He reached down and inched her dress up. "Does it turn you on?"

"Yes." Her heart was beating fast. He could feel it against his lips.

Jeremy continued teasing her dress up until he could feel skin. Skin and lace.

He groaned against her neck. "I have to see."

She turned around and sat on the edge of the bed. "So see."

Jeremy knelt down and spread her knees. "Fair is fair, Miss McKinnon."

"I love that your pants are hanging open and you're still wearing your bow tie."

"Yeah? I love..." He pulled her dress up to her waist and stared. "Fuck."

She was wearing black lace thigh-highs and even lacier panties. They were practically see-through. Her thighs were thick and smooth.

She propped herself up on the edge of the bed. "You love what?"

He blinked. "I forgot what I was going to say."

"That is exactly the right response."

Jeremy licked his lips. "Keep that water bottle close by. I'm going to need it after I get done with you."

———

TAYLA WOKE UP WITH A SMILE ON HER FACE. SHE AND Jeremy had spent a couple of hours reenacting "everything but" teenage antics before he'd gone home for the night.

It was perfect.

She'd been more than satisfied while still hanging on to the delicious anticipation growing between them. There was something to be said for sneaking around like teenagers.

Besides the sexual satisfaction, she was aglow with his sheer goodness. Jeremy was fun and funny. He told great stories and wanted to hear hers too. He was curious and imaginative.

Yes. She smiled. Plenty imaginative.

She reached for her phone and texted him. *Good morning.*

A few minutes later he responded. *Very good morning.*

Did you sleep well?

I'd have slept better if I'd been able to use your thighs for a pillow. He followed that with a strawberry and a "yum" emoji.

Tayla felt her face turn red at the memory. *Plenty of time for that.*

Dinner this week? He sent sushi emojis.

Did he want to go out for sushi, or was he just dirty texting now? It was impossible to tell. *I'm going to SF this week, remember? Interview.*

Right. When do you leave?

The reminder dulled her glow a little bit. *Wednesday.*

You're going to kill it.

Thx. She included a blowing-kiss emoji. *What are you doing today?*

In the shop. If it's slow, I'll do inventory and orders.

Sexaaaaay.

If I let myself think about last night, it will be. Might scare Jarrod tho.

Tayla laughed. Jarrod was one of the college kids who helped Jeremy out a few times a week. He had a rotating staff of college students who were passionate about comics and games, but none of them stuck around for very long.

The crack in her emotional armor was growing. She felt a soft ache that she knew would only get worse they longer they spent together.

Why do you have to be such a good guy? She sent the message before she could think twice.

Too much effort to be an asshole, he wrote back. *I'm kind of lazy.*

You're kind of perfect, Jeremy Allen. She didn't type it. It was bad enough that she was thinking it.

I better get some coffee.

See u later.

Tayla went to the bathroom and took a quick shower before she got dressed. Before she could make it out to the kitchen for coffee, she saw another message on her phone.

You didn't post any pictures last night. It was from Emmie. *So???*

She'd forgotten to post pics? She'd looked amazing last night. She definitely should have posted pics. How could she have forgotten? She'd have to post pics this morning.

Everything went great. Had an amazing time. We fooled around in the kitchen. I'll clean up before you get back.

You better be joking.

I am not.

You are.

Tayla started her morning coffee before she started her makeup. She tried to go light since she'd kept her face on for too long the night before. She was a firm believer in giving your skin at least eight hours every night for it to breathe, but some days that just didn't work out.

When she was finished with her makeup, she sat at the kitchen table and sorted through her schedule for the day.

A nine-thirty hair appointment and helping Emmie in the shop were the only things on her calendar. It was Saturday, after all. Most people didn't do bookkeeping on Saturdays or Sundays, which meant she was free to help Emmie on the busiest day at INK.

She scrolled through her pictures from last night. She only had five. FIVE? How had she slacked off so bad? She should have been promoting the clutch she'd worn and the dress designer and shop. The escape room could have used a shout-out too. Had Jeremy taken any? Maybe. She'd have to ask.

She was slacking. All she had was a selfie they'd taken in the escape room, holding old-fashioned magnifying glasses up to their faces, and a few more pics of Jeremy being sexy in his bow tie.

"Nothing by the car," she muttered. "Nothing in the restaurant."

What had she been thinking?

She hadn't been thinking about pictures or product placement or expanding her reach.

She'd been thinking about Jeremy Allen.

This was going to be a problem.

CHAPTER TWELVE

THE TRAIN from Metlin left at one thirty on Wednesday. Tayla had packed three carefully chosen interview outfits to match any unpredictable weather and a few casual outfits for a weekend in the city. She'd show up in Richmond during rush hour, but she could take BART into the city and get off at the Embarcadero to find a car to her parents' house.

If she was lucky, they'd both be at a social event and wouldn't return until after she'd already hidden in her room. If Mena, the housekeeper, was in a sympathetic mood, she'd help Tayla.

If she was unlucky, her mom would be sitting drunk and sad in the garden and guilt her into staying more than one night.

Either way, her dad would be out, so he wasn't an issue.

She stowed her bag in the overhead bin and grabbed a seat by the window before she put her headphones over her ears and closed her eyes. She'd chosen the east side of the train compartment so she didn't bake, but she wished she could close her eyes and lie in the sun. She wanted to soak in the heat of the valley before she reached the Bay Area.

This time of year, it was just as likely to be cold and foggy as warm and sunny. Forecasts meant nothing there, hence the three outfits.

She dozed intermittently as the train worked its way north. The rocking motion always lulled her to sleep. People sat next to her and left. The slow shuffle of humanity moved on and off as they wound closer to San Francisco. Families and singles. Elderly couples and college kids. She changed trains in Martinez, finally heading west.

She owned a car, but it was impossible to park it in the city. When she lived in San Francisco, she'd shamelessly used her parents' garage. They had room for three cars, after all, and she rarely used her car unless she wanted to take a weekend trip.

Since moving to Metlin, she used her small car more, but she still didn't like driving in the city. She'd rather take the train.

She carried her bag from the platform in Richmond and looked for the Millbrae train platform, joining the few commuters heading her direction. The crowd of people in the station made her smile. She'd missed the energy and the pace.

The train into the city was uneventful, and she stepped off at the Embarcadero just as the sun was setting. She walked across the street and caught a cab.

"Russian Hill," she said. "Francisco and Hyde."

The cab driver gave her a low whistle, but Tayla kept her sunglasses on and ignored him. She wrapped a sweater jacket around her shoulders and watched the flow of traffic out the window. The cabbie immediately turned right and started working his way through the financial district until he reached the Transamerica building and pointed the cab northwest on the familiar flow of Columbus Avenue, heading toward what was—for better or worse—her childhood home.

TAYLA TURNED HER KEY IN THE LOCK AND ENTERED HER personal security code, which let her parents, the security company, and the household staff know she was in residence. As expected, by the time she walked from the street entrance to the foyer, Mena was there to greet her.

Mena Wright was a pale Englishwoman who was a professional household manager in the classical sense. Mena ran her parents' home, had since Tayla was a child. She scheduled staff, arranged social events, appointments, meals, and everything else her parents might need. She was tall and rail thin with a regal bearing and impeccable grammar.

"Hey, Mena."

"Miss Tayla, we didn't realize you were coming for a visit."

"We" could mean the household staff—three were full time—or it could mean Mena and her mother, who were joined at the hip. Mena's voice was cool—not because she was unhappy to see Tayla, that was just her voice.

"I'm here for an interview. I won't be more than a few days. Are my parents home?"

"I believe your father is at the club tonight..."

A sinking feeling in her belly.

"...and your mother is in the upper garden." Mena's smile was tight. "Reading."

Drinking.

"Got it." Tayla started toward the stairs.

"Let me get Charles for your bag."

"Please, Mena." Tayla's shoulders slumped. "I've got it. You don't need to bother Charles."

"It's his job," Mena said quietly. "He'll be irritated if I don't call him."

"He's got to be seventy now."

"And it is still his job," Mena said. She got her phone out and sent a quick text message to Charles, who was the gardener, her parents' chauffeur when needed, and general handyman around the giant Victorian house. "He'll take your backpack and bag up to your room. Would you like a drink in the garden?"

Tayla wasn't going to get away with avoiding her mother, so she nodded and pulled her sweater more tightly around her body. "What's she drinking?"

"Red wine."

"I'll have the same."

Red wine was her mother's booze of choice. Bianca Reyes McKinnon had long claimed wine ran in her blood. And in a sense... it did. She'd been born in the Sonoma Valley to one of the oldest winemaking families in California. During Prohibition, her family had even fermented sacramental wine to sell to the Church in order to keep their vineyards.

An alluring mix of Spanish, Italian, and Hungarian blood, Bianca had been known as one of the leading beauties of San Francisco society when she was growing up, and she'd quickly caught the eye of Aaron McKinnon, a newly arrived financial genius who'd grown up in Philadelphia and attended school at Stanford.

Her parents met, married, and partied through the 1980s until Tayla's birth brought their high-flying lifestyle to an abrupt crash landing.

Bianca had never been suited for motherhood, despite her traditional Catholic upbringing. And Aaron? Aaron worked. They did their social duties, sent their daughter to the right schools, and went through the motions even though it was obvious both of them were miserable.

Tayla walked up the stairs to the third floor where a terraced garden had been carved into the hill where the house was built. Overlooking the deep blue of San Francisco Bay, the yard was Charles's masterpiece, though her mother liked to putter around and pretend to tend it when the weather was nice.

Tayla saw her mother sitting on the far end of the patio, a glass of wine in her hand, wrapped in a thick Pendleton blanket, watching the lights blink on the bay. Tayla ignored the buffet of wind and walked across the gravel. Her mother turned when she was only a few feet away, and her eyes widened in surprise.

"Tayla!" The smile came quickly, as did the shadow at the back of her eyes. "I didn't know you were in the city. When did you get here?"

"Just now." She bent down and gave her mother an awkward hug. "How are you?"

"Fine." She waved her wineglass in the direction of the Golden Gate Bridge. "Beautiful night. Just watching the sunset. Enjoying a cab from 2005. Excellent year for deep reds in the valley. Daddy got some top-ranked wines that year. He won an award or two, I think..." Her words were only a little slurred. It was early. "Sit, baby. I like your hair. It's not purple or anything."

"I know. I'm trying something more conventional." Her mother's approval made her want to dye it fluorescent green just for spite. Tayla closed her eyes and forced the contrary urge back. "I like yours. Did Charity add highlights?"

"Just a few." Bianca patted her dark brown hair. Tayla's coloring came from her mother. Bianca's vivid blue eyes were famous. "Our hair is almost the same now."

"Close." Tayla glanced at her mother's glass and the bottle, which was almost empty.

"Where's Mena?" Bianca craned her neck and almost fell off the bench. "Why isn't she bringing you a glass? And this bottle is almost gone, but she'll bring me another."

"I'm sure she's on her way." Because Mena was all knowing and accommodated every whim her mother had, including drinking massive amounts of wine and vodka.

It was hard to fault the woman. It was Mena's job to work for her mother. If Bianca ordered another bottle of wine, Mena opened a bottle, even if Bianca was roaring drunk.

Mena came moments later with a fresh glass and a new bottle of red. She poured Tayla a glass and set the bottle on the garden table.

"Is there anything else you need, Mrs. McKinnon?"

"That's all, Mena. Thank you."

"I'm going to retire for the evening." Mena shot Tayla a glance that said *your turn*.

"Fine." Bianca waved a careless hand. "I'll see you in the morning."

Mena turned to Tayla. "Do you need me to arrange anything for your appointment in the morning? Gloria or I could press any clothing you might need. Will you need Charles to drive you?"

"I'll be fine, Mena. Thanks. I don't need anything."

"Very well." Mena left without a backward glance.

"What's she talking about?" Bianca poured herself another glass, nearly spilling the wine. "You have an appointment? For what? Are you *finally* moving back?"

Her mother's voice was the familiar odd mix of hopeful and reluctant. Bianca wanted to be happy Tayla was living closer, but in a way, Tayla living at a distance was a buffer.

Your daughter avoiding you was easy to explain when she lived a couple hundred miles away. It was a lot harder to dismiss when she was in the same city.

"I'm not sure of anything yet," Tayla said. "It's just an interview."

"What's the company? Another accounting firm?" Bianca's eyes went wide. "If you take another job at a rival company—"

"It's not a rival to Dad," Tayla quickly volunteered. "It's not even in the same vein of what I've been doing. It's a fashion thing."

"Fashion?" Bianca's smile was sincere and unshadowed. "Tayla, that's wonderful. Is it with one of those companies for... um, average-sized girls?"

Tayla tried not to cringe. She reminded herself that this was actually an improvement for Bianca. Tayla was built like the women on her father's side—sturdy, stocky women of Irish descent, born to work on farms, survive famines, and run from English invaders.

Her mother had struggled. Tayla had been put on her first diet at age nine. Every year after that had been another diet. More tears. Another fight and another series of doctors all insisting to Bianca that Tayla was perfectly healthy and nothing was wrong with her thyroid gland.

She was just a big girl.

Bianca had spent so much time tiptoeing around the word "fat" or "big" or "plus-sized" that "average" was nearly progressive. After all, Tayla was pretty sure the average size for a woman in the United States was something like a fourteen. Technically, Bianca was probably correct.

Tayla nodded slowly. "Uh... kind of. It's called *inclusive* sizing. They carry things from retailers who cater to bigger women and also some who carry clothing from a two to a thirty-two. It's a little bit of everything."

"Thirty-two?" Bianca was mentally trying to do the calculations. It was painful to watch.

Tayla tried to change the subject. "It's actually more like a tech start-up. Dad should love it. It's an online marketplace for international designers."

Bianca's laugh was brittle. "Don't tell him that part. Just say it's in fashion and he'll only ever half listen to what you're saying. If you tell him it's in tech, you'll never hear the end of it."

"Yeah, I figured." For the thousandth time, Tayla wished her mother would just leave. She could move back to Sonoma and start painting again. She could move into her own place in the city and hang out with interesting people.

Bianca wasn't a bad person. She was a privileged person who'd never been forced out of her bubble. Sometimes Tayla imagined her mother as a hippie in the Haight or as an artist in Marin. Bianca had a beautiful way of seeing the world when she wasn't miserable and drunk.

"Hey, Mom, why don't we go in?" Tayla shivered. "It's getting cold."

"You go ahead, sweetheart. Mena will help me to bed when I'm ready."

"Mena turned in for the night, remember?"

Bianca blinked. "Did she?"

"Yep." She stood and tried to help her mother to her feet. "Come on, Bianca."

"I don't like it when you call me that."

"But everyone says you're too young to be my mom." Which was true. Botox and very good cosmetic surgery had frozen Bianca in her early forties. "Come on. Want to leave the blanket?"

"S'cold." She pulled the wool blanket closer around her shoulders.

"I know." She helped her mother stumble to the door and toward the elevator. The house was four stories, and her mother's bedroom was on the top floor. Her father kept a separate bedroom on the third floor next to Tayla's room. That is when he wasn't sleeping at his club in Union Square.

When Bianca slumped against her, Tayla was more grateful than ever that her father had had the elevator installed. When she was a child, Tayla had nightmares about her mother falling down the stairs and dying. The elevator was a prudent decision.

She helped her mother into bed and tucked her in with a glass of water and a bottle of aspirin on the bedside table. She also cleared out any medications in the small drawer that could interact badly with alcohol. It was something Mena probably did regularly. She stowed the various sleep aids and anxiety medications in the guest bathroom on the second floor before she made her way up to bed.

The bed had been turned down and a gas fire was lit in the fireplace, ridding her room of the chill that came with a San Francisco night. The queen bed in the center of the room had been updated with smooth cream bedding and new pillows. The curtains around the antique four-poster bed were fresh too, a verdant green velvet that reminded Tayla of the hills around Lower Lake.

Her bag was unpacked and her clothes hung up in the closet. Her toiletries had been unpacked and organized in the adjoining bathroom. A fresh decanter of water and a bowl of fruit had been placed on the table in the sitting area.

Mena wouldn't have considered any of those things an invasion of privacy. She was hired to see to guests and make them feel at home. The fact that Tayla hadn't wanted her underwear unpacked was beside the point.

Ah, home. Cozy, friendly home.

Tomorrow couldn't come soon enough.

CHAPTER THIRTEEN

THE BUILDING that housed the offices of SOKA was a restored Victorian house in a mixed residential and commercial area of the Mission District. Located just off a main road, it had light traffic when the car dropped Tayla off. A small diner was on the ground floor of the building to the left, and a dry cleaner sat on the other side of a narrow alleyway to the right.

The brass plate near the door was the only indication it was a business. A simple plate.

SOKA.

Tayla knocked, hearing music drifting from the interior. It was something fast and bright with a Caribbean beat. A few moments later, the door opened.

"Tayla?" A smiling woman greeted her. "Welcome to SOKA. I'm Kabisa." She held out her hand. "Please, come in."

Tayla followed her into the small foyer of the Victorian house. "Thank you for inviting me."

"It's a pleasure to meet you." Kabisa's accent was as crisp as the brightly patterned shirtdress she wore.

Tayla felt a bit starstruck. Kabisa Nandi's biography said she had a background in modeling, and Tayla wasn't surprised. She had deep brown skin and dramatic features, most notably a vivid smile. Her hair was twisted into bantu knots, and she wore a purple headband that drew attention to her incredible cheekbones. Tayla blinked. "You are absolutely beautiful. Your pictures don't do you justice."

"Thank you! That's always lovely to hear. I think you're very beautiful too. I've been looking at your Instagram. I love the way you accessorize."

"That's a great compliment. Thanks."

"Is there anything you'd like to leave by the door? Your coat maybe?"

Tayla saw a rack of coats, umbrellas, and random bags in the entryway. It reminded her more of a home than an office. "I'll leave my coat. Thanks."

"It looks like it will be sunny today. I'm so relieved. I am very ready for summer." Kabisa ushered her up the stairs and into what looked like a slightly messy living room. "When Azim and I bought this place, we wanted to incorporate the concept of common spaces for our staff to encourage creativity and collaboration, but it's ended up being a little bit more like a family home."

Tayla loved it. She saw folders scattered around and various samples draped across the back of a chaise. Two coffee cups sat abandoned on a side table.

"I'd like to tell you it's usually cleaner than this, but I can't." She shrugged. "We tend to have one day a month or so when we do a dramatic cleaning, but Azim read a study about how chaotic work spaces promote creativity, and ever since, he's been very reluctant to ask people to clean up."

A heavy step bounded down the stairs, and a young Latino man with a long Mohawk and multiple facial piercings thundered into the room. "Hey! I'm Rudy. You must be Tayla. Nice to meet you."

"Rudy is our tech wonder, Tayla." Kabisa pointed to the coffee cups. "Are those yours?"

"I was coming to clean up," he said. "Promise, mom."

Kabisa rolled her eyes and raised her hand as Rudy laughed. "The younger members of the staff like to tease me."

"No." Rudy gave Kabisa a side hug. "She's just the best."

"Are you and Azim at a good stopping place?"

"Yeah, he's in your office." Rudy waved up the stairs. "I was going to make more coffee. Tayla, would you like some?"

She couldn't help but smile at the young man's friendliness. "Yeah. That would be great. Thank you." He looked like he was no more than eighteen.

"Cool." He pushed through a swinging door. "Cool, cool, cool."

Kabisa pointed to the kitchen. "I'm old-fashioned. All important decisions for our first business in Nairobi happened around my mother's kitchen table, so we still hold staff meetings over meals. We try to all eat lunch together once a week."

Tayla's heart was flying. So far it was a dream office. The people were nice. The atmosphere felt like a cool collective, not a corporate office.

"Let's go up to meet Azim." Tayla walked up the staircase. "I hope you don't mind stairs."

"I grew up in Russian Hill, so everything was a climb," Tayla said. "No problem."

"That's a beautiful area, but we love the Mission. There is so much energy here."

"I agree."

Kabisa showed her into an office that looked over the alleyway. There was a small balcony with various plants growing. In fact, the entire office was filled with plants. They hung in the windows, and an indoor palm grew between twin desks on the longest wall.

Unlike the rest of the house, this space was impeccably neat. Organized bookcases filled one wall, and two mustard-yellow chairs sat in front of them, lined up in perfect symmetry. The room was painted a soothing blue, and the scent of lemon filled the air.

"This is a great office." Tayla looked around. Though the room was neat, it was filled with art and photographs of all kinds.

"Azim and I work in here, and as you can see, we like things a little neater. But all our employees are allowed to personalize their spaces."

"How many employees do you currently have?"

"We have five still in Nairobi because we have a physical store there. We have another two setting up a satellite office and probably a physical store in Chiang Mai, Thailand, right now, and then five here." She sat in one of the yellow chairs and motioned for Tayla to take the other. "Expansion is inevitable. Not because we're anxious for the business to be bigger—we actually liked being a smaller company—but because our market is growing, and without expansion, our customers are going to become dissatisfied. The upside is that we're going to be able to highlight artists and designers from new markets like South America, where we haven't been able to travel much in the past."

"So you and Azim do all the research yourselves? Finding new artists and companies?"

"Not entirely, though that's how we started out. We get a lot of referrals now from existing relationships. Most of our new artists come via word of mouth."

"That's so cool."

"And now with the app launching—"

"Hi." A tall man stood in the doorway of the office. "I see Kabisa has already started."

"Azim!" Kabisa rose and Tayla joined her. "Meet Tayla. Tayla, this is my husband, Azim, the business brains of SOKA."

"Don't let her fool you," he said. "Her brain is plenty business-minded.

"It's very nice to meet you." Tayla shook his outstretched hand. "I really like your office."

"Thank you." Azim had a much lighter accent, and he looked Indian, not Kenyan. He was as tall as Kabisa but had a slim runner's build like Jeremy. He wore glasses and was clean-shaven. He was also incredibly handsome. He didn't look like a tech nerd. He looked like a Bollywood star playing a tech nerd. Tayla tried not to stare at the two ridiculously pretty people she might be working for.

"Was the office easy to find?" he asked.

"So easy." She pulled out her phone. "But I can't lie. I use my phone to find everything."

Azim smiled. "Then you are our target demographic."

Tayla and Kabisa sat, and Azim pulled up a chair. They continued the meeting, talking about the development of the app, which was a fairly open secret in the online fashion world. Kabisa talked about her ideas to create community on the app with chat rooms and profiles where users could post pictures and keep fashion journals.

"I think that's a great idea," Tayla said. "Think about how many times you've been shopping and tried something on, taken a picture, and had to wait for friends to get back to you if you want a second opinion."

"Exactly," Kabisa said. "Imagine if you could join a group on the SOKA app specifically for clothing opinions. It wouldn't have to be related to our inventory either. It could be for any clothing. But you'd have a built-in community of people ready to give you advice on fit or suggestions if you don't know what would be good for an event. Things like that."

"So it's going to be a combination of social network and shopping app?"

"Yes," Azim said. "But curated, like it is now, and we're already working on filters and moderation, because we want the chat rooms and forums to remain positive and constructive."

"Will people have the option of creating a private profile and limiting what is available to see?"

"Absolutely," Kabisa said. "I think that's essential for user trust."

"We all agree with that," Azim said. "And since we're a retailer and we'll be charging a small yearly subscription for the app after a trial period—we're thinking under five dollars—we won't be collecting data for use by anyone but us for internal marketing and suggestions."

Tayla nodded. "I think most people can live with that."

"The position we're thinking about you for would be influencer outreach," Azim said, "though we'd obviously be looking for input on other aspects as we go."

"As a social media user," Kabisa said, "I think some of the metrics companies are currently using for marketing aren't what we're looking for. Our customer isn't always following fashion blogs or influencers. Often they're following travel. Or photography. Or art. Music. Social justice. It's not all about the models."

"I can see that," Tayla said. "But fashion is still a huge community online."

"I agree," Azim said. "And the numbers don't lie. Inclusive sizing and diversity in marketing are keys to reaching that community."

Tayla said, "I'm really happy to hear you say that, both from a professional and personal standpoint."

"We encourage all our retailers to offer clothes in a wide variety of sizes," Kabisa said. "After all, if all we had to offer was clothing for women my size, my sisters would *kill* me."

Azim smiled. "You think she's exaggerating, but I can confirm that. My sisters-in-law have no mercy."

"Good to know." Tayla was impressed. More than impressed. For the first time since she'd sent in her résumé, she realized she wanted this job. Really *wanted* it. Not just for benefits or salary, but because they were doing something extraordinary, opening online retail to designers and customers of all kinds.

"Okay," Tayla said. "You've sold me on your company vision. Let's talk about specifics."

———

TAYLA GROANED INTO HER HANDS. "TOBIN, WHY DID you send me this job listing?"

Tobin sipped his margarita. "Told you. And clearly, I want you to move back to San Francisco. That's why I sent you the job."

"It's perfect. It's like the perfect company."

"Nope." He raised a hand. "I guarantee it's not perfect. No job is perfect. Things you think are amazing right now might eventually get on your nerves. Doesn't mean it's not great though. And the two of them are so..."

"Hot?"

Tobin laughed. "Yeah. Pretty much. Everyone is buzzing about working for them. Everyone wants in."

"Okay, you know I have no problems with my self-esteem, right?"

"I have known this for some time, yes."

"But seriously, why are they that interested in me? I'm a small-to-medium-level influencer; I don't have the biggest follower count. Not even close."

Tobin frowned. "I think there're two things you're not seeing. One, you have a business background and an accounting degree. More than one tech start-up and fashion company has been doomed from the start because they can't balance a basic budget. So that's one thing you have going for you. The other thing is, look at your friends."

She frowned. "What about my friends?"

"I don't mean real-life friends. I mean online friends. You may not have the highest follower count, but the people who do follow you are some very big names. You know the people with the high counts and they respect you. The people with the biggest following aren't interested in outreach. They're interested in raising their profile. You, on the other hand, know everybody. At least you know them online. You're the model other models like."

"I guess so." She finished her martini and waved at the waitress to order another one. "I've never thought about that. A lot of those girls I just know because we all started blogging around the same time."

"Yeah, but you're a serious person and you don't chase drama. And now some of those early contacts are *huge* names. That's valuable. I think SOKA was brilliant to spot your potential." He glanced to the side and eyed her legs. "I spotted it years ago."

She laughed. "Never going to happen."

"Why?" He reached for her hand. "We don't work together anymore. All the reasons you gave me for not hooking up aren't reasons anymore."

Tayla slipped her hand from his grip. "Because... of other reasons. And I'm kind of seeing someone right now."

"I don't mind. I wasn't asking to marry you." He frowned. "Wait, where? Where are you seeing someone? In that little town?"

"Yes, in that little town. And I know *you* don't mind, but he would. I don't think he's a casual-fling kind of guy."

"Are you serious?"

"It's not serious, but..." She was at a loss. How did she explain Jeremy to someone like Tobin, who thought buying an Android over an iPhone was cheating, but dating three women at the same time without telling them was no big deal? "We're seeing each other. It's fun. I don't have time to juggle. It just doesn't work for me right now."

Tobin blinked. "That sounds like... Dare I say it?"

"Don't be a shit, Tobin."

"It sounds like a *relationship*." He took her hand and pulled her closer, staring into her eyes. "Who are you, and what have you done with Tayla?"

"Didn't I tell you to not be a shit?"

"I do what I'm good at, which you'd know if you slept with me." He shrugged. "So tell me about Mr. Wonderful."

"No."

"Why? Are you embarrassed? Is he a cowboy? Please let him be a cowboy."

"He's not a cowboy." Though his grandfather was. "He owns a comic and game shop. He's an old friend of Emmie's. He likes the outdoors a lot. He's a mountain climber. He—"

"Hold up." Tobin smiled. "He does what now?"

"He's a mountain climber. And he likes the outdoors."

"Oh my God, you're dating someone crunchy." His eyes went wide. "Does he wear deodorant? Does he have back hair? I'm so curious now."

"Of course he wears deodorant."

"There is nothing *of course* about the crunchy kind! I hooked up with a rafting guide once when I went up to Tahoe. She was super-hot, but you should have seen the hair on her legs." He shuddered.

Tayla finally got the server's attention and ordered another drink. "You're such an ass, Tobin."

"Why?"

"When was the last time you shaved *your* legs?"

"Uh… never."

"But a woman has to or she's…" Tayla pantomimed his shudder. "You suck. That is another reason I'd never hook up with you."

"Fine, I suck. But does your mountain man wear deodorant or not?"

"Yes. He smells very nice." She leaned closer. "And he smells even nicer when he's worked up a sweat."

"Lucky bastard," Tobin muttered.

She'd only said it to irritate Tobin, but Tayla realized it was true. Jeremy *did* always smell nice. Even when they'd been hiking. She put it down to good body chemistry and diet, because no man she'd ever met smelled nice *all* the time.

And now she was thinking about Jeremy after she'd just had

one of the best business meetings of her life. The server set down another dirty martini. Jeremy liked dirty martinis.

Shit.

Tobin must have picked up on her sudden melancholy. "So what is your mountain man going to think about you working at SOKA, huh? You think you could get him to move to San Francisco with you?"

Jeremy in San Francisco? Tayla let out a hard laugh. "Yeah... no. I don't think that's on the table."

"Poor little rich girl." Tobin leaned back in the booth as Tayla started her second drink. "So many choices. Looks like you have some decisions to make."

CHAPTER FOURTEEN

AFTER TOBIN PROPOSITIONED HER, Tayla hadn't wanted to crash at his place. She'd racked her brain for more options, but she couldn't come up with anyone who would let her stay with them at the last minute, so she decided to remain at her parents' house. She'd been there for three days before she saw her father.

They nearly ran into each other walking out their bedroom doors.

"Oh." Tayla blinked. "Hi."

"Tayla." Her father frowned. "I didn't realize you were home."

"I didn't realize you were home either. How's the club?"

He was oblivious to sarcasm, as usual. Or he simply didn't acknowledge it. "It's fine. Why are you in the city? Have you moved back?"

"No. I was here for a job interview with a new fashion company."

He straightened his cuffs. "That sounds fun. Does it pay as much as an accounting position at my firm?"

"I have no idea, but since I'm still not interested in an accounting position at your firm, I don't really see the relevance of your question."

His stiff smile was as familiar to her as his indifference. "I noticed you haven't touched the balance in your trust fund lately."

"Not since I bought the car." The trust fund was something her father brought up often and she tried to ignore. "Did you have a question about the management of my personal finances?"

"Just a curious inquiry."

"I see."

Her father resented that her maternal grandparents had set up sizable trust funds for their four grandchildren and Tayla had no need for her parents' money. She didn't have any resentment about her trust fund—her grandparents had been good people and had earned honest money—but she didn't think about it much.

The trust fund wasn't enough to live on for the rest of her life or anything—especially not in San Francisco—but it meant she could take a shit job every now and then without having to worry about it. She'd always imagined that when she wanted to buy a house, she'd tap into it. Until then, it sat quietly accruing interest.

She wasn't an idiot. She knew how fast money could fly away. No one outside her family knew about her money. Not even Emmie.

"So what are you doing today?" she asked her father. "Mom was talking about an exhibit she wanted to see at the botanical gardens."

"That sounds like a nice thing for you to do."

"What about you?"

Her father looked at her as if she were speaking a foreign language. "I'm working, Tayla."

"Of course you are." Tayla often wondered if her mother left the house if her father would even notice. "Okay, see you."

He frowned. "How long are you staying?"

"I'm leaving tomorrow." Or maybe today if she couldn't take it anymore. She'd talked to Emmie last night, and she missed her best friend. She missed the bookshop, and she'd missed Friday lunch with Daisy and Emmie. She didn't want to go out to another club and play Tobin's wingman. She didn't need to see another concert. She didn't want another silent brunch in the morning room.

She wanted to sleep in her own bed.

She wanted to see Jeremy.

She wanted to think about this whole SOKA thing without her mother's depression hanging over her like a cloud.

Tayla got on her phone and reserved a ticket for the afternoon train, breathing a sigh of relief when her email dinged in confirmation.

———

EMMIE MET HER AT THE TRAIN PLATFORM. IT WAS already nighttime, and Tayla didn't feel like walking the eight blocks to the store in the dark, so she was grateful.

"Yeeeeah!" Emmie ran toward Tayla. "You're back. Were you bored? Please tell me you were bored."

"Your encouragement is overwhelming. Stop. Please stop." Tayla hugged her back and tried to act annoyed, but she was too happy to see Emmie. "I wasn't bored. You know the train is a nightmare on Sunday afternoon. I just wanted to beat the rush."

"Sure." Emmie picked up her bag. "Come on. I borrowed Ox's truck. How did the interview go?"

"Do you really want to know?"

Emmie took a deep breath. "Yeah. I do."

Tayla waited for Emmie to throw her bag in the truck bed. They hopped in the cab and buckled up.

"It was great," Tayla said. "It was really, genuinely great. The owners are amazing. The office is super chill and really friendly. Honestly, I know it's not what you want to hear, but I really hope I get this job."

Emmie's smile was tight, but Tayla could tell it was sincere. She swallowed hard and nodded. "I'm happy for you. I really am.

And I'm excited for you. I'm thrilled you found something that sounds so perfect for you. Did they offer the position to you?"

"Not yet. And thanks." She leaned over and gave Emmie a hug. "The worst part about this job would be leaving you."

"And Jeremy."

Tayla sighed. "I'm not thinking about that right now."

"You have to stop pretending this isn't real." She started the truck and headed toward the exit of the parking lot. "He was mopey the whole time you were gone."

"I texted him."

"Yeah, he told me." She turned left, then made a quick right. "What are you going to do?"

"Nothing yet," she said. "They haven't offered me the job. They were up-front about interviewing other people. They had a list of five or six, I think. It's entirely possible that I won't get this, and then I'll never take another job because nothing will ever compare with the perfection of working for SOKA. I'll stay in Metlin forever and slowly be consumed by a massive cloud of pollen."

"Ha ha." Emmie stared at the road.

"Just say it."

"I don't have anything to say. Honestly. I'm thrilled you found something so incredible that makes you sound happy and excited. And I'm also heartbroken because Metlin can never compare with the perfect job in your hometown."

"I'm not... I'm not being sentimental about the city." She stared into the oncoming lights. "Trust me, that's not it."

"How's your mom?"

Tayla shrugged. "The same."

"And the paternal unit?"

"Only saw him once." She glanced at Emmie. "In passing."

"His loss."

"No loss. You can't feel a loss if there was never a relationship to begin with."

Emmie sighed. "Yeah. You can."

They drove in silence back to the bookstore, and Tayla waited for Emmie to pull around to the east entrance. Ox usually parked his truck on the side of the building in a spot reserved for residents. Tayla parked her tiny Fiat next to it. Emmie jokingly called the two cars David and Goliath when they were both at home.

"Anything exciting happen while I was gone?" She hopped out of the truck and immediately felt her eyes start to water.

Ah, Metlin.

"I texted you about the bike race downtown this morning, right?"

"Yeah. Sorry I wasn't here to help out."

"That's okay. I didn't even know about it until Friday when they started cordoning off Main. We got some good traffic, but nothing Ox and I couldn't handle."

"He helped out in the shop?"

Emmie chuckled. "Dude. He sells so many books. So many. Especially anything he suggests in romance."

Tayla grabbed her bag so Emmie could open the door. "Do you ever feel like you're taking advantage of your boyfriend's many muscles and tattoos for purely monetary purposes?"

"Don't be ridiculous." She turned to Tayla. "It's for *literacy*."

"Keep telling yourself that, you pimp."

"Hey, I didn't know you'd be back today, so we kinda planned a morning hike for tomorrow with Cary and Jeremy. They want to scout out a new camping spot that has a rock nearby they've been wanting to climb. It's not far, maybe five miles total. You want to come?"

Hmmm. Did she want to spend all morning staring at Jeremy's ass as they hiked up a trail in the mountains? "How much up and down is there?"

"The trail? It's fairly flat, but there's some slope going up. Would be downhill on the way back."

Tayla nodded. "I can do that. I might bring that new yoga mat and gear Outdoor Om sent last week. That's right up their alley, and I'm sure there'll be a good location at some point."

"Oh! Great idea. I could pack a couple of those middle grade adventure books too. Do some pictures of great outdoor books in the great outdoors. Ox is reading *Hatchet* with the kids in book club next month."

"Emmie, what have you done? That man is getting so wholesome he could be a dairy product."

———

THE FIRST THING JEREMY DID WHEN HE HOPPED OUT OF his truck Sunday morning was head straight to Tayla and pull her around the corner of the building to kiss her. He pressed her against the red brick, warm from the morning sun, tilted her chin up, and took her lips in a long, slow, lazy kiss.

Her heart was racing by the time he let her go. "Hi."

He smiled. "Hey. Missed you. How was San Francisco?"

She almost said *who?* "Uh, it was fine. Great. The interview went really well."

"How's your family?"

"Ha. The same. How's Pop?"

"Up at my parents' place still. I think he and my dad have been hitting the spring fishing hard. They've both been muttering about bass for weeks now."

"Your family cracks me up."

"There's nothing funny about bass fishing, Tayla." He teased a piece of her hair that had fallen out of the messy bun she'd created that morning. "This is cute."

"I'm going to take some pics with the new yoga stuff."

"You know, if you learned how to rock climb, you could do yoga at the top of the cliff."

She pursed her lips. "Hmmm. Let me think about that.

Balancing in sometimes precarious positions along the edge of a very tall cliff…? No thank you—I like my skull intact."

He slid his hands down her back to cup her ass. "I'd hold on to you."

"That would make for a very different kind of Instagram account." She couldn't stop her smile. "I'm doing all the outdoorsy things now, you know. I'm practically a nature girl. Can't you just be happy with that?"

"I am." He bent down and kissed the side of her neck. "Very happy."

"Hey!" Ox yelled from the truck. "Can we get going please? Cary's meeting us at the trailhead."

"Spoilsport," Tayla muttered. "I never liked him."

"Yeah, you do." He took her hand. "We can make out later. After we climb to the top of the hill."

She spotted Ox securing a bundle of ropes in the back of the pickup truck. "You're climbing today? I thought we were just hiking to the place where you were climbing later?"

"Cary and I wanted to scope it out some. See what kind of permanent anchors are there and what their condition is, what we might need to bring if we wanted to take a new route. Stuff like that."

"So you *are* climbing today?" For some reason, the thought gave her a shot of panic.

"Just a little bit. Cary'll lead. He's more experienced than I am."

"Hey!" Emmie called. "You guys ready or what?" She was wearing a pair of long hiking shorts and a T-shirt that said I'm Sorry for the Things I Said when We Were Pitching the Tent.

"Yeah, we're coming."

"Too much information," Ox muttered.

"Ha ha." Tayla whacked his arm as she climbed into the back

seat of the pickup. She always volunteered to sit in the back since she had short legs and didn't get carsick.

Jeremy climbed in beside her.

"What are you doing?"

"Emmie's feeling sick," he said. "I can sit back here."

"With those legs?"

"I'm not feeling sick," Emmie said. "He completely made that up."

Jeremy stretched his legs across to her side. "I guess we'll have to cuddle."

Tayla smiled and decided to go with it. Ox pulled away from the curb and put James Bay on the radio. They drove into the light as the sun rose behind the mountains in the east.

Tayla closed her eyes and felt all the tension from the visit home dissolve. Her mother's misery drifted away. The pressure of her father's expectations flew from her mind. Lounging against Jeremy Allen's chest in the crew cab of a pickup truck while he played with her hair wasn't something she could complain about.

The morning was cool, and the mountains would be cooler. Tayla had dressed in the clothes the Outdoor Om had sent her— long, stretchy shorts with pockets, a long-sleeved shirt, and a thin vest that moved easily with her body. It was comfortable in the valley, but she knew she'd be chilly until the hike started.

"This is cute stuff." Jeremy plucked at her shorts. "You taking pictures?"

"Yeah, it's kind of perfect. I just got this box of stuff from a company that specializes in outdoor yoga gear. A whole bunch of it. It's really cute."

"What's the difference between outdoor yoga gear and regular yoga gear?"

"Heavier-duty mats, for one. More cushioned. And specialized backpacks that have a pocket for a yoga mat. And this." She gestured to her clothes. "Clothing that's flexible enough to move easily in but also sturdy enough to hike in. I wouldn't want to hike in most yoga pants."

"They kind of remind me of climbing pants."

"That may be where they got the idea. I think some climbers do yoga, right?"

"Lots." He bent down to her ear. "You'd love climbing."

"I wouldn't."

"Just you and the mountain. The quiet. The wind. The views."

She shivered. "So you're saying that I can't blast my K-pop playlist while you're stuck to the side of a mountain?"

"What if I promised to teach you fun things to do with ropes?" he whispered.

Her eyes went wide. Was Jeremy revealing a kinky side? "Uh…"

"You know, climbing harnesses—"

"You know we can hear you back there, right?" Ox broke in. "No offense, J, but I do not want to hear where this conversation is going."

"Jealous much, Ox?" Tayla asked.

"Intrigued." Emmie tapped her chin. "Tayla, let me know if you want book recommendations."

She laughed as Jeremy covered his face.

"I'm shutting up now," he said.

"No, no," she said. "I'm very curious where you were going with that."

His cheeks were dark. "I'll tell you later."

"Don't worry. I'll remind you."

———

THEY ARRIVED AT THE TRAILHEAD AN HOUR AND A HALF later. The air was cool and crisp, and the dogwood trees were blooming along the road.

Tayla squeezed out of the truck and took a deep breath.

Fresh air. Pine. A little dirt.

"No pollen." She sighed in relief. "Okay, this is my favorite place to be in the spring."

Jeremy bent and kissed her cheek. "My mom says the same thing. She lectures me about the air quality in the valley all the time."

"Do you have one of those air filters in your bedroom?"

He grinned and nodded as he bent over to lace up his hiking boots. "Christmas present from her a few years ago."

"I need to get one," Tayla said. "And in the meantime, maybe I'll just spend more time up here." She batted a fly buzzing around her face. "Or maybe not."

"Come on." Jeremy twisted a bandana and tied it around her neck. "It's not that bad."

It wasn't bad; it was great. The air was clear, the sun was warm. The quiet was unexpectedly soothing. But she couldn't give in that easily.

She bent over and dusted off her cute green hiking boots. "I can't believe they're already dirty."

Jeremy laughed. "They're hiking boots."

"Yes. And I clean them every time I use them. Just because you wear something in the great dirty outdoors doesn't mean it shouldn't be cute and well cared for."

"*Cute and Well Cared For* should be the title of your album."

She smiled. "Yeah, it should be."

"Come on." He reached in the back of the truck. "This one yours?"

"Yep." Tayla put her phone in the long zipper pocket on the side of her thigh and held her hand out to take her backpack. It was aqua blue and summer yellow, pretty colors that went well with the flower pattern on the pocket of her shorts and the fitted T-shirt they'd sent.

"You know, if all brands sent stuff this coordinated, my job would be so much easier." Tayla slung her backpack over her shoulder. She'd have to keep that in mind if she went to work for SOKA.

"Can I ask how much you make for something like this?" Jeremy asked. "They send you free stuff, obviously, but do you make actual money from brands for posting their stuff?"

"Yeah, a little." She put her sunglasses on. "The free stuff accounts for a lot more. I looked on their website and all this stuff together would cost well over three hundred dollars if I ordered on my own. But I get it for free and then a hundred dollars or so for the post."

"A hundred dollars?" Jeremy's eyes went wide. "Maybe I need to start doing Instagram."

She pointed to all the gear around his waist. "I'm guessing all that stuff is pretty expensive. You might get free stuff with enough of a following. You're a good-looking guy."

"And black." He smiled. "Advertisers might not go for that, especially in climbing, which isn't exactly the most diverse sport out there."

"I've noticed that." She'd maybe been doing a little research on rock climbing. Just out of curiosity. "Seems like it's mostly a lot of skinny white guys."

Cary walked up. "And a few skinny Asian dudes. More and more women all the time, which is nice to see."

"And twelve black people," Jeremy said. "In the entire world. There's only twelve of us."

Tayla laughed. "That can't be true."

He smiled. "It's not, but there aren't too many. More all the time, which is cool. I'm not the only black guy at the gym anymore."

"And not many big girls, I've noticed." Tayla looked down. "But I guess that kind of makes sense. I don't think these boobs would work with rock climbing."

Cary frowned and studied her body. "Yeah, that could be an issue, but you've got great legs."

Jeremy punched his shoulders. "Hey."

"What?" Cary shrugged. "She does. They're strong and she's got a low center of gravity. You could climb, Tayla. You'd just have to wear a really good sports bra." Cary frowned and stared at her boobs. "Probably. I don't have any, so I can't speak with authority on that."

"Dude. You can quit staring at her tits anytime."

Cary shook his head and looked up. "Just trying to help."

Tayla bit back a laugh. She'd normally have been offended, but Cary really did seem to be evaluating her from a technical perspective. "I'm really okay with not climbing, but thanks for saying I have great legs."

"Sure. You guys ready to hike?"

"Yep."

Jeremy nodded at the truck. "I got a little more gear to pack."

"Then stop flirting with your girlfriend and pack your shit up, dude." Cary and Jeremy walked away, and Tayla stood frozen in the middle of the woods.

Girlfriend?

She'd avoided being a girlfriend for twenty-eight years. What was happening? Jeremy hadn't objected when Cary said it. Did he think of Tayla as his girlfriend? Had she agreed to any of that? Didn't that have to be a mutually-agreed-upon label?

"What's wrong with you?" Emmie walked up to her. "You look like you feel sick."

"I'm okay." She forced one foot in front of the other. "Just… fine. I'm fine."

"Yeah, you sound like you're totally fine. Sure." She started walking. "Just let me know if I need to kill someone."

"See? This is the reason you're my best friend."

CHAPTER FIFTEEN

JEREMY WATCHED from the base of the rock as Cary hooked another nut in the seam of cracked granite. The soft metal square stuck in the rock as Cary tugged on it. He clipped an extender into the metal loop and hooked the rope into the carabiner.

"There's a bolt up here," he called down, "but it's old."

Jeremy quickly made a notation in his climbing journal, keeping one hand on the belay rope. "Got it."

Cary worked his way up the granite face. He was almost to the crux of the climb, a sheer, crumbly stretch of granite with very few holds. It was a good section to practice on, however. The rock wasn't that high, but it was more challenging than what they'd done in the past.

"I'm glad we came up to check this out," Cary yelled. "A lot of information on that website is old."

"There's been a lot of snow the past few seasons."

"Yeah."

Snow and ice led to widening cracks and rusted bolts. Rusted bolts could be deceiving. Jeremy glanced over his shoulder to see Ox arranging a rough camp stove with rocks and a folding metal grate Cary had brought. Tayla and Emmie were off near the creek, taking pictures of Tayla doing yoga.

"You with me down there?"

"Yeah." Jeremy looked back up at Cary. "I'm here."

"This stretch is deceiving. Lotta holds."

"Crimps?"

"Mostly, but they're decent."

Jeremy made another note in his journal and watched Cary as he set the last two anchors before he reached the top. "Nice, man."

Cary disappeared past the edge of the rock only to reappear a few moments later. "Safe! Nice permanent anchors up here."

Jeremy kept the rope in his hands as Cary began to pull it up to set the belay for Jeremy to climb.

"Ready?"

"On belay?" He tugged on his harness and checked the knot for the third time.

"On belay. Climb when ready."

"Climbing." Jeremy turned his face to the cool granite, dusted his hands with chalk, and began to climb. Everything but the rock fell out of focus. There was only the mountain, the rope, his body pressed against the rock. His lead's occasional direction as he pointed out anchors.

The stretch of every muscle came into sharp focus. The complete and utter awareness of the mountain, the rock, and his body. Balance and focus.

Reach, grip.

Shift, unclip. Clip.

Reach. Shift.

Hold by hold, Jeremy lifted himself off the ground and up the face of the rock, removing the anchors as methodically as Cary had placed them.

Nothing cleared his mind like climbing.

Cary stepped back as Jeremy pulled himself over the edge. He felt the surge of adrenaline and the rush of pleasure when he looked out over the tops of the trees.

"Damn." He let out a long breath and slapped Cary's hand in a firm grip. "That was awesome."

The rock stretched back in a long, easy slope away from the face that jutted up through the forest. A long black granite slab warmed by the sun. Jeremy stretched out and let the wind cool the sweat over his body as Cary got out his camera and began to take pictures.

"The guide was right. Great views of Grand Sentinel."

"Uh-huh." Jeremy didn't care about taking pictures. For him, the thrill was being in a place few others could reach. It was about the quiet and the focus of the climb. He rolled over and pressed his cheek to the granite.

"Gonna take a nap now."

Cary chuckled. "Okay. I'll wake you up when I'm ready to go."

"Cool."

He closed his eyes and drifted for a while, listening to a pair of hawks as they hunted. The sun was fully overhead when he realized he could smell the scent of meat cooking below them.

Emmie had packed kebabs, fruit, and a pasta salad. Tayla had said something about brownies.

"Cary!" Jeremy sat up. "You about ready to head down?"

"In a few. Smells good."

"I know. We need to climb with girls more often," Jeremy said. "The food is always better."

"We *could* pack food and cook like grown-ups."

"But we always end up grabbing beef jerky and trail mix instead."

"True."

Jeremy took a deep breath. "Hey, Cary?"

"Yeah?" The older man was still taking pictures.

"I'm falling hard for this girl."

Cary walked back up the granite slope and started packing up his camera. "Dude, you've already fallen. Bad. This has been going on for months."

"But it's only getting worse. And she's moving to San Francisco."

"You don't know that yet."

"She said the interview went really well."

Cary paused and looked at him. "Really?"

"Yeah."

Cary took a deep breath. "I don't know what to tell you."

"I can't leave Metlin." His shop was here, but even more, his family was here. He couldn't leave his pop. He couldn't leave his parents, his sisters, his nieces and nephew. Not even if he was falling in love with Tayla.

"No." Cary shook his head. "You can't leave Metlin."

"And I can't ask her to stay."

"I wouldn't advise it. If she stays, it has to be her choice." Cary looked down at him. "Be careful, man."

Jeremy had a feeling that being careful with Tayla wasn't in the cards. He was nuts about the girl. Every moment he spent with her made him fall harder. In rock climbing, you anticipated a route, saw what falls could happen, and changed course to keep yourself safe. Any other attitude meant you were dancing with death.

With Tayla, he could see the route, see where the problem was, but he couldn't seem to change direction. He didn't want to, even though the fall would crush him.

Jeremy and Cary readied for their descent, checking anchors and counting nuts and cams to make sure Jeremy had grabbed everything on the way up. They double-checked, rechecked their harnesses and knots, and then carefully rappelled down the cliff.

When they reached the bottom, Tayla was standing at the base of the rock, scrolling through pictures on her phone. "I got some great shots of you—"

Jeremy bent down, hooked an arm around her waist, and brought his mouth to hers.

She tasted delectable. Like mango and chili pepper. He licked the bottom of her lip. "Hi. You're sweet."

"Hi to you. I was eating fruit salad." She hooked her thumbs in his climbing harness. "You hungry, mountain man?"

"Yes."

"Then unstrap all the... things and come eat. Lunch is ready."

He smiled. "I will unstrap all the things and come eat."

She walked away, turned back, saw him staring. "You okay?"

"Yeah." *I'm just in love with you and pretty convinced this is all going to end with my heart at the bottom of a cliff.* "I'm good."

———

THE SHOTS OF JEREMY AND CARY RAPPELLING DOWN the cliff had garnered more likes and comments on her feed than anything since she'd posted about finding a vintage Alma bag at a yard sale.

Hawt.

Mmmmmmountain men. Yes plz.

#silverfox

#rockzaddy

Where are u finding these men?

I'll take both. Is both an option?

And many, many fire emojis.

She bit her lip and decided to wait to post the yoga shots. She didn't even want to attempt to compete with shirtless Jeremy and Cary. She scrolled through the pics of the hike on Sunday while she waited for coffee to brew.

Jeremy, Cary, and Ox standing against the cliff, Jeremy and Cary still in climbing harnesses, laughing at Ox in his apron and grilling tongs.

Jeremy and Ox holding Emmie between them, raising her like they were overhead lifting.

Tayla and Jeremy holding warrior pose at the base of a sequoia tree.

Cary crouched by the fire, poking at the coals with a come-hither look. He'd been looking at the brownies. The man liked brownies a lot.

Ox wandered out of his and Emmie's room, scratching his unshaven face.

"Hey," he grunted. "Coffee?"

"Making." She continued to scroll through the pics. "I got a bunch of cute ones of you and Emmie yesterday."

"Send 'em to me."

"I will."

Tayla didn't mind Ox as a roommate, mostly because he was minimally social before he got his coffee. He wasn't a morning person. He didn't attempt interaction when he wasn't caffeinated, which suited Tayla just fine.

They each poured a cup of coffee and doctored it to their liking, black with a lot of sugar for Tayla, cream and no sugar for Ox. They sat at the counter, checking their phones and drinking coffee for a good fifteen minutes.

"Emmie still sleeping?"

"Yeah. She woke up last night. I think she came out and read for a while."

"I heard her."

He took a few more gulps of coffee. "Is it stress?"

"I don't think so. She just does that. Always has, as far as I know."

He frowned. "Huh."

"Yeah, she's weird."

"Aren't we all?"

"Touché."

Tayla got up to refill her mug, feeling slightly more social. She silently offered a warm-up to Ox and he held out his mug.

"So what are you going to do about Jeremy if you get this job?"

"Are you actually asking me about my love life?"

"You've grilled me about Emmie roughly a million times. It only seems fair."

Tayla put the carafe back in the coffee maker. "I don't know what I'm going to do. It'll end. I don't think there's any point in trying to maintain something long distance when our lives are going in two different directions." The thought made her queasy. Or maybe she just needed to eat something. She was drinking coffee on an empty stomach.

She opened the fridge and got out a cup of yogurt.

"That's it?" Ox asked. "'It's been fun. See you on the occasional weekend and at Christmas'?"

She set her mug down. "What do you suggest I do, Ox?"

"Don't leave Metlin. What's so great in San Francisco that you can't get here?"

"Uh, a job—"

"You have a job."

"A better job." She picked up her coffee again. "And... culture. Art museums. Plays. Concerts."

"We have concerts here."

"GrizzlyFest doesn't count."

He frowned. "Why the hell not? And you're talking about stuff you do like... a few times a year. Why would you move for stuff you're going to do a few times a year?"

"I used to *live* by the Palace of Fine Arts. I went at least once a week."

"So here you can drive up to the mountains instead. You trying to tell me art is more beautiful than nature?"

She let out a breath. "It's just different. I'm more of an art museum girl than a nature girl. That's all. There's nothing wrong with Metlin, it's just not home."

"I think you're wrong." He reached for the bread box and got

ELIZABETH HUNTER

out a bagel, then bit into it.

Tayla's jaw dropped. "What are you doing?"

He looked at the bagel. "Eating."

"What is wrong with you?" She grabbed the bagel from his hand and walked to the knife block. "You can't just eat an untoasted bagel."

"You can, actually. I was doing it."

"Not in front of me, you heathen."

Ox watched her cut the bagel and toss it in the toaster. "I think you do think of this place as home. I think you're being stubborn because this isn't how you imagined your life going. But stuff that's unplanned can be just as amazing. Sometimes it's more amazing. You think I ever imagined opening a bookshop with Emmie?"

"That was serendipity."

"Yeah. And what if your meeting Jeremy is just as serendip..."

"Serendipitous."

"That. What if this is your destiny?"

"You think my destiny is being a bookkeeper in Metlin, California?"

He leaned across the counter. "What's wrong with being a bookkeeper in Metlin, California? A bookkeeper with great friends who are there for each other and have a lot of fun on weekends. A bookkeeper who does yoga in sequoia groves and learns how to rock climb with her boyfriend. And hosts a book club for cool teenagers who think she's the shit. What's wrong with that life? Other than it wouldn't shove success up your parents' collective asses?"

"You know what?" She popped the still-cold bagel out and put it on a paper towel. "Toast your own bagel, Ox."

"You know I'm right. That's why you're pissed off right now."

Tayla walked to her room and shut the door, taking her coffee with her.

Stupid Ox. She'd never liked him.

160

CHAPTER SIXTEEN

JEREMY and his pop were talking on the front porch of his parents' cabin.

"You leave me with them another week and I'm gonna go insane," Pop said. "I want some damn bacon, and your mother is convinced my sodium is high."

"To be fair, we probably all eat too much sodium, Pop."

"I am eighty-five years old, Jeremy Augustus Allen. You think I give a damn about my sodium? I want a piece of bacon with my eggs in the morning."

Jeremy shuffled his feet. "Mom and Dad already planned for you to visit for another week." It was Monday night, and his mom had asked him to bring up some groceries from town. He hadn't realized his pop was going to ambush him. He should have been clued in by the tofu his mom had included on the list. "Is the only issue the food? You and Dad are catching a ton of fish." Jeremy had an ice chest full of bass and early trout.

Gus crossed his arms. "There's only so much a man can fish."

"And now you're just talking bullshit." He looked over Gus's shoulder to the dim cabin. His parents were already getting ready for bed. "I'll call Mom in the morning. Convince her that you've had your... score... I can't remember what it's supposed to be."

"Three score and ten! It's biblical, Jeremy."

"Fine, fine." Jeremy backed toward his truck. "I'll mention the biblical reference and remind her that you're a grown man who can pick his own food and if she wants you to keep visiting them, then she needs to let you have bacon."

"See that you do."

Jeremy stopped before he opened the truck. "Do you really want me to take you home?"

His grandpa had given up his license a few years back, when driving at night became too difficult. He'd been placated by the fact that he liked walking, he lived close to all the places he liked to go, and Jeremy was always willing to cart him around. At times like this, however, Jeremy was reminded how limiting it was to be without a vehicle, especially for an independent man like Gus.

"I'll be fine." Just venting about the diet seemed to have assuaged him. "You climb that new rock?"

"Yeah. Went well. There are a few different routes we want to try next month when we have a couple more people, but for now we got a good feel for the lower level and what we need."

"You be careful." Gus was the only one in Jeremy's family who asked him about climbing. His mother claimed she didn't want to know. His father made the right noises, but Jeremy could tell it wasn't his thing and he didn't really get it. "And how's that Tayla?"

"She's great." He forced a smile. "Her interview in San Francisco went really well. She's waiting to see if they call her back."

Gus's eyes didn't waver. "I don't understand wanting to haul yourself up a mountain," he said. "I don't understand the desire for it. I worry about the danger. But I'd never ask you to stop."

His pop wasn't talking about mountain climbing. He was talking about dreams. "I know."

"Take care of yourself, son."

"I'll call you tomorrow, Pop."

"Drive safe."

Jeremy slammed the door and started down the hill.

———

WHEN HE PULLED INTO HIS DRIVEWAY, HE SAW A DARK figure sitting on the porch. He pulled all the way up to the garage and got out cautiously but relaxed when he saw who it was. "Tayla?"

"Hey."

"Hey." He closed the door and walked around the truck bed. "What are you doing here?" He frowned. "We were supposed to—"

"No." She stood and brushed off her pants. She was wearing a pair of skinny black jeans he loved, a T-shirt, and a long cardigan that brushed her knees. "It's still cold at night."

"Yeah." He walked over and leaned against a porch post. "What's up?"

She looked at him, then away. "You know I like it here, right?"

"Yeah, but it's not San Francisco."

"And that's fine. I don't think there's anything wrong with Metlin, okay? I'm not being a snob. I'm not being a big-city shit about small-town life or anything. I don't want you to think I'm being a snob because I want this job."

His heart twisted in his chest. "I don't think you're a snob." He nodded toward the garage. "I really need to hang my equipment from yesterday before it gets tangled and—"

"I can help."

He didn't really want to continue a conversation where she justified all the reasons she was going to leave him, but he couldn't bring himself to tell her to go. "Yeah, okay."

They walked back to the garage, and Jeremy walked around to the side door and flipped on the lights. Pop's woodworking bench lined one entire wall, each tool, saw, and clamp hung carefully on a pegboard. On the opposite wall, closest to the house, Jeremy had created something similar for his outdoors equipment. A rack of fishing poles hung high, a kayak was hoisted to the ceiling, but most of the wall was lined with hooks and small shelves to store his climbing gear.

"You have a lot of outdoor stuff," Tayla said. "This looks like a scaled-down REI."

"They have a lot of climbing stuff," he said. "Cary buys most of his stuff from them."

"Where do you get yours?"

"Local shops up near Yosemite. REI sometimes. A couple of places online." He lifted the end of one rope and began to loop it around his palm and elbow.

"What can I do to help?"

"You don't have to help."

"No, I'm really good at organizing stuff," she said. "You should see my closet."

He smiled. "I have."

The slight red tinge to her cheeks told Jeremy she was thinking about the night they'd spent together in her room. She glanced at the house. "Where's your grandpa?"

"Up in the mountains. He and my dad are trying to outsmart bass."

"Is that difficult? Outsmarting bass?"

"Harder than you might think." What was he doing? Why was he torturing himself? He should be the one to end it. She was going to leave, which would just leave him... where? Looking like the small-town chump the glamorous heroine leaves behind. In the movies, she changes her mind and comes back, sets up shop in the small town, and marries the chump.

Life wasn't a movie.

"Tayla—" He was about to turn and tell her to go when he felt her arm sneak around his waist and a carabiner clip onto his belt loop.

"Gotcha."

Jeremy could hear the smile in her voice. It was irresistible. She was irresistible. He slowly turned. She had backed away to the other side of the garage, holding the end of the rope, a smile on her face.

"You've hooked me." He crossed his arms over his chest. "Now what are you going to do with me?"

She hopped up on the woodworking bench. "I'm reeling you in."

"Is that a figure eight knot?" *A really good figure eight knot?*

"I told you I took a lot of classes at the yacht club. They occasionally come in handy."

He unlatched the carabiner from his jeans when he reached the bench and hooked it in her belt loop. "There. Hooked you back."

"Yeah." Her voice was breathless. "You have."

Jeremy took her mouth in a hard kiss that left no room for argument. She kissed him back, digging her fingers into his neck. The edge of her nails hurt, but Jeremy didn't care.

Fuck it.

He was going to get hurt either way. While she was still here, he wanted to do everything, feel everything, indulge in everything.

If it was going to hurt, at least give him the thrill.

He released her mouth. "Come inside."

"Yes."

———

THEY LEFT THE ROPES IN THE GARAGE, AND SHE followed him into the dark house; he locked the door behind him. Tayla walked upstairs and into a spacious bedroom on the second floor that smelled like clean linen and cedar.

She watched him in the darkness, her emotions a riot inside her.

This is a bad idea!

This is a great idea.

You should tell him before you—

Shut up, Inner Tayla. I've been listening to you all day.

She wanted him. She wanted him with no reservations, no second thoughts. He was good and sweet and sexy as hell. Jeremy Allen was the guy romance books made you dream about. The thought made her simultaneously giddy and irritated.

Stop being so perfect!

Maybe he's bad in bed.

She found the idea improbable, based on their earlier recreational activities, but maybe that would be his one imperfection. He had come awfully fast the one time before. Granted, she'd been teasing him all night and she'd been giving him a blow job.

Stop thinking so much!

Jeremy turned on a lamp beside the bed while she lingered in the doorway. Then he walked back over to her, doing the reach-down-and-take-the-shirt-off-in-one-sweep thing that was so damn sexy her mouth went dry.

He'd been mostly clothed the night of their escape-room date. Part of the fun was making him come in formal wear. This time his body was on full display.

The dark curl of hair across his chest wasn't heavy, but it begged for her fingers. His body was exactly like she'd imagined. Lean and long, every muscle defined from climbing. He wasn't bulky—far from it—but he was so strong.

He flipped open the button on his jeans and unzipped them, reaching inside to allow his pants to gape and rubbing a hand over what was already a very hard erection.

Jeremy walked back to Tayla, pulled her inside his room, and shut the door. He cupped her face with both hands and proceeded to kiss her in a way that left little room for doubt that he was very good in bed, he'd been imagining this for a while, and he was going to take his time.

She stroked his tongue with her own and allowed her hands to run up and down his back, giving herself over to the familiar rush.

Excitement, desire, hunger, trust—

Fuck.

Her breath caught. The trust was new.

She pushed back the creeping doubt in her heart and focused on his hands cupping her ass, her fingers teasing the button of her jeans. He tilted her chin up and tasted her neck, running his tongue along the line of her collarbones, his beard roughing up the delicate skin above her breasts.

Jeremy took her by the waist and walked her backward until she felt the bed hit the back of her knees. She sat and looked up at him, her mountain man. The sexiest man she'd ever met. A rock in a tumbling, twisting world that most of the time made no sense whatsoever.

He made sense.

Warm skin stretched over lean muscle, long arms reached down to tease her nipples through her shirt. Jeremy took a single finger and ran it around her lips. She opened for him, and he dipped his thumb inside. She sucked on it, scraped her teeth along the flesh, and he tapped her cheeks in soft reprimand. Her tongue licked out and soothed his thumb. Her hands reached for his waistband, but he batted them away.

"You want to taste me?"

She couldn't do anything but nod.

"Not tonight." He nudged the sweater off her shoulders. "I want to see you. Every inch." He took her hand and pulled her to her feet. "Take off your shirt," he whispered.

Tayla did, and her skin had goose bumps from the chill in the air and the rush of desire.

"Jeans." Jeremy gripped his erection through his boxers, watching her as she shimmied out of her pants. He stepped closer and ran a hand over the pink satin panties covering her ass, the pink lace covering her breasts. "You wear matching lingerie every day, don't you?"

Her cheeks went hot, and her chin went up. "Just because no one sees it but me doesn't mean it doesn't need to match."

Jeremy chuckled, his chest moving against her breasts. "I love it." He bent down and kissed her, long and sweet. "I do appreciate the effect, but it's in my way."

He reached back and ran his fingers along the hooks holding her bra closed. "Hmmm. Four."

"You don't hold these girls up with anything less, Mr. Allen."

"I love it when you call me that." He started unhooking her bra, kissing along her shoulder. She felt the release when her bra came off. His warm hands cupped her breasts.

So good. So very good.

He bent down to taste them. "Delicious."

Tayla's heart started to race. "Jeremy—"

"Don't rush me," he whispered in her ear. "I promise I'll make it worth the wait."

Fuuuuuuck. How was she supposed to keep her emotional distance when he said things like that?

Her back hit the bed. Her panties slid down her legs. He lay beside her, hands everywhere. She wanted his hand between her legs, but he didn't oblige her. He teased the back of her knees and her ankles. He ran a single finger up the inside of her thigh. He licked just under her belly button and tasted the soft flesh with a playful bite. He spent a lot of time on her breasts.

Sweet mother of dragons. He was going to make her insane.

"Jeremy—"

He kissed her again, moving his hand from teasing her nipple to the inside of her thigh. His finger slid inside, and his thumb teased her clitoris. She moaned into his mouth.

Jeremy moved in a slow, torturous rhythm, clearly in no rush. He brought her to the brink and backed off, playing with her. He brought her up again, just to the edge of climax, before he moved his hand, taking it away from the one place in the world that Tayla wanted it.

She nearly cried in frustration. "Jeremy Allen, if you don't—"

He laughed and kissed her again. "I like having you at my mercy."

"Just remember it's my turn next."

"I'm counting on it."

He bent down, sucked her nipple into his mouth, and put his hand between her legs, finally throwing her into a climax so hard she felt tears come to her eyes. Every muscle in her body tensed and released at once. Tayla yelled so loud the neighbors probably heard her. Her hands gripped the sheets of the bed. Eventually she had to force his fingers away.

"Too much," she panted. "Jeremy, too much."

"Never too much," he whispered. "I told you it'd be worth it."

Despite her earlier threat, she felt too boneless to move. It was her turn, but she was going to need some recovery time. Jeremy shoved his pants and his boxers down his legs and lay on his side, facing her, one hand on his cock.

He smiled. "You okay?"

"You ask that, knowing how hard you just made me come," she muttered. "That, Mr. Allen, is gloating."

"Maybe a little."

She rolled toward him and looked him up and down. "Have I told you that you're a very attractive man?"

"You have."

"And I would very much like to have sex with you now."

"Since you asked so nicely, I think we should do that."

"I'm so glad you agree." She draped her leg over his hip. "I am assuming you have protection."

He reached back and opened the drawer on his bedside table. "I do believe I can take care of that, Miss McKinnon."

"That's excellent news."

He took her mouth, making love to it as he rolled the condom on and scooted closer. He nudged between her legs and Tayla opened more, hitching her leg higher so he could slide inside.

Oh. There was nothing like that feeling. She was full, her mind clear, her body moving as one with his.

"Fuck, you're sweet." He bit his lip and closed his eyes. "Tayla, I need to…"

She rolled to her back, bringing him with her. "Move."

"Yes."

Jeremy propped himself on his elbows, his body weighing hers down as he moved his hips. They were so close, his rhythm was hard and deep. He took her mouth again, and Tayla wrapped her legs around his waist, angling her hips up.

"Fuck." He grunted. "You're flexible."

"Yoga."

"Yoga's awesome." Jeremy moved from his elbows to his hands, bracing himself above her as his hips rocked harder. He closed his eyes. "I could stay inside you forever."

"Sounds complicated, but we could probably work something out." What was she saying? She was babbling nonsense. Why did sex with Jeremy make her so stupid?

Shut up, Tayla!

Jeremy grinned for a second before pleasure overtook him. He mouthed the word *fuck* one more time before he came hard. His face was frozen in satisfaction, his mouth open, his muscles tense. A few moments later, a look of utter bliss stole over his features and he lay beside her, running his hands up and down the skin of her naked back.

It was like a full-body sigh.

Relax. You're safe here. You're safe with him.

Tayla fell asleep with her face pressed to Jeremy's neck, the scent of him filling her senses.

CHAPTER SEVENTEEN

SHE WOKE in a dark room lit by a small lamp. She panicked for a moment until she caught his familiar cologne.

Jeremy.

She blinked her eyes open and turned to the side. He was lying next to her, a blanket pulled up to his waist, his arm stretched over his head. Tayla was on her side, somewhat shocked she'd fallen asleep so quickly.

It was a point of pride for her that she did not stay over. She had a normal, active sex life, but she also had her independence. She didn't stay at men's houses, not even for a night or a weekend.

But...

She only lived a couple of blocks away. If she went home right now, she'd wake up Emmie, who was going through a stretch of insomnia. She could leave in the morning and not cause a scene if she was careful.

You want to stay with him.

You're fooling yourself.

You know this isn't going to last.

For the hundredth time, Tayla hushed the internal voices that were warning her away; she reached over and turned off the lamp. She scooted closer to Jeremy, and his arm fell around her waist as he snuggled closer.

They were skin to skin, lying next to each other with nothing between them.

It was the most intimate moment of Tayla's life.

Bathed in darkness, she was lulled back to sleep by the moonlight and his even breathing.

———

A KISS ON HER BARE SHOULDER. THE SUN IN HER FACE.

"Hey." Jeremy's rough morning voice was a thing of manly, growly beauty. "I'm making coffee."

Tayla blinked her eyes open. "You are a god among men."

"So last night didn't give me the 'god among men' designation, but coffee does?"

The sun was too bright; she decided to hide her eyes in the pillow. "I spoke too soon, because it'll actually depend on how strong you make it."

He chuckled and kissed her shoulder again. "I make it pretty strong. Cream or sugar?"

"No cream but a lot of sugar."

Jeremy reached down and pinched her bottom. "So... strong, black, and sweet?"

She couldn't stop the smile. "I didn't say it."

"You like your coffee like you like your men? Strong, black, and sweet?"

"You made that joke, not me." She couldn't stop laughing. "And I don't really have a *type* of man, okay?"

"No?"

"Over the course of my dating life? No. Currently, I'd say my type is a man who makes me coffee in the morning and doesn't harass me."

"But it's such a nice ass to harass." He ran his hand over her bottom. "I like having you in my bed, Miss McKinnon."

She tried not to squirm. "It's a very comfortable bed."

"You snore a little, but you don't kick. You're welcome anytime."

"I do not snore!" She rolled over, prepared to hit him with a pillow, but he'd already slid out of bed. He stood in the doorway, grinning at her, shirtless and wearing a pair of baggy sweatpants low on his hips.

Wrong. You have a type. It is him. Him is your type and every other man pales in comparison and you are thinking with your ovaries because what are you doing, Tayla?

"Just a little." He held his fingers a fraction of an inch apart. "I set a clean T-shirt out for you if you want to borrow it."

"Thanks." She glanced at her phone when he left the room. There was a text message from Emmie. *Since your phone is at Jeremy's house, I'm assuming you are too.*

She typed back. *I knew letting you use the Find My Phone app would avoid awkward conversations.*

Tayla got up and used the attached bathroom, washing her face and grimacing when she saw her reflection.

This. This was why she didn't stay over. There was no reason that Jeremy needed to see her in this condition. Her mascara was flaking, her foundation was probably rubbed into his pillow. No highlighter. No eyeliner. She looked like she'd stayed all night at a goth Halloween party.

Disaster.

Her carefully prepared public face was completely gone. Now she had to walk home with blotchy skin. She didn't even have her purse with her, which would have had an emergency makeup kit with the basics. Skin balancing cream, a tube of highlighter, brow gel, and mascara.

Jeremy had a good array of products on the counter. Coconut oil, shea butter, an oil that looked like it was for beards, and a fragrance-free moisturizer. She found a tissue and used the coconut oil to remove her scary eye makeup. She used a bit of the moisturizer and sniffed the oil.

That was the scent she'd assumed was cologne. It was perfect for him. She dabbed a tiny bit on her wrist before she put it back.

When she walked out, her phone was lit up with a new text message. She sat on the edge of his bed to read it. She could hear Jeremy whistling downstairs.

Did you tell him yet?

No.

You better.

She hated putting dirty clothes on, but she didn't really have a choice. She got dressed and put on the T-shirt Jeremy had laid out for her. She only had a couple of blocks to walk home. She could do this. Why hadn't she thought about all this last night?

Oh right. Rendered stupid by sex with Jeremy.

Damn it.

She walked downstairs and immediately smelled coffee, which made life so much better. Even more, she saw two mugs sitting out on the counter, a regular mug and a travel mug.

Oh, you wonderful man.

"Hey." He looked up from the toaster and smiled. "Nice shirt. I'm sure it's driving you crazy to be in dirty clothes and without a toothbrush, so if you want to grab your coffee and run, it won't hurt my feelings. You are also welcome to stay and hang out. I can make you breakfast."

Stay!

Eat breakfast!

Have more sex!

"Uh, thanks. I appreciate it." She looked down at herself. "If you really don't mind, I think I'll take the coffee to go. Honestly, it's the dirty socks that are bugging me the most, but yes, it all feels kind of gross."

He laughed. "Completely get it." He poured black coffee into the travel mug. "Next time you should bring a change of clothes and a toothbrush. That way we can sleep in."

Okay! Let me go get that now, I only live a couple of blocks away!

Tayla walked to the counter and added sugar from the blue-and-white speckled enamel bowl on the counter.

Jeremy put his arm around her and kissed the top of her head. "You know, you still look gorgeous even without all the makeup."

"I like makeup."

"And you look great with it. I'm just saying you still look sexy as hell in my shirt and not much else. You sure you don't want to—"

"SOKA called me back yesterday," she blurted out. "They want me back for another interview on Thursday."

His silence was like a gut punch.

Tayla blinked back unexpected tears. "Jeremy?"

He backed away and leaned against the counter opposite the coffee maker. "Did you come over to tell me that last night?"

"I don't know why I came over last night. I wasn't thinking—"

"But you could have told me last night." His face was carefully blank. "And instead you flirted with me and had sex with me and stayed over and you didn't tell me that you got called back for another interview at a company two hundred miles away."

"I'm sorry." Regret sat like lead in her stomach. "I told you from the beginning—"

"I know." His voice was bitter. "Trust me. I know."

She didn't know why she asked the question, but she had to. "Do you regret last night?"

Jeremy didn't speak. He walked over, poured a cup of coffee, and picked it up. "I don't know how I feel." He started toward the stairs. "I need to take a shower. Just shut the door on your way out. I'll see you, Tayla."

He walked upstairs, and he didn't look back. Tayla sipped the coffee he'd poured for her.

Black, strong, and sweet. Exactly like she wanted.

The bitterness in her mouth was all her own doing.

———

Jeremy drove out to Cary's farm after the shop closed that night. He was supposed to do orders, but he couldn't think straight. He didn't get a dozen flirty or funny texts from Tayla. He hadn't texted her. She hadn't texted him.

He was organizing his climbing gear when he realized he had a set of cams and a rope from Cary's stuff.

"You drove all the way out here to give me three cams and a rope?" Cary frowned when Jeremy handed his stuff through the truck window.

"Yeah."

"Bullshit."

Jeremy put his truck in park and turned off the engine, listening to the wind sweep over the orange groves. The scent of blossoms was heavy in the air. It smelled like one of Tayla's perfumes.

"I'm all fucked up, Cary."

"Yeah, I figured." Cary stepped back. "Come on. My mom will feed you, and then we can talk."

"I don't want to inter—"

"She made beef stroganoff."

Jeremy hopped out of the truck. "Yeah, that sounds good."

An hour later with his belly full and his heart a little patched up by Mrs. Nakamura's beef stroganoff and noodles, Jeremy felt a little better. He knew his mom and dad loved living in the mountains—it was their dream—but sometimes Jeremy missed having his mom close by.

He and Cary took two bottles of beer out to the porch and sat on the rocking chairs Cary's dad had made.

"What's up?" Cary asked.

"They called Tayla back for another interview in San Francisco."

"Okay." He sipped his beer. "That wasn't exactly a surprise, right?"

"She told me this morning after she stayed at my house all night."

"Ah." He nodded. "I'm guessing you weren't playing Scrabble."

"No."

"And she could have told you the night before, but she didn't, and you feel like she sprang it on you this morning while you were thinking you'd dazzled her with your sexual prowess, won her heart, and everything was going to fall into place."

"One, I never want to hear the phrase 'dazzled with sexual prowess' from you ever again."

"Hey, Emmie convinced me to read romance. You should too— you might learn something."

"And two…" Jeremy shrugged. "I don't know. Maybe. Kinda."

"Dude, this isn't a Hallmark movie."

"Okay, I know that but—"

"No. You can't be a dick about this. She told you everything up front. You told her you were going to… I don't know exactly what you said or anything. We're not girls."

"I told her I wanted to be with her." The memory put a sour taste in his mouth. "That I didn't want to think about the future."

"Okay then." Cary gave him a decisive nod.

"Okay what?"

"You told her you were all about the moment. Own it or let her go now. Don't be a dick."

"You know, you used to be my teacher. I'm not sure you're supposed to be calling me a dick."

"I'm not calling you a dick." Cary pointed his beer bottle at Jeremy. "If you get pissed at Tayla for taking you at your word, *then* I'll call you a dick. And it doesn't matter that I used to be your teacher. I'm not looking for a reference."

Jeremy swallowed the lump in his throat. "I'm in love with this girl, Cary."

Cary sighed. "I wish I could just be happy for you, J. I really do. I'm not counting you out yet though. They haven't offered her that job, and she hasn't said yes. You're a good guy. She's not gonna find better anywhere. Be her reason to stay."

Jeremy nodded, but he couldn't find anything to say.

Cary was right. He couldn't be a dick about Tayla moving, even if he wished she'd had better timing about telling him about the second interview.

"You know, maybe the fact that she *didn't* want to tell you about it means she's more invested than you think, okay?" Cary finished his beer. "I don't want to give you false hope or anything, but I've seen you guys together. She's not playing you. There's not a lying bone in that girl's body."

"No, sometimes she's painfully honest."

"The only danger I can see with Tayla is… she might have a hard time being honest with herself," Cary said. "So my advice is to be a safe place for her to be herself. Listen to what she's saying and what she's *not* saying. And don't be a dick."

"Yeah, I think I got that part. Thanks."

————

HE DROVE BACK TO TOWN AND WENT IMMEDIATELY TO the bookshop. He parked in front and texted her. *U home?*

A few minutes later, he saw a light turn on. She walked to the door and opened it. Her eyes were wary, and he hated that he'd been the one to cause that.

"Hey," she said.

Jeremy spread his arms out. "I was a dick."

She took a deep breath and let it out. "I should have told you before we—"

"I don't regret last night. Not a single minute of it. Not a second. If I made you think that, I'm sorry. That was shitty of me to do."

"Okay." Her eyes softened.

"But also, I wish you'd felt like you could tell me about the second interview, because yeah, it surprised me. And I didn't react well."

She leaned against the door. Her hair was up in a messy bun, she was wearing leggings and a sweatshirt, and as always, she looked gorgeous. "Truth time? I don't know what I'm doing here," she said quietly. "I don't date, Jeremy. Not like this. You are like the complete opposite of the kind of guys I usually hang out with."

Damn right I am. "Good."

"And don't pretend I'm like the girls you've dated either. We are *so* different."

"I like that about us," he said. "You keep me sharp."

She stuck her hands in her pockets. "I'm breaking all these rules for you, and I don't know why I'm doing it. It's probably a really bad idea. For both of us. So if you want to stop seeing me—"

"I don't."

She bit her lip. "I don't know what you want from me."

"Why don't we talk about that over dinner tomorrow night? At my house. I'll cook. And you bring a bag."

She let out a breath and gave him a reluctant smile. "See? This is another rule. I don't stay over at guys' houses. Ever."

"You're not staying over at some guy's house." *Not ever again, if I have anything to say about it.* "You're staying over at *my* house. You know I make good coffee, and my *chilaquiles* are even better."

"I don't know what that is."

"It's really good. Trust me."

"I do." Her smile was tentative. "That's kind of the problem."

Oh Miss McKinnon, I see you now. He stepped toward her. "Come over tomorrow."

She whispered, "Okay."

"Stay the night."

She nodded.

Jeremy bent down and kissed her softly.

Stay the night.

Stay in Metlin.

Stay with me.

180

CHAPTER EIGHTEEN

THURSDAY MORNING, Tayla was sitting with her parents in the morning room, eating a silent breakfast and wondering why she was there. She should have just gotten a hotel room. Her father was reading the financial section, and her mother was tuned to a small television on the buffet. Tayla was staring out the sunny window, watching the boats sail across a crystal-blue bay.

The color of your beautiful eyes. She remembered her father saying that to her when she was a girl. When had his interest in her waned? When she'd started developing a personality? They asked her nothing about her life in Metlin. Probably they assumed it was a phase like pink hair or the peasant shirts and Birkenstocks she'd worn for a solid year in college.

It was an experimental year.

She took a drink of the weak coffee their cook had brewed that morning. "So, I'm seeing someone in Metlin. It's kind of a regular thing. His name is Jeremy, he climbs mountains, he's really fun, and also he's black."

Her mother looked up and blinked. "Are we supposed to be shocked? This isn't 1980, Tayla. And your father and I don't see color."

So much to unpack there, but she didn't have the time that morning. "Just wanted you to have the correct mental picture because sometimes people assume everyone in small-town California is white, and that's really not the case."

Her father didn't look up from his paper. "What does he do?"

"He has a degree in finance from UCLA."

Her father raised one eyebrow.

"But he hated LA and hated working in finance, so he runs a comic book shop in Metlin and takes care of his grandfather."

Her father's eyebrow went down and the newspaper went up.

"I thought you said he was a mountain climber," her mother said.

"He only does that on the weekends."

She looked confused. "But you hate camping. We tried to send you to a summer camp in Lake Tahoe one year, and you called a cab and stayed at the Ritz-Carlton for a week."

Ah yes, summer camp. Tayla had dozens of fond childhood memories of the lakefront view and the room service. "I still hate camping, but I like Jeremy. So... I might try it. If he really, *really* wants me to."

Her father put the paper down. "You have a second interview with the international fashion company this afternoon, correct?"

"Yes."

"So is this young man interested in moving to the city with you and running his comic book shop here if you get the job?"

Tayla felt the color drain from her face. "I doubt it."

"So why did you bother telling us about him?"

Because he's important to me. Because I want you to know I have a life outside your tiny orbit. Because I want you to care.

Tayla didn't say any of those things. It wasn't worth the effort. She'd tried in the past to start fights with her parents to see if they cared.

They didn't.

Her mother just drank more and her father would go to his office.

Tayla stood. "I'm going to get more coffee."

"We have staff for that." Her father rang the crystal bell in the middle of the table.

"He sounds very nice," her mother said. "Would you like to bring him up to the city for a visit?"

In my nightmares. Tayla walked out just as their cook, Gloria, was walking in.

"What can I get for you, Mr. McKinnon?"

"Tayla," her mother said, "don't leave. We can have more coffee here."

"It's fine." She walked to the kitchen and set her cup on the counter before she started up the stairs.

Why did she bother? Why did she even try?

———

Tayla was sitting with Kabisa and Azim in the garden of the SOKA office. It was a lush green space that spread along the side of the building, cut off from the alley by a fence covered in greenery. There was a grill and an outdoor dining table, but Tayla was in the sunny sitting area with a gas firepit in the center.

She'd created an idea board for her second interview, detailing some of the outdoor-living ideas she'd collected from her own research, along with a few of the social influencers she thought they could target.

"...so a lot of whom we'd be going for are not the big-name interior design people, but the garden niche, environmental, and travel crowd. Look at this chair, for example. The wood is reclaimed from Vietnamese fishing boats. And the company that makes them is a collective of former boat builders who are making furniture now instead. It's a fair trade company using recycled materials that are, honestly, stunning."

"I love all the colors," Kabisa said. "The variety. We'd have to check their references, but they sound like exactly the kind of company we'd like to work with. And their prices are within our target area."

"It's not cheap, but these are boat builders. The quality is going to be very good, and it's wood furniture that will be able to stand up to the elements."

Azim looked around. "A few of those pieces would look great right here actually."

"I was thinking the same thing," Tayla said. "And look at these influencer ideas." She handed them printouts of screenshots she'd taken of the profiles and a sample post. "They're nicely photographed. Not the highest follower counts, so sponsoring posts for them would be cost-effective."

"And look at the comments." Kabisa's eyes lit up. "Great interaction."

"That's what we're looking for. Accounts with lower followers but high interaction. Real dynamic. Word of mouth. A lot of these influencers are also really active on other social networks where we could include direct links to SOKA's site. And we can target the travel accounts depending on where the products are sourced. People who have stayed at a cool local hotel in Ha Long Bay, for example, might be drawn to remembering that amazing trip with a chair or a table made from wood that reminds them of the boats they saw. Play on ideas like that."

"This is very good, Tayla." Kabisa paged through the proposal Tayla had put together. She exchanged a look with Azim. "And we've tossed around the idea of including more housewares on the site, but I think the outdoor-living aspect presents some intriguing tie-ins and possibilities we hadn't considered. Thank you."

"I hope that gives you an idea of where I think we can go with this. And obviously a lot of these ideas translate to fashion, accessories, all the other products you guys are currently offering."

Azim was nodding silently, still paging through the papers. Tayla had debated going with electronic presentations, but Jeremy had encouraged her to give Kabisa and Azim something to hold, to engage more than a single sense to make herself more memorable.

"I think that's all we need from you for the interview," Kabisa said. "But Azim and I are cooking lunch tomorrow for all the staff. Would you be interested in joining us? We'd love for you to meet everyone."

Tayla's heart sank. "And I'd love to meet them, but I have to head home in the morning. Tomorrow is the monthly art walk in Metlin, and we're doing a book club party for the high school book club I've been leading. I promised the kids I'd be there for the party."

Kabisa's face lit up. "That sounds so cool! What a great thing to be involved in. Of course you can't miss that. You can meet the staff another time."

"How did you get involved in that?" Azim said. "It's lovely you have a bookshop in your town. You work there part time right now, correct?"

"I do. It's my best friend's bookshop. She reopened it after her grandmother passed, and I moved down to help her out because I was looking for a new challenge. She's started a bunch of reading groups and clubs that meet in the store, and she hosts events there. We even had a baby shower a couple of weeks ago! Her partner is a tattoo artist, and he has a shop within the shop, if that makes sense. It's been really successful."

"That is so intriguing," Kabisa said. "We may have to come visit Metlin someday to see it."

"If you're interested in seeing the Sierra Nevadas, it's the perfect place to stay."

Azim smiled. "It sounds like it could be hard to say goodbye."

Tayla quickly schooled her expression. "It would be. But it's not far to visit, and I'm always looking for a new challenge. A company like SOKA presents me with an ongoing challenge, so it's very much what I'm in the market for."

"Excellent." Kabisa clapped her hands. "Tayla, it was so lovely to see you again. Shall we grab another coffee before you have to leave?"

"I'd love that."

———

TAYLA WAS BATTLING A HEADACHE ON THE TRAIN. SHE'D left as early as she could after another tense evening at her parents' house. Her father was gone, of course. Her mother was drunk. Tayla had spent the evening in the sitting room with Bianca as she belligerently watched international real estate shows.

Tayla's phone buzzed. Jeremy was calling.

A little of the headache lifted. She tapped the Answer button. "Hey."

"Hey. You on your way home?"

"Mm-hmm." She leaned against the window, glad for the morning sun. "Train's pretty quiet."

"Good. You sound tired."

"I didn't sleep great."

Silence on the other side. "You said the interview went really well."

"It did. They invited me to a company barbecue today actually. But I told them I had to head back."

"We could have covered for you."

"I wouldn't want to disappoint the kids." She'd been having too much fun reading their newest book, *When the Stars Go Blue*. The protagonist was a talented dancer struggling with hard choices, first love, and the future. The parallels were hitting a little close to home. "And there's the dance performance outside the theater. Some of the girls want to go to that, and Emmie can't leave the shop on art walk night."

"Okay. So what's the headache for?"

I miss you. I don't know what I'm supposed to do. You're messing everything up by being wonderful. Also, my parents are assholes. "Probably just tired." She thought about Jeremy. "And probably not drinking enough water."

"I told you." Jeremy told everyone to drink more water. "Coffee doesn't count. The most common cause of headaches is not drinking enough water. You have your bottle with you?"

She smiled. "Yeah."

"Drink it all. And text me when you get to Fresno. I'll meet you at the station."

"Okay. I'll see you in a couple of hours."

"See you."

As soon as she put her phone down, the headache returned.

Great. She was suffering from Jeremy deprivation.

Fuck my life.

———

Tayla walked down to the theater with eight fourteen- to sixteen-year-old girls, all of them jumping up and down with excitement to see the dance team from Fresno perform in front of the old Fox Theater. Like many other towns in Central California, Metlin had an old art deco–era theater that used to be for movies. Now it hosted concerts, the local symphony, and a few big-name artists that passed through.

Main Street was teeming with artists and crafters showing their stuff, street musicians performing on each corner, and food vendors pushing carts down the center of the street, which had been cordoned off for six blocks.

Once a month, Metlin turned into the place to be in the valley. Street artists exhibited at an old warehouse on 7th Avenue, shops stayed open late, and the whole town and the surrounding area turned up for the party.

Tayla and Jeremy walked with the girls to the front of the theater where the modern ballet company from Fresno would be performing in a few minutes. They were drinking bubble tea from the Thai restaurant and shepherding the girls, who were giggling and walking in a tight pack.

"Do you think they're talking about us?" Jeremy whispered loudly.

The girls giggled and stole glances over their shoulders.

Tayla shook her head, but she was smiling. "Since you insisted on holding my hand, I think they probably are."

"I can't help it. You're cute and short. I might lose you in a crowd."

"In Metlin?"

"Have you seen how many people came tonight?"

It *was* pretty crowded. The art walk grew every month, but this month must have broken records. "You think it's the dancers?"

"And the band maybe?"

It was the first time the theater was doing a public performance to tease an upcoming show like this. They were doing two fifteen-minute previews of coming attractions on the sidewalk outside the theater, and people were crowded around.

Tayla and Jeremy managed to find a space for the book club near the front of the theater, and the girls waited, bouncing on their toes, for the dancers to start. Jeremy stood behind Tayla, his arms around her waist and his chin propped on her head.

"Comfortable?"

"So much." He bent down. "You staying at my place tonight?"

"I shouldn't. I need to do laundry and catch up with Emmie. Tomorrow?"

"Going up to the mountains to grab Pop tomorrow. I'll be back Sunday."

"Okay. Well… we'll figure it out." Tayla's heart sank.

"No worries. And no worries about Pop. He knows I'm an adult, and he turns his hearing aids off at night. Trust me."

Tayla laughed. "Your senior roommate."

"I can't complain. He makes a mean bacon sandwich."

"Definitely can't complain about that."

"Play your cards right, and he'll make one for you someday."

"I'll remember that."

She was back, so why did she feel like she was already saying goodbye? And why did it feel so wrong? She wanted to move back to the city. She was thrilled with her interview. She was nearly certain she had this job. And it was a dream job!

What is wrong with me?

She plastered on a happy face and fought back tears. The laughter and joy of the crowd around her was bittersweet. The smiling faces of the book club should have lifted her spirits, but Tayla couldn't help but think about their next month's read, *The Hate U Give*. Would she be there to talk with them about it? Would she have to move before they finished?

"Stop thinking so loud," Jeremy said in her ear.

"Sorry."

He tilted her chin up until he could read her eyes. "And stop saying goodbye already."

"I'm not."

"Mm-hmm." His tone was doubtful.

Intro music started and everyone clapped when the dancers came out. They bowed, the music changed, and they threw themselves into the dance. It was passionate and arresting. The two principals at the center of the group moved together in a graceful union before they were torn away from each other by the other dancers in the company. Over and over, they struggled to stay together only to be dragged apart.

Did everything *have to be a sign today?* Tayla focused on the girls in the book club, who were riveted to the performance. One of them had tears in her eyes.

Nearly twenty minutes later, the dancers were taking their bows and the book club—along with the entire crowd—erupted into applause and chatter. Jeremy and Tayla guided the girls back to the bookshop where most were being picked up by their parents. Then they walked over to Jeremy's shop where Cary was watching the counter.

A selection of his photographs was also hanging on the walls because he was one of the featured artists that month.

Tayla and Jeremy nearly ran into Ox's sister Melissa while she was walking out of the shop. Her cheeks were red and her eyes were wild.

"Melissa?" Jeremy put a hand on her shoulder. "You okay?"

"Fine!" she nearly shouted. "I'm fine. Have you seen Ox?"

Tayla pointed across the street. "I think he's over at INK with Emmie. Unless he went out to get food. He was just finishing up with a client when we left and he mentioned he was hungry."

"Okay. Great. Thanks." Melissa had always struck Tayla as a force of nature. She was a widowed mom who ran her family's ranch and orange groves nearly single-handedly. She rarely came into town, probably because she was constantly busy with her daughter, her mother, and her cows.

She was beautiful in a Western, outdoorsy way. Honestly, if Tayla imagined Jeremy with a woman, it would be someone like Melissa. Her blond hair was streaked gold from the sun, she was tan, and her body was lean and muscled from days on horseback working with cattle.

Melissa crossed the street, her commanding stride making people move out of her way without her saying a word.

"What was all that about?" Tayla asked. "I've never seen her upset like that. She was upset, right?"

"Yeah, she definitely was." Jeremy frowned and walked inside the shop.

Along the far wall, Cary's photographs stretched across the display area, framed and lit like they were hung in a professional gallery. Most were vivid landscapes of the mountains or the foothills. A few animal prints. Some really excellent shots of cowboys kicking up dust in a corral. A few portraits.

"Those are from the Oxfords' branding day last year." Jeremy pointed to the ranching pictures. "And— Oh shit."

Tayla followed his gaze and saw what might have caught Melissa's eye. It was the central picture of the ranching series, larger than the rest and centered on the wall.

The shot was taken in profile, an intense moment captured in the middle of chaos. Dust kicked up around her, her hat at an angle, a boot propped up on a split-rail fence—the portrait was a full-body shot of Melissa, her gaze intent on something in the distance and her mouth hanging open a little. Her skin was flushed, sweat beaded on her forehead and chest. Sunlight made her tan skin glow. Her body was twisted, and the wind plastered her shirt to her body so her waist and breasts were clearly outlined.

It was dynamic and beautiful, a woman in command, intent on her work. Her jeans were dirty, her boots covered in dust. It was both utterly powerful and achingly feminine at the same time. Though the setting was public, the lens had captured an expression that felt intensely intimate.

Tayla looked at the caption: *Cary Nakamura. Beauty. Digital photograph.*

"Oh," she breathed out. "He is *so* in love with her."

"Yeah."

Jeremy walked to the counter where Cary was paging through a catalogue and very definitely not watching Melissa walk across the street. His expression was tense.

"Did you ask her?" Jeremy asked.

"She knew I was taking pictures at their last branding. I asked if I could exhibit some tonight. She said no problem."

"But did she know about *that* picture?"

He continued to flip pages. "I told her that she and some of the other cowboys were in the pictures. She said, and I quote, 'No problem.'"

"But she's mad about that picture."

He shrugged. "Don't know. She wouldn't talk to me. First time in the past five years the damn woman doesn't want to give me a piece of her mind."

Tayla and Jeremy exchanged a look. It might have been the first time Melissa was confronted by the undeniable fact that Cary Nakamura clearly had feelings for her past professional admiration.

Tayla said, "It's a beautiful picture, Cary."

He looked up. "Thank you. I thought so too."

Jeremy asked, "You okay here?"

"Yeah. I'm fine."

They walked back to mingle with patrons in the shop, but Tayla kept sneaking glances at Cary.

He was not fine.

CHAPTER NINETEEN

THE FOLLOWING WEDNESDAY, Tayla walked into Bombshell Tattoos only to be hit with the intense smell of stale beer combined with disinfectant. Ginger's employee, Russ, was mopping the floor, so the stale beer smell was gradually being drowned out by the disinfectant.

Tayla set her books down on the desk in back where Ginger's computer lived. "Hey, Ginger?"

"Be down in a sec!"

Like Emmie, Ginger's apartment was above her shop. Also like Emmie, Ginger had once lived with Ox. Awkward? Maybe. But you had to get over all sorts of things when you lived in a small town, even exes living right across the street and working at rival businesses.

Not that it was all that dramatic a year and a half after the initial conflict. Ginger was never going to be Emmie's favorite person, but they weren't enemies or anything.

Tayla had developed a sudden interest in relationship dynamics. Why did Ox and Emmie work but Ginger and Ox didn't? Were they too much alike? Maybe. When Tayla thought about it, more couples she knew were different than they were alike. Ox and Emmie. Daisy and Spider.

Speak of the devil.

Spider walked into the shop and bumped knuckles with Russ. He smiled when he spotted Tayla. "Hey, gorgeous girl."

She walked over and gave him a hug. "Hey yourself. How you doing? Haven't seen you in a while."

He shrugged. "Busy at home. Refinishing the woodwork in the front bedroom."

Spider was one of the preeminent tattoo artists on the West Coast, regularly visited by very picky clientele and regularly profiled in national magazines and trade journals.

But his face was never shown, and he kept a very low personal profile. The man didn't even have a mobile phone. He was like the opposite of a marketing genius. He had no social media. No website.

The mystique had become his brand.

"What are you doing here?" she asked.

He lifted his arm and Tayla saw an outline of flowers spreading from below his elbow and wrapping around his wrist. "Working with Ginger on a new piece."

"I didn't know you got your tattoos from her."

"Not *just* her, but…" He lowered his voice. "Ginger's better than Ox. Especially with color."

Russ laughed in the corner. "It's true."

"Shut up, Russ."

Tayla examined his arm. "Daisies?"

Spider's harsh face broke into a grin. "Gotta get my woman on my skin, no doubt."

"That's gonna be beautiful." She dropped his arm and walked back to the desk just as Ginger came downstairs.

"Hey, Spider."

"Hey." He handed her a coffee. "Large caffe latte, as requested."

"You're a saint." Ginger reached for the coffee.

"I'm the opposite." Spider sat down on Ginger's rolling stool. "Ready when you are."

"Get outta my chair. This isn't your place. We doing all the fill today?"

"I think we have time." Spider smiled and moved to the client chair. "The area's not that big."

"Let's do the main fill, then we'll talk about shading when that's done. Just because it's flowers doesn't mean it's not worth the time to do it right."

"Damn straight."

Tayla broke into their conversation. "Ginger, I'm probably going to have the occasional question while I do the books since we're new. Is that cool, or am I going to be distracting you?"

"Nah, you're cool." She nodded to a blank workspace. "Just move the computer there. Cash won't be in until after lunch today, and he actually cleaned his shit up."

"Perfect." She moved her stuff from the back desk to the currently empty station. There was plenty of room to spread out. "Spider, how's Daisy?"

"She's good. Busy. She told me your second interview in that shithole city went well."

"Yeah, it did. Can you stop calling San Francisco a shithole?"

"I will if you agree to stay in Metlin."

"Fine. Keep calling it a shithole. I don't care."

"You leaving us after all?" Ginger sat down and pulled on her gloves. "Damn, Tayla. I'm gonna have to get another bookkeeper?"

"And I'm gonna have to find somebody else for trivia night," Spider grumbled. "Ethan doesn't know history for shit."

"Nothing's for sure," Tayla said. "Yet. They haven't offered the job to me."

"But they invited her to a company barbecue," Spider said. "So they're going to."

Ginger pursed her lips as she filled small plastic cups with ink.

"That sucks. I mean for us. I'm sure Tayla's thrilled to get out of here."

"I'm not *thrilled*," Tayla protested. "I like Metlin. I'm not dying to leave or anything."

In fact, more and more she had to admit that Emmie and Ox had a point. She didn't have many friends left in San Francisco. Most of her social life had moved away. Other than Tobin, and he hadn't even returned her text when she was in the city the week before.

Asshole.

Why was she moving away from Metlin again?

"She likes Metlin a little." Spider spoke from the chair as Ginger cleaned his arm and inspected the outline. "She likes Jeremy a lot."

Ginger's needle began to buzz. "Jeremy Allen is hot as shit. I was tempted to hit that, but he's too damn sweet. I would ruin that man."

Tayla felt an unexpected stab of jealousy. After she left, maybe Ginger would "hit that." The flare of anger surprised her.

"Relax." Ginger smiled. "I don't poach men. Especially not from people I like."

"Especially from people who could mess your financial shit up," Spider said. "Tayla holds the *power*."

"Shut up, Spider." She opened Ginger's computer and started to examine the happy rows of numbers. "I would never be unprofessional with someone's private financial information."

Ginger cackled and put the needle to Spider's skin.

Tayla liked numbers. They didn't argue. There was no grey area. Numbers added up or they didn't. Accounts were reconciled or they weren't. Nothing was subjective.

"So if you like Jeremy so much, why are you leaving?" Ginger asked.

"This job isn't just a job. It really is my dream job."

"Doesn't sound like your dream job," Ginger muttered. "Not when you're having to leave a place you like."

"Good point," Spider chimed in.

"It *is* my dream job," Tayla said. "Every opportunity means sacrifice."

Ginger snorted. "Who told you that shit?"

Her father. She'd heard it so many times she didn't even question it. "I just mean... the world isn't going to lay everything out on a silver platter, is it? You have to take opportunities where you can find them. There's never going to be a truly perfect job. You have to sacrifice to get what you want."

What had her father sacrificed?

Family. A relationship with his wife. His daughter. Did he think it was worth it in the end? He'd reached the height of success at his firm, and yet he slept alone at his club most nights with no one but a bunch of other rich assholes to keep him company.

"I don't believe in sacrifice." Ginger was curled over Spider's arm. "I mean, I believe in working your ass off. That kind of sacrifice. And I believe in going after what you want. Personally, I think if the world isn't going to give you what you want, then you make the world your bitch until it gives it up."

"That's poetic. Thanks, Ginger."

"Hold up," Spider says. "She's got a point. I mean, how great a job is it if you have to give up living in a place you like that has a better cost of living and is where most of your friends live? Sounds like you'd be happy at work and nowhere else."

Tayla sighed. "It's not that I don't like doing people's books and being my own boss and working with Emmie sometimes and leading book club and all that stuff. But I cannot tell you how excited I am about this company. For real, it's not just a normal job. It's like... a mission. It's being part of something big. Who's to say I won't make new friends at this job? They seem like really cool people."

"Yeah, okay." Ginger shrugged. "Whatever works for you. If you feel like settling, settle."

"It's not *settling*."

Ginger lifted the needle. "Tayla, everyone in Metlin likes you. You're practically a celebrity here. Don't pretend you don't like it. Your best friend is here, and she's not leaving. And added to all that, you're banging Jeremy Allen, who is about the sweetest damn man in this town, and he looks at you like you're a fucking goddess."

"You also dominate on trivia night," Spider added. "There's no guarantee you would in San Francisco. There's probably more book-smart people there."

"Thanks, Spider, that's helpful." Ginger shook her head. "Remind her she's surrounded by numbnuts here."

"I said *book* smart. Not real smart."

"I like Jeremy." Tayla felt her cheeks flush. "More than like him, maybe." *Definitely.* "But Ginger, you of all people cannot be telling me I should give up an amazing job opportunity to stay in Metlin for a man."

"I'm not saying that." She turned the needle on again. "I'm saying I think you should get everything you want."

"Life doesn't work that way."

"Says who?" She glanced up. "In a dream world, what would you want? Emmie to move back to the city? Would you want Jeremy to move up to San Francisco with you?"

The thought was tempting, but also impossible. "Neither of them can move, Ginger. And Jeremy would be miserable there. He hated living in LA."

"I agree. So... I don't know. Don't settle, and figure out how to get everything you want. That's my advice. You're a smart girl. Work it out."

Tayla turned back to the computer while Ginger continued filling in Spider's tattoo.

Just figure out how to get everything you want.

Sure! Why not? I mean, why wouldn't SOKA move their entire operation to Metlin? Give up their amazing office in the city? Move away from a large international airport and down to Bumfuck, California?

Made total sense.

———

TAYLA ALMOST SNORTED ICED TEA THROUGH HER NOSE. "He did what?"

Gus smiled. "So I told his mother there'd been a little complication and we'd be late for dinner."

"Getting stuck fifty feet up a pine tree isn't a little complication! Did you tell her about the tree?"

"If I'd told her about the tree, she'd have tried to keep that boy in town, and he wasn't made for town." Gus winked. "I knew that much when he was a little bug."

Jeremy had his hand over his face. His cheeks were dark red. "Pop, you've got to stop telling people this story."

"We managed to get him down. I knew a forest service guy with a cherry picker."

"How long was he up there?"

Jeremy said, "About five hours."

"I told him if he could climb up the tree, he could climb down. I was too old to go get him. I had arthritis by then."

"He told a five-year-old that it was up to him to find his way back down a fifty-foot-tall sugar pine," Jeremy said. "This family has no mercy."

"It was a damn fool thing to do, bug."

Tayla's eyes were the size of saucers. "How did you even get up that high?"

"I had no fear on the way up," Jeremy said. "When I got to the top branch, I got a little freaked out."

Gus reached for another slice of pie. "We should have known then about the mountain climbing thing."

Tayla shook her head. "I guess so." She held up her hand when Gus offered her another piece. She'd accepted Jeremy's invitation for dinner, and Gus proceeded to make a delicious tri-tip dinner followed by dessert and all sorts of embarrassing stories about Jeremy. "Does it bother you?"

Gus frowned. "What?"

"The rock climbing thing?"

"I'm his old grandpa," Gus said. "He doesn't listen to me. Does it bother *you?*"

"A little." Tayla glanced at Jeremy. "I don't love the idea of him getting hurt."

"That's the truth." Gus cleared his throat. "But you know why he does it?"

"I think so." She stole a glance at Jeremy, who was watching her with an unreadable expression. "I know he says it centers him. The way yoga does for me."

"I'm guessing with yoga you keep your damn butt on the ground though," Gus said.

"Well, yeah." She looked at Jeremy. "But I'd never ask him to stop."

He mouthed the word *thanks.*

"Besides, it isn't my place," she said.

"Sure it is," Gus said. "Look at him."

"Pop, enough." Jeremy stood and reached for the plates. "Tayla, you want anything else?"

She shook her head. "I'm good. The food was great. Thanks, both of you."

"The pie came from Daisy's café. Do you know it?" Gus's eyes twinkled. "Café Maya. She makes me a fresh blueberry and sour cream every week. That was my wife's specialty. Did Jeremy tell you that? Blueberry sour cream, and sweet potato. That was my other favorite pie. Every church picnic, she'd bring a sweet potato pie. Everyone wanted her recipes. She only gave them to Maya though. Daisy's grandma. They were friends."

"Wait, so Daisy's grandma—?"

"Maya. She was friends with Louisa, my wife. When Maya and Enrique first moved here, they didn't speak a lick of English. Enrique worked on the ranch for a while. He was a damn good worker and knew his horses, that's for sure. We managed, even though I didn't speak any Spanish back then."

"Wow. What year was that?"

Jeremy said, "Probably around 1955? 1956?"

"It was 1957 when they moved to the United States. And none of the white teachers in town had classes for the Mexicans who wanted to learn English. The schools had some classes for children, but they wouldn't take adults. Now, my Louisa's mother was a school teacher back in Georgia and she had that teacher's spirit. Do you know what I mean?"

"I do."

"So she started a class after church on Sunday. And all the Mexicans who wanted to learn English would come to learn at the church. That's how she and Maya got to be friends. They stayed friends their whole lives. It was hard on Louisa when Maya passed. She passed young."

"So did grandma," Jeremy said.

"Not as young as Maya," Gus said. "Daisy's mama had all her recipes though, so they kept up the café. And my Louisa's pie recipes are the ones they still use, isn't that right?"

Jeremy smiled. "Yeah, Pop. Daisy's added a few new ones, but the older ones are all grandma's."

"That's amazing." Tayla marveled at the long ties of friendship and family. She had family history on the Reyes side, but her mother didn't talk about it. Her grandparents had passed. She didn't really know her aunts and uncles in Sonoma. Her father's family back east were a video chat once a year, and no more than that. "That's really special, Gus."

"Special and delicious." Gus gave a decisive nod.

"That's our family motto," Jeremy said, wiggling his eyebrows. "Special and delicious."

Tayla burst into laughter.

Gus rose to his feet. "And that is my cue to leave you two young people, because I don't want to hear anything about that business, Jeremy Allen."

"Turn your ears off then."

"You know I will." Gus took his cane and paused by Tayla's chair. "Young lady, thank you for joining these two old bachelors for dinner. There's hope for this one, huh?"

"Good night, Gus." Tayla kissed him on the cheek. "Thanks for the steak and the stories."

"See?" Gus turned to Jeremy. "*That* is our family motto: Steak and stories."

"Go to bed!" Jeremy kissed the top of Gus's head. "I'll clean the kitchen."

"You better."

Gus walked down the hall and into his bedroom, leaving Tayla and Jeremy alone.

"Special and delicious, huh?" Tayla raised an eyebrow.

"Give me a hand with these dishes and I'll tell you all about it."

CHAPTER TWENTY

THEY WERE LYING naked in bed, and Jeremy was using Tayla's scarf to demonstrate his knot-tying skills.

"The figure eight you know..." He held her wrists together. "But do you know how to tie a figure *nine* loop?"

"I don't." She batted her eyes. "Thank you so much for teaching me."

"You may need to practice."

She leaned over and lightly pulled on his chest hair with her teeth. "You may need to let me go first."

He lifted her hands over her head, making her breasts arch up to his mouth. Taking one of her nipples in his mouth, he scraped it with his teeth before he laved it with his warm tongue. "I don't know," he murmured against her skin. "I kind of like practicing on you."

"I feel like, at some point, a climbing harness is going to get involved here."

"Holy shit." He turned his eyes upward. "Do you think I can secure a pulley to the ceiling?"

Tayla burst out laughing. "I was joking."

"I'm not. I think." His eyes narrowed and he turned back to

her before kissing over her breasts and belly, tickling her neck with his beard, and generally making her laugh more than she ever had with a man.

Jeremy wasn't only a great lover, he was fun. Tayla had never been able to let go like this in the bedroom. Sex was usually an intense, serious "let me show you how hot I am" display of manliness. Making love to Jeremy was easy and fun. He was confident without being cocky, though… he could be a little cocky too.

He enjoyed teasing her. He liked it when she teased him. If something awkward happened—and something awkward always happened with sex—he laughed and then proceeded to make her come, even while she was laughing. His knee slipped off the bed once, and they both went down. They tumbled onto the floor in a heap. Tayla pulled a groin muscle, but she couldn't be mad, especially when Jeremy massaged it very thoroughly.

"For medical purposes."

Right.

He tied another loop on the end of the scarf and hooked it over a corner post. "So, while I have you here—"

"Teaching me knots?"

"Exactly." He kissed up her body. "I thought you could give me your opinion on an important discussion topic."

"Really?"

"Really." He reached under her and arched her back up, bringing her breasts back to his mouth. "I mean…" He licked between them. "There's a lot of discussion about positive female representation in comics these days. And because you are female—"

"I'm so glad you noticed." Her voice was high.

"—I thought you might have an opinion."

"Okay." She could hardly breathe. "Um… did you have a specific concern?"

He moved down her body and got to his knees. Then he pulled

one of his casual He-Man moves and flipped her onto her stomach, her hands still tethered over her head.

"Oh!"

He bent down to her ear. "You good?"

"Yeah." He was driving her crazy, but she was happy to play along.

Jeremy smoothed a hand over the small of her back and along the curve of her bottom. "This area, for instance."

"Yeah?"

"It provokes a lot of debate."

"Really?" She could feel his hands along the outside of her thighs, tracing the round flesh. "Um... what do people debate?"

His hands massaged her ass, thumbs tracing the sensitive line where the curve of her bottom met the back of her thighs. "Some critics think that comic book depictions exaggerate the proportions of the female buttocks. They think artists oversexualize female characters."

"Really? And what do you think?"

"Me?" Jeremy straddled her, his knees on either side of her thighs. He lowered himself until his chest touched her back. "I find it very difficult to complain about a generous ass on a woman, but I can't argue that it isn't overtly sexual in nature and therefore possibly objectification."

Tayla was panting. "Did you know that feminist criticism of comic book culture turns me on?"

He reached down and felt between her thighs. "I had no idea."

Fuck. She bit into his pillow. "Jeremy—"

"You still comfortable with your arms up there?" he asked again, his beard tickling her neck.

"Yes, just stop torturing me or I swear—"

He shoved her knees open, brought her hips up, and slid inside.

Fuck yes.

Tayla sighed in relief. Then she wasn't sighing at all. She was moaning into his pillow. She was begging. She was yelling his name.

At one point she was pretty sure she blacked out.

And when she woke, he was untying her hands and kissing her wrists, whispering sweet things against her skin and cuddling her against his chest.

"You staying the night?" He played with a lock of hair that had fallen across her cheek.

"I brought a bag."

"Good." He kissed her temple. "I'll make you breakfast in the morning. Sleep."

————

WHEN SHE WOKE, IT WAS TO THE SOUND OF HEAVY breathing near the bedroom door. Tayla pushed her hair out of her eyes. "What are you doing?"

"Practicing my golf swing." Jeremy looked over his shoulder and grinned as he did another pull-up. His knees were bent and his arms extended as he raised and lowered himself on the pull-up bar over his doorway.

"You know, for some reason I thought that bar was a kinky sex thing or something related to rope storage."

"It is a kinky sex thing. I just use it for pull-ups too."

Sweat was dripping down his back, which flexed and bulged with every extension.

She looked at the clock. It was barely seven a.m. "Do you do this every morning?"

"Every other morning." He did two more pull-ups. "Arm strength is really important for bouldering."

She sat back and relaxed against his headboard. "I fully approve of this activity."

Jeremy laughed. "I'm glad."

HOOKED

"Not at all because it's sexy. I'm only thinking about your health. And bouldering of course."

"You're so thoughtful, Miss McKinnon."

"I try."

"Give me a few more minutes to finish up and take a quick shower. Then I'll go make you breakfast. You want the shower first?"

"Sure." It all felt so domestic. Like she was playing house or on vacation with a boyfriend. Only she'd never had a boyfriend. She'd never wanted one.

But she wanted Jeremy.

"Shower?" He nodded toward the bathroom, still pulling his body up with only his arm strength.

"Yeah." She hopped out of bed, buck naked, watching him as he watched her. "Like the view?"

"It's a nice way to wake up in the morning."

She glanced at his gym shorts. "You're insatiable."

Jeremy grinned. "He knows what he likes."

"Shower." She grabbed her bag and ducked into his bathroom, flipping on the light. She fiddled with the faucet handle and turned it all the way to hot, guessing that like the bathroom at Emmie's place, this one also took a while to heat up.

Old houses. Old plumbing.

She tied her hair up and put on some music to shower to. A thumping piano and the cheerful beat of "No New Friends" put a smile on her face. Then she locked the door.

There was seeing her naked, there was sex, then there was watching her shower. She wasn't a bathroom sharer, not with Jeremy. Not with *anyone*. Some things didn't need to shared: bathrooms, toothbrushes, excessive baby pictures on Instagram. There were rules about things for a reason.

Tayla rinsed off, dancing a little as she showered.

When was the last time I was this happy?

207

The thought bumped into her head like an obnoxious pop-up ad.

When was the last time you were this happy, Tayla?

She didn't know.

Don't you think it has something to do with Jeremy?

Great sex always made her happy though. It was great sex. The whole purpose of it was to make you happy.

It's more than the sex.

It *was* more than the sex.

It was definitely... more.

What would she do when it was time to leave? She was already suffering from headaches and withdrawal symptoms when she spent a few days away from him. It was becoming a serious problem. What was she going to do?

What will he *do?*

What would Jeremy do? Jeremy would be fine. He was well-adjusted. He was *wonderful*. Once Tayla was gone, he's probably find a real girlfriend. Someone who wanted marriage and babies and all that stuff.

Fuuuuuuck that.

She felt her jaw clench. Her fingernails bit into her palms. The unexpected surge of anger made her blink. *What was happening to her?*

Tayla shut off the water and listened for Jeremy in the bedroom. He was humming along to Pink, occasionally singing along, and he obviously knew the words.

"Of course he does," she muttered. "He's perfect." He read feminist comics and had crazy, sexy muscles and ate ethically sourced beef products. "He probably knows all the dance moves to 'Single Ladies' too."

"Tayla?"

She was mental. "Yeah?"

"I'm gonna go downstairs and start the coffee, okay?"

"Okay." Suddenly Tayla didn't want to leave the bathroom. If she didn't leave the bathroom, maybe she wouldn't have to confront the terrifying idea that she might just be falling stupid in love with Jeremy Allen.

She waited to hear the door shut before she poked her head back into the bedroom. Nothing looked different, but everything had changed. Jeremy had made the bed and folded her scarf neatly on the side table.

She could smell the coffee brewing downstairs. Could hear the low rumble of male voices. Pop was awake. Jeremy was probably cooking, making sure his grandfather took his medication, and mentally getting his day in order.

He would make a wonderful father.

What? Why had she even thought that?

She didn't want children... probably! Her parents were nightmares, and she had no idea what to do with kids. Sure, she liked teenagers, but they didn't give you a teenaged kid at the hospital. They gave you a little squirmy one that didn't talk and pooped all the time. Did she know how to teach a baby how to poop in a toilet? Of course she didn't. Her parents had probably hired someone to do that.

Why was she thinking about children? And pooping?

"Tayla?"

"I'm coming!" She paced around the bedroom, her heart starting to race. "I'll just be a minute." She paused in front of Jeremy's dresser and opened the top drawer. It was a little messy, but he had his socks folded. And underwear. He even had a row of cotton handkerchiefs in the corner.

"Of course he does." She slammed the drawer shut.

Jeremy would want children. When Jeremy Allen fell in love with someone, he would want to marry that someone and stay married and celebrate a golden anniversary or whatever prize you got when you stayed married for a *really long time*.

He would want the wedding and the house and camping trips and drink-your-milk-before-school and good grades, and he'd probably volunteer to be a soccer coach or something. He'd live his life, running his shop in Metlin and climbing mountains on weekends and raising a family and being a happy, contented, perfect grown-up.

That's why you're freaking out, Tayla. He's not some shallow little boy you can play with and leave behind when you get bored.

What the hell had she done? Tayla sat on the edge of the bed and clutched her phone like a security blanket when she realized the truth.

She'd gone and fallen in love with an actual man.

She didn't want to leave him, but she also wasn't sure she wanted the same life he did. What were you supposed to do with that? And she wasn't feeling philosophical about their eventual separation. The phrase *c'est la vie* had not crossed her mind. In fact, she was *pissed* just thinking about it.

She was pissed about something that hadn't even happened!

But it would.

Her phone buzzed in her hand. She slid it open and saw the notification of a new email. A sense of dread hit her stomach when she saw who it was from.

"Dear Tayla, We wanted to make the formal offer in writing. Azim and I are so excited to offer you a position…"

The offer that would have made her dance a month ago suddenly felt like a burden she didn't want to carry.

They needed an answer within a week.

The salary was… far more generous than she'd expected.

Medical.

Retirement matching.

She heard his footsteps on the stairs.

"Tayla?" Jeremy cracked the door open. "Hey."

"Hey."

He knelt down in front of her. "What's going on?"

I'm in love with you.

You probably want marriage and children.

I don't know what I want.

Except you. I want you.

Tayla held up her phone. "SOKA offered me the job. I need to give them an answer by next week."

Tayla saw everything in his eyes. Panic. Pride. Fear. Determination. She blinked back tears, resenting their intrusion.

Jeremy leaned forward and kissed her. "Congratulations, Miss McKinnon. I knew you'd kick ass."

She threw her arms around his neck and clutched him tight. "You're not going to ask me to stay in Metlin, are you?"

His fingers dug into her back. He kissed her neck. "You know I can't."

"Dammit."

"Whatever you want, Tayla." He kept kissing her neck. "You have to do what's right for you."

You're right for me.

So was this job.

How could she make a choice between the life she always wanted and the life she'd never imagined she'd want?

Tayla wanted it all.

Impossible.

CHAPTER TWENTY-ONE

TAYLA FLIPPED the sign over at Café Maya and pointed to Adrian Saroyan, who was still sipping his coffee and reading the paper.

"Out," she said.

He frowned. "This place closes at four. It's only three forty-five, and I want to sit, enjoy my paper, and—"

"So help me"—Tayla leaned over and put her palms flat on his table—"if you don't get your skinny little suit-clad ass out of here in the next five minutes, I will make your life a living hell, Adrian."

His eyes went wide.

"I am having a personal crisis," Tayla said. "And you are not part of my girl gang. So leave."

He gulped. "Is it a financial crisis, because I'm really good with—"

"I appreciate that you're trying to be relevant, but I have an accounting degree from Stanford and was raised by Aaron McKinnon, founding partner of McKinnon, Foster, and Smith. I do not need your financial advice, and I do not want you here. Leave."

He got to his feet and straightened his tie. "I was just trying to help."

"You can help by *leaving*." She walked him to the door, opened it, and shut it behind him. "Daisy!"

The girl behind the counter watched her with wide eyes. "She just took the trash out to the alley."

"Are you done here?"

"I need to wash the dishes."

"Do you know Jeremy Allen?"

She frowned. "Who?"

"Fine. You can stay."

Daisy walked in the back door. "Hey, Ronnie, can you check the storage room? I think we need to order more— Tayla? Hey!"

Tayla walked to her and held out both hands. "I need advice from a grown-up. And you're the most grown-up person I know that I can still talk to about my sex life."

Daisy looked over Tayla's shoulder. "Ronnie, you can clock out early today, hon."

"Okay." The girl scurried away.

"Tayla," Daisy said softly, "she is a junior in high school."

"You think she doesn't know what sex is? I guarantee she does."

"Sit." Daisy went behind the counter. "Coffee or tea?"

"Vodka?"

"No vodka." Daisy laughed. "What is wrong with you?"

"I'm in love with Jeremy Allen, and I have no idea how to teach a baby how to use a toilet."

Daisy blinked rapidly. "Wow. There's so much going on there."

"Do *you* know? Do babies even use toilets? What age does that happen? See, these are things that adults should know, right? I thought I was an adult, but clearly I am not."

"Are you pregnant? Is that what's happening? If yes, *please* tell me Jeremy is the father."

"Because *he* is a grown-up who would know how to handle this shit, right?" She walked to a table. "And I am a grown-up who knows how to contact a Kardashian if I really, really wanted to.

Not that I *do* want to. I'm just saying that if I called in a few favors, I could probably—"

"Tayla!" Daisy walked over and shoved her into a chair. "Sit. Chill. I'm calling Emmie."

"Fine! But I have seen her checkbook. She is no more prepared for adulthood than I am." Tayla rapped her fingers on the table and stared out the window. It didn't help that Top Shelf Comics sat almost directly across the street. "Also, I'm not pregnant."

"Good. Especially if you're thinking about turning to vodka."

Jeremy was probably inside, helping a customer find the newest edition of their favorite superhero comic or helping a mom buy a game for a picky fourteen-year-old. He was good at that stuff, helping people get what they needed. His encouragement was probably one of the reasons she was offered the position at SOKA. She'd been drinking more water. He was the one who suggested paper handouts for her presentation even though she'd only been thinking digital.

And now she was going to leave him.

She laid her forehead on the table. "My life is a mess."

Daisy put a mug of coffee on the table and patted her hair. "I thought things were going well. Did you hear about the job?"

"Yes. They offered it to me."

"That's amazing! Congratulations! Did you tell Jeremy?"

"I was at his house when I got the email. That was right after I realized I am in love with him and I do not actually believe in serial monogamy because I would destroy any other woman he tried to sleep with ever again in any foreseeable future."

"Okay, well, that is a violent reaction to realizing you're in love." Daisy cleared her throat. "Maybe take a deep breath. Emmie's on her way over. What we need to do is make a pros and cons list for—"

"I tried that." Tayla sat up and pulled a piece of paper out of her pocket. "I already tried that. In fact, I wrote it all out." She smoothed the paper and spread it on the table. "See? On this side,

I wrote down all the great things about working at SOKA. And on the other side, all the great things about Jeremy." She shoved the paper in Daisy's face. "See? They're the same!"

Daisy's eyes went wide. "Wow. I didn't ever need to know some of that."

Tayla glanced at the paper. "Oh. Yeah, I included some sexual positions that were pretty unique, but the point is"—she crumpled the paper up—"it doesn't matter! Because not all data points have equal value. How do I weigh 'has good health insurance' on the same line as 'is sincerely kind to old people'? One of these things is fundamentally more important than the other in the grand scheme of life."

The bell over Daisy's door rang and Emmie walked in. "What's going on?"

"Existential crisis," Daisy said. "Tayla realized she's in love with Jeremy, SOKA offered her the job in San Francisco, and she's having some surprising issues with toilet training."

Emmie's eyebrows went up. "That *is* surprising."

"Not *me!*" Tayla threw her hands up. "I'm concerned that I am not a fully equipped adult person capable of having a mature relationship with someone like Jeremy, who you both cannot deny will fully expect a serious relationship to eventually result in marriage and children and things like that."

"Aren't you jumping ahead a bit on this?" Daisy said. "I mean, there's a difference between admitting you believe in true love and jumping into a full-on relationship with a man—admittedly a really great man—but you haven't been dating that long."

"If I am this conflicted about taking a job that pays a *very* generous six-figure salary because it will be the end of my relationship with this man, it *better* be a serious relationship." She dug her fingers into her hair and pulled. "If it's not serious, then what the hell are we doing?"

"Hey." Emmie eased Tayla's hand out of her hair. "Stop. Don't start with the hair pulling again, okay?" She took her hand. "And for what it's worth, I know Jeremy is serious about you. He's not someone who just puts himself out there like this unless he's serious."

Panic subsided and fear crept in. "Emmie, what am I going to do? My dad was right. Opportunity doesn't come without sacrifice. So am I supposed to sacrifice my career? Or am I supposed to sacrifice Jeremy?"

Emmie sighed. "I think—"

"Your dad is full of shit." Daisy grabbed the coffee she'd brought for Tayla. "You don't always have to give up something you love to get the right opportunity. That's zero-sum thinking and it's lazy."

Tayla blinked. "Okay." She sat up straight. "Okay. Ginger told me something the other day that might be relevant."

Emmie crossed her arms. "Well, this should be good."

"It was something along the lines of 'If the world isn't giving you what you want, then make the world your bitch.'"

"Yeah, that sounds like Ginger."

"Okay yes," Daisy said. "But she's right. In a sense. Have you even tried to think what a compromise might look like? Why can't you keep your relationship with Jeremy and also take this job in San Francisco?"

"First," Emmie said, "I don't think commuting two hundred and thirty miles every day is practical. Not until transporter technology has been developed, and we all know that's a ways off. We can't even build high-speed rail."

"It's a question of fiscal priorities, Emmie. The state of California— Wait!" Tayla shook her head. "I'm not having this discussion right now. I don't think anyone is suggesting that I commute to San Francisco. That's not going to happen."

"What about telecommuting?" Daisy said. "Lots of people do these days, and you're talking about a company that operates in the online world. That seems like the most practical solution."

"Emmie and I already talked about that. It's a great idea, but

SOKA's whole deal is that they want that personal connection. They have company dinners and communal break areas. They're all about spontaneous collaboration. It's hard to have spontaneous collaboration when one person lives hundreds of miles away."

"Okay." Daisy took a deep breath and let it out. "Fair enough. That's actually kind of admirable."

"I know," Tayla said. "The whole company is amazing, and I would love to work there." Her forehead fell back to the table. "I'm screwed."

Daisy said, "I know this seems out there, but have you thought about asking Jeremy to move up to the city with you? He has a degree. I'm sure he could find work in finance or investment somewhere."

"And he'd hate it. Can you imagine him up there? There's no way. He's built a business here. He can't just leave that. And besides, even if he didn't have the shop, he can't leave his grandfather."

Daisy sighed. "You're right."

"Stop." Emmie held up a hand. "There's a much bigger question we need to ask before we keep going with this." She took Tayla's hand. "When you first applied for this job, you were adamant that you wanted to leave Metlin. It wasn't just the SOKA position, it was moving on, returning to the city, picking up your life there. I know it's hard to imagine now, but if Jeremy didn't exist, if you never had a relationship or you were only friends... would you want to stay in Metlin?"

"Oh. Good question." Daisy sat back. "If you and Jeremy broke up—it happens even when people love each other—if you broke up, or things didn't work out, or whatever... would you want to stay in Metlin? Because life is unexpected. Trust me."

Tayla thought about traffic and museums and symphony concerts. She also thought about walking to work, biking for tacos, art walks once a month, and open mic night at the Ice

House. She thought about where her friends lived and what she liked to do.

And yes… she even thought about the mountains.

"I like it here," she admitted. "It's small, but there are still lots of things to do. And a lot of the people I was friends with in the city have moved on or moved away. The people who are left are… kind of assholes. I mean, except for Tobin. Tobin is a borderline asshole, but he volunteers at an animal shelter, so I don't think he can be one hundred percent asshole, and I'm getting off track."

Daisy was smiling. "So you like Metlin."

Emmie grinned. "I knew it."

"Don't celebrate yet," Tayla said. "We still haven't figured out how this is all going to work."

"But we will," Daisy said.

"I have an idea." Emmie raised her hand. "But you're not going to like part of it. What if you compromised with SOKA? Spend one week a month up there and three weeks down here? You'd still have lots of face-to-face time. You could still collaborate. But you could live here most of the time."

"That sounds nice on paper, but think about the realities of that situation. Can you imagine living in a hotel for a week every month?" Tayla asked. "It would get expensive as hell. Not to mention annoying to have to live out of a suitcase like that."

"What if you got an apartment?" Daisy asked. "It wouldn't have to be big. Just someplace to put your stuff."

"Have you seen the prices for studios in San Francisco?" Emmy grimaced.

"You could buy a fixer-upper in Metlin for what you'd pay in one year," Tayla said. "Not to mention, most of my income would be going to a place where I was only present one-fourth of the year."

Emmie raised her hand again.

"Why are you raising your hand?" Tayla asked. "This isn't school."

"Because you're going to hate my idea and I'm trying to be adorable?"

"Just throw it out there. Can't be worse than what we've already thought up."

"You could keep a room at your parents' house."

No one spoke.

"I know it's not ideal. But Tayla, think about it. They have room. It wouldn't even be a question whether you could live there one week out of the month, and the commute is completely reasonable."

Tayla felt sick to her stomach. "On the surface, that might seem like a good idea, but I think you're forgetting that my main objection to my parents' house is that *my parents live there.*"

Daisy was wincing. "Emmie, I don't think—"

"You have one set of parents," Emmie broke in. "One. Bianca and Aaron are the only parents you have. And they're still living. At some point you're going to have to come to terms with them."

"Why? I've spent years trying to move past them."

"You can't pretend they don't exist."

"Really? Because I've been doing that pretty successfully for years."

"Your whole reluctance toward adult relationships has been because your parents are so unhappy," Emmie said. "Don't you think it might be good to examine that—possibly with them— before it causes you to sabotage something that's important to you?"

Daisy wrinkled her nose. "I hate to tell you this, but Emmie has a point."

"You're going to have to deal with your parents someday," Emmie said. "And maybe you'll decide that you truly want nothing to do with them, but it won't be this avoidance tactic you have going right now. You don't hate them, Tayla. Especially not your mom. And at some point you're going to want to introduce Jeremy to them. You might have children someday, and they're going to want to know who their grandparents—"

"Okay, okay, okay." Tayla waved her hand at Emmie. "Let's not get too crazy with the kids thing, okay? I'm still getting used to admitting I'm in love with Jeremy."

Daisy leaned forward. "Would you consider this as an option? In theory? If you can sell this idea to SOKA—"

"Which is a huge 'if.' *Huge*."

"But not impossible," Emmie said. "I'm just saying this could be a good opportunity to make some positive change, both for you and your parents. You could be with them for a week, come back home and take a break. But you'd go back. And they would know you'd be coming back. It might be what they need to start talking to each other."

Tayla pursed her lips and considered what Emmie was proposing.

One week in the city. Meetings with SOKA. Employee dinner. Collaboration meetings. Maybe grab a concert or a museum exhibit. Three weeks in Metlin. Nights with Jeremy. Weekends with her friends. Trivia night.

She could do it. In fact, it would be everything she wanted. The question was: Would SOKA be interested?

"If I proposed this," she said, "I'd have to convince SOKA they would be getting a better employee in the process. Otherwise, what's in it for them?"

"A happier Tayla. A more productive Tayla."

"You could also bribe them with food," Daisy said. "We grow everything around here. Pistachios. Almonds. Grapes. Oranges. And don't forget the cheese."

Emmie asked, "Where are their other offices?"

"Nairobi and Chiang Mai, Thailand. And then the main office in San Francisco."

"All big cities."

"Yep."

"But you living in Metlin not only makes a happier Tayla, it also keeps you in touch with a more rural market. Lots of people only buy clothes and house stuff online around here because the choices are limited in the shops."

She nodded. "That's a good point."

"You can sell this." Emmie leaned forward and put a hand on her arm. "Tayla, you can sell *anything*. You've sold thrillers to little old grandmas and young adult fiction to farmers. You can sell staying in Metlin to SOKA."

CHAPTER TWENTY-TWO

JEREMY HOOKED himself into the anchors at the top of the cliff and turned to yell down. "Safe!"

He started to pull the rope up, taking his turn to belay the next climber coming up the rock. Cary had introduced Jeremy to Ashley and Dave the night before. They'd hiked the trail to the rock, eaten dinner and set up camp, then Cary led them up the rock face the next morning.

"On belay?" Ashley called from the bottom of the cliff.

"On belay," Jeremy called. "Climb when ready."

"So Tayla's up in the city this weekend?" Cary watched Ashley and Dave check her harness.

"Yeah. Said she wanted to talk to her parents about something."

"About the job?"

"Climbing!" Ashley called.

"Okay, climb." Jeremy watched Ashley start up the rock face. "I'm not sure what the thing with her parents is about."

"She seemed weird on trivia night."

"She's just got a lot on her mind right now."

"But I heard her refer to you as her boyfriend. That's new."

Jeremy kept his eyes on Ashley, but he couldn't stop his smile. "Yeah, I heard that too."

"Congrats?"

Jeremy tried not to let his heart get heavy. "Might be too soon for that."

"She hasn't said yes yet."

"She's not going to say no." Jeremy kept his eyes and his focus on Ashley. He was responsible for her safety, and it wasn't fair that he was so distracted by Tayla being gone. Luckily, Ashley was an experienced climber. She was a tiny girl who looked like she was about sixteen, but she moved like a monkey. She made it up the cliff in short order and clipped on, taking the rope from Jeremy to belay Dave up the wall while Jeremy collected their gear.

"Beautiful day." Ashley was panting and smiling. "Wow, this is a great spot."

They were a fun couple, newly arrived in Fresno from somewhere back east. New York maybe? New Hampshire? Somewhere around there. Ashley still had that pale not-enough-sun look, but Dave had clearly spent some time out of his office. He'd said something about agricultural marketing, but Jeremy hadn't been paying attention.

"It's really nice," Cary said. "If we hike a little farther along this ridge, there's another wall around this height I think we could get to today. Some nice bouldering along the base and great seams right up to the top."

"I'm game if Dave is," Ashley said. "It's early; we've got time."

"Sounds good."

They waited for Dave to make it up the cliff and gather their anchors where Cary had placed them. After all four climbers were safe, they spread out, exploring the giant slope of granite that protruded from the forest. Jeremy was first to walk along the ridge that Cary had mentioned, curious about the next rock.

The route Cary had mapped out was a variation of one they'd found online. Again, it would be a little challenging for them, but still well within their skill level. Jeremy eyed the sloping base of the climb, eager to try some bouldering.

He glanced over his shoulder, curious what was taking Cary, Ashley, and Dave so long. Wanting to keep his body loose, he dusted his hands and climbed low along the wall, heading for a ledge he saw ten or twelve feet up. The holds were easy and the height was low enough that it was an ideal practice area. Also, the ledge was in the sun, a perfect spot.

His muscles were warm and quick, his fingers hardly sore. He needed a board for crimp training. His pull-up bar was good, but it didn't give his fingers any practice. He focused on moving along the rock face, reaching for each new hold, enjoying the scrape of cool granite under his fingers and palms.

His right foot reached for a nice crevice just a few feet beneath the ledge, and he shifted his weight when his toes felt secure. His hips nicely balanced, he reached his right hand up and over the ledge, testing his grip to make sure it could take the shift he would need to move his left foot off the jug it was resting on.

His right hand secure, he lifted his left foot and boosted himself up. His face cleared the ledge and everything happened at once.

His eyes registered the bared teeth first, but he didn't hear the snarl until it was too late for him to retreat safely.

"Shit!"

The mountain lion had been sunbathing on the ledge Jeremy was headed for, its back against the rear wall, invisible from the ground.

"Jeremy!"

Their voices only registered faintly. Jeremy's right hand let go of the ledge when he saw the giant cat's paw go up. His left hand was too low to hold his weight. His left foot was unsteady.

The shock of the cat's appearance drove the air from his lungs.

He fell.

———

"Jeremy!"

The sound of shouting made Jeremy sit up straight, and he immediately regretted it.

"Whoa." Cary pushed him back down. "Relax. Dave was just scaring off the cat."

Jeremy drew a harsh breath in and everything hurt. His chest hurt. His head hurt. His right arm was numb. He could feel the blood pulsing through his body.

"Lion!" he gasped.

"It's gone," Ashley said. "It ran off. Dave threw a few rocks at it, but you surprised him as much as he surprised you, I think. How's your head?" She was probing around his hair.

Usually that weirded him out—white people could be strange about black people's hair—but he could tell Ashley was checking him for injuries.

"I'm not feeling anything swollen and nothing is bleeding." She snapped her fingers and he looked at her. "Follow my finger, okay?"

"Okay." His gaze tracked her finger as it went right and left. Up and down.

"Cary, what are you doing?" He was watching Ashley, but Cary was messing with his right arm, the numb one. "My fingers hurt."

"Your fingers are pretty torn up, my man, but I'm a little more worried about your ulna."

Jeremy looked down his arm. It was bleeding, and he saw a bone protruding above his wrist. "Oh fuck." Bile start to rise as the feeling began to return. "That's not good."

"No, it's not," Ashley said. "Cary, let me look at the bleeding. Come hold his head, okay?"

"Are you a nurse?"

Dave crouched down beside him. "She was an EMT before our daughter was born. How you doin', man?"

"Been better. Big cat."

"Yeah, he was a big one. Lazy though. I think you interrupted his siesta."

"My mother is never going to shut up about this."

Dave grinned. "No class prepares you for interrupting a mountain lion's nap. Is it shitty that I'm kind of thrilled I saw one? We don't have 'em back east."

"Uh… yeah, it's maybe a little shitty. I have a bone sticking out of my arm."

"You only fell about ten feet. Unfortunately, your arm hit at exactly the wrong angle."

"The bleeding isn't out of control," Ashley said. "Dave, get me my first aid kit."

"On it."

"Is anyone's phone working?"

"No reception for a couple of miles," Cary said. "We'll have to tie him up and lower him down the cliff. Jeremy, you trust me to tie you on and get you down? The other option is two of us boogie out of here and hike back to call search and rescue."

"Fuck no." He was going to throw up. There was no avoiding it. "Get me on my side."

Ashley and Cary rolled him over, and he upchucked the oatmeal he'd eaten for breakfast. He felt better, but the nausea only yielded to waves and waves of pain. "I think I did something to my shoulder too."

"You may have a partial dislocation." Ashley was feeling along his neck. "No pain here?"

"No."

"Any numbness anywhere?"

"My arm was numb. Not anymore."

She winced. "Yeah, your nerves have caught up with the break. I don't feel anything along his spine or his head, Cary." She took something from Dave and poured it onto his arm before she started wrapping gauze around the bone. "Jeremy, you think you can walk? Are your legs okay?"

He flexed his knees up. "Yeah, they're good."

"I think it's more important that we get his arm taken care of as quickly as possible. I'm gonna wrap it up and make sure the bleeding is okay, but I don't want to mess with it. I'm not a doctor. We need to get him down the mountain."

"Okay." Once they made it down the cliff, it was a two-mile hike back to the car. "This is gonna suck."

"Yeah." Cary put his arm around Jeremy and helped him to his feet. "It really, really is."

———

TAYLA HAD FORCED HER PARENTS TO SIT IN THE LIVING room. Together. Or as together as they ever were. Her mother was on the chaise near the bar, and her father was impatiently steaming in a wingback chair.

"Tayla, what is this about?"

"I have been offered a job at SOKA, the international trading company I was interviewing with."

Her father was mollified. "That's excellent. I'm glad you're finally putting your degree to proper use."

"I'm also excited about it. However, I'm not thrilled about moving back to San Francisco. Partly, to be frank, because of you two."

Bianca put on her best wounded face while Aaron looked bored.

"Darling, I don't know why you're—"

"Mom, I don't want us to be this way." She waited until her father met her eyes. "I really don't. And I don't think you want us to be this way either. We're not a family. Not even close."

"I suppose your friends down in that little town have some-

227

thing to do with this." Aaron sighed. "Tayla, I'm not going to justify my work or the life I've provided for you."

"Fine." She clapped her hands. "Don't justify it. But also don't pretend you have to work as hard now as when I was a kid. You don't. You're at the point where you could be semiretired if you wanted to be. You and mom could travel. You could pursue... I have no idea what you like other than being at the office."

"Sailing," Bianca said.

Aaron picked at a piece of lint on his pants. "I haven't sailed in years."

"But you liked it. That's why I wanted to get a membership at the yacht club, Aaron. You were happy when you were on a boat."

"I thought you liked the brunches."

Bianca rolled her eyes. "Those people are so boring. I always assumed you'd eventually get a boat. God knows we have enough money for it."

Aaron looked uncomfortable.

"This is good," Tayla said. "See? We can talk about things. Maybe we're not like close families. But Mom knows things you like. And Dad, you know things that Mom likes too."

"Wine."

Bianca's eyes turned cold. "Fuck you, Aaron."

"Such lovely language," he said. "Such a society girl."

"Have I told you lately—?"

"Redirecting!" Tayla shouted. "Mom, you do have a drinking problem. You know it as well as we do. We can work on that. We can talk. Dad, you don't have to be an asshole about it. And yes, that's my society language coming out too."

Aaron frowned. "Are you moving home? Are you planning to live here when you take this job? Is that why we're having this conversation?" He didn't look as negative about the idea as Tayla had expected.

"I want the job. I don't love living in the city the way I used to. I'm thinking about a compromise. I'll be counteroffering to SOKA, proposing a one-week-here, three-weeks-in-Metlin plan to combine telecommuting and on-site work. They may not go for it, but I want to try, and I'm willing to take a slightly lower salary to account for cost of living."

"Don't go too low." Aaron frowned. "Let me know if you want some studies on the fiscal benefits of telecommuting. Our firm has seen good returns, and I can give you some data."

Tayla was shocked. "Thanks, Dad."

"So you'd be living here one week a month?" Bianca was smiling. "That would be lovely, Tayla. Where is the office?"

"In the Mission."

"Charles can drive you and your father together."

"Or I can take the bus."

"The bus?"

"These are details!" She tried to stop the train from derailing. "Mostly I wanted to talk to you both about the idea of me living here. We haven't had the easiest adult relationship, but I would like to make that better."

Aaron cleared his throat. "That's admirable."

"Thank you. So part of me living here would be that all three of us would go to family therapy with a professional."

"Absolutely not."

"Do you really think that's necessary?"

Tayla raised her voice. "Why would you want to keep going like this?" She looked between her parents. "Dad, you're barely sixty. Mom, you're only fifty-seven. You really want to live like this for the next thirty years? Miserable together?"

Both of them were silent.

"Listen, it's obvious you're not going to get divorced at this point. You're not going to start over with someone new. And you've only got one kid. Me. So you can be miserable, lonely old people, or you can try my idea." She put her hands on her hips. "What would you rather do?"

They glanced at each other, then looked away.

"Just... think about it, okay? Or we could continue living like strangers in the same house, our only point of contact the household staff. I don't want that. I really don't. I'd rather we have something... warmer."

"Is this a result of this young man you're seeing now?" Bianca said. "Why are you suddenly so adamant about this?"

"It's not because of Jeremy. Or not *only* because of him. But yeah, it's partly because he has a nice, normal family of people who talk to each other. And someday I'd like him to meet you both, and I don't want him to think we're aliens, okay?"

Aaron shrugged. "I don't think we're that unusual."

"That's because you hang out with a bunch of rich old men who also have messed-up families and estranged children. Let's aim a little higher, okay? Because all those people refer to their children as vultures. Let's not consider them the standard."

"Fine." Aaron stood. "If you insist on this... I am willing to consider it."

"Thank you." Tayla was genuinely surprised this had gone as well as it had. "Thanks, Dad." Her phone had been buzzing in her pocket over and over. "I'm sorry, I better check this. I don't know who..." She glanced at the phone and saw twelve calls from Emmie and a dozen frantic texts from Daisy.

Where are you???

Tayla called Emmie back immediately. "What's going on?"

"Where have you been? I've been trying to call for an hour—"

"What is going on, Emmie?"

Tayla's stomach dropped as Emmie told her what had happened. "Where is he?" She swallowed hard. Her heart was in her throat. "I'm coming."

"Tayla, what's wrong?" Bianca rose to her feet.

She ended the call and turned to her father. "I need to borrow your Porsche, and I really don't have time to argue."

CHAPTER TWENTY-THREE

TAYLA BURST into the waiting room. "Where is he?"

"He's still in surgery." Cary rose to his feet. "Calm down. Crap, how fast did you drive? Emmie said you were in San Francisco."

"I was." She looked around the waiting room of Metlin Regional Hospital. Then back at Cary. There was blood all over his shirt. "Emmie said it was a broken arm? Why are you covered in blood?"

"It was a compound fracture." Cary put a hand on her shoulder when her knees went weak. "He had two bones sticking out, so it bled a lot, but there were no arteries broken. And Ashley's an EMT, so she got him stabilized before we lowered him down the cliff. He was mostly able to walk out on his own."

"Mostly? Who's Ashley?"

"One of our climbing partners." Cary pointed to a smiling couple sitting on the far side of the waiting room.

"Hey." They waved.

"Hi. Thank you for stabilizing my boyfriend and making his bleeding stop." Tayla felt her stomach go queasy just thinking about the pain. "Oh my God."

"Dave and I had to carry him a little toward the end. Two miles is a lot when you've got a bone on the outside."

Tayla felt like she was going to be sick. "But he's going to be okay?" She looked around. "Where is everyone? Where's Emmie?"

"She went to the house to stay with Gus. His parents are back with the doctors. I'm sure they'll be coming out soon, so why don't you just—"

The doors opened in a rush.

"Where is he?" Melissa Rhodes swept into the waiting room. "Where's Cary?"

"Missy?"

She locked panicked eyes on him. "Cary?" Her cheeks were red. "Ox said there was a climbing accident." She looked him up and down. "Why are you covered in *blood*? What happened? Why didn't you call me?"

He stepped toward her, hands raised. "Jeremy is the one who got hurt. He has a compound fracture in his right arm, that's why there's blood. Ashley, Dave, and I got him down the hill. We're fine."

"You're fine?" She was still in panic mode. "The blood...?"

"Not mine."

"Oh my God." She covered her face and burst into tears.

Cary's eyes went wide. "Missy?"

Without another word, she turned and raced out of the waiting room.

Cary turned baffled eyes to Tayla. "What the hell was that?"

She shook her head. "Dude. *Go after her*."

"Right." Cary ran out of the room, chasing Melissa.

Tayla walked over and sat next to Ashley and Dave. "So, this is a weird way to meet."

"Are you Tayla?" Ashley asked.

"Yeah."

"Jeremy talks about you a lot."

"He does?"

"He's a hell of a guy," Dave said. "Tough as nails. He'll be fine."

"Yeah." Tayla took a deep breath and settled in to wait. "He'll be fine."

———

JEREMY FELT HER SKIN AGAINST HIS. SHE WAS SO SOFT. What did she use on her skin? Was it lotion? Was it oil? Some kind of special soap?

"He's waking up."

"Mmmup."

"What?"

"Jeremy?" His mom's voice was brusque. "How are you feeling? Tell me your pain level from one to ten."

"It would be so useful to have a mom who was a doctor."

It wasn't useful. It was horrible. His mom was the most unsympathetic mom ever and he could never fake being sick.

"Jeremy, pain scale."

"Fnnn."

"What was that?"

"Did he say he was fine?"

She was holding his hand. That was nice. God, she smelled so good. Was it the lotion again? Why did she always smell so good?

"If I'd been here before they started, I could have told them to go light on the anesthesia. He's very sensitive." The sound of paper flipping. "It'll take him a bit longer to come out of it, that's all."

His dad's voice. "The surgeon said they used two pins?"

"Yes. Not bad considering the break."

"And a lot of stitches. It was so many stitches."

"That's an average amount for an injury like his."

"Really?"

233

"Mmmmm."

In his somewhat conscious mind, Jeremy realized he was hearing his parents' voices and Tayla's. Which meant that his parents had met Tayla when he was unconscious.

Not ideal.

Or maybe it was fine. They seemed to be friendly. He'd certainly told his parents enough about Tayla.

Wait, had they told Tayla how much Jeremy talked about her?

Did that matter?

"Jeremy Augustus Allen, you need to wake up."

He blinked his eyes open. "Okay." He couldn't keep them open for long. It was just an automatic reaction to his mother's voice.

"Hey bud." His father patted his arm. The one without bandages. "I heard you had a run-in with a bobcat, huh?"

"Lion," Jeremy muttered. "Wzzz... lion."

"He always did like correcting me."

"Hey." Her soft lips touched his cheek. "Hey, handsome. Wake up. I want to see your eyes. I broke about eighty traffic laws to get here before you woke up, okay? So wake up."

"That's a really beautiful vehicle, by the way."

"Thanks, Mr. Allen."

"You can call me Doug."

Oh thank God, because Jeremy really liked it when Tayla called him "Mr. Allen" during sex, and that had been about to get really weird. His mother better not make Tayla call her Dr. Washington. She'd pulled that with one of Jeremy's girlfriends in college. That one hadn't lasted.

"I think he's just sleeping now."

"He's probably eavesdropping on us," Tayla said. "Gathering blackmail material." She ran a hand over his cheek. "I'm so glad they didn't shave his beard."

"I would have."

His mother hated his beard.

Jeremy took a deep breath and opened his eyes. "Thirsty." His voice was scratchy. "Can I get some water?"

Tayla pressed her cheek to his, and he could feel tears against his skin.

"Hello, beautiful." He tried to lift his arm, but it was heavy. Way too heavy.

"Don't move your cast." Tayla sniffed. "Just let your arm rest. They had to put all kinds of equipment in it. Pins. Screws. I'm sorry; you're half robot now."

He reached across with his left arm and tucked a piece of hair behind her ear. "So I'm like Robocop? Is that what you're saying?"

She pulled away. "Yes. I'm so sorry."

"Don't. That means I'm a badass." He wanted to flex his fingers so badly, but they were taped to a metal brace on his cast. He wanted to touch her. "My fingers are all taped up."

"You broke some of those too."

"Three, to be exact." His mother stepped back to let the nurse in.

"And my chest hurts."

"You broke two ribs, your ulna, and three fingers. Your shoulder was partially dislocated. Be glad you don't have any head injuries. Cary said you weren't wearing a helmet."

"Sorry, Mom."

The nurse checked his vitals and made notes on his chart. Asked him a bunch of questions that made him tired. Then she handed him a pill and held out a cup of water with a straw.

"Pain killer," the nurse said. "You're going to need them until tomorrow at least. After that, you can probably switch to over-the-counter."

"Okay."

His mother waited until the nurse had left the room. "Cary also said you were climbing without ropes or anchors. You told me you didn't do that, Jeremy."

"I was bouldering about ten feet off the ground, Mom. If I hadn't been surprised by a mountain lion, I'd have been fine."

"And did you have bear spray?"

"Cary had some, but we didn't need it."

His dad sat in the chair opposite the bed and stretched his legs out. "Good thing that Dave guy has a good rock-throwing arm. I'd have brought my shotgun."

Jeremy frowned. "On a climb?" He sipped from a cup of water that Tayla held out. "Thanks. When did you get here? You weren't supposed to be back until tomorrow."

"Seriously?" She gave him angry eyes. "My boyfriend breaks his arm, partially dislocates his shoulder, has to have surgery, but you think I'm gonna wait until tomorrow to head home?"

He was still a little loopy. So was his grin. "I like it when you call me your boyfriend."

Her cheeks went red. "Well, you're the first man to have the title, so congratulations."

"Only man to have the title," he muttered. He was so tired. He closed his eyes and felt his head drifting. "Did you bring a bag?"

"It's in the car." She smoothed a hand over his cheek. "If you're tired, sleep. I'll stay here."

"You met my parents without me."

She brushed a thumb back and forth over his cheek. "No, you were there. You were just unconscious."

"They know about you," he muttered. "Told them all about you."

Her voice was soft. "Yeah, I heard."

"You going to stay?"

"Didn't I tell you I brought my bag?"

"So cute." He turned his face into her hand and closed his eyes. "Love you, Tay."

———

Love you, Tay.

Her breath caught. She'd known it. How could she not know it? Every move he made spoke his love to her. Every sweet, supportive encouragement. Every tender kiss.

Her eyes filled with tears. She looked up at Jeremy's parents and wiped her eyes. "Sorry."

Jeremy's mom, Patricia, was crying too. "Don't be sorry."

Tayla cleared her throat. "I don't think anyone has said that to me before. Except my best friend, Emmie. She has."

"Oh, Tayla." Patricia walked over and enveloped her in a hard hug. "I don't understand how that could be, but I know you must be a wonderful person if Jeremy loves you. He's a good judge of character."

She sniffed and hugged Patricia back with one arm. The other one stayed on Jeremy's cheek. She didn't want to let go of him. Not even for a minute.

"Did he tell you I got this job offer in San Francisco?"

Doug said, "Yeah. He was excited for you, but…"

"I'm gonna figure out a way to make it work," Tayla said. "A wise woman once told me that if the world isn't giving you what you want, then you have to make the world your bitch." She froze. "I probably shouldn't have said that in front of you."

Patricia let go of her and laughed. "The language may be harsh, but the sentiment isn't far from what my mother told me before I came out to California." She took Tayla by the shoulders. "She said, 'Don't wait for life to come to you. Work hard and never settle for almost perfect when perfect is what you want.'"

"That's right." Doug stretched his arms up and crossed them behind his head. "She waited for perfect, and perfect was what she got."

Patricia's eyebrow went up in a very familiar arch. "I was talking about my job, Douglas."

"And yet you somehow found a perfect husband too." He smiled.

Tayla was gobsmacked by their easy and affectionate teasing. "You two are wonderful."

Doug smiled. "We do all right." He stood up. "Now, Patty, if you're done second-guessing every medical professional in this hospital, why don't we head over to Pop's? He's going to want an update now that the boy's awake."

"But are you sure—?"

"Tayla's with him. She'll call the house if anything comes up."

"Write down your numbers." She wiped her eyes and held out the pad sitting on the tray. "I'm not supposed to turn my phone on in here, but I'll call you if he needs you."

"Thank you, sweetheart." Doug gave her a one-armed hug. "It's been a long day. You try to get some rest, okay?"

"I'll try."

————

JEREMY WAS LUCKY ENOUGH TO BE IN A DOUBLE ROOM with no one on the opposite bed, so Tayla stretched out next to him and a sympathetic nurse brought a couple of extra blankets.

She was a mess. She'd brought her bag in from the car and washed her face before she slept. She tied her hair back in a couple of braids and tried to sleep with nurses coming in and out through the night, checking on Jeremy's vital signs, the drainage on his arm, and helping him to the bathroom when he woke up at midnight.

The male nurse who helped him was taller than Jeremy and built like a football player. Tayla half listened to them while she dozed.

"Rock climbing accident, huh?"

"Yeah." Jeremy's voice was rough.

"You know, we're the hospital that search and rescue brings all the climbers to. Could have been a lot worse."

"I keep telling myself that."

"That your wife?"

"Girlfriend."

"She's cute. Seems nice. Might be a good idea to try to stay in one piece for her."

"That's definitely the plan."

After the nurse left, Jeremy dragged his IV stand over to Tayla's bed, lowered the railing, and climbed in beside her.

"Hey. Aren't you supposed to—?"

His kiss cut off her protest. He kissed her long and hard, his cast arm draped over her waist. When he let her go, Tayla was silent.

"My bed is cold."

"I can get you more blankets."

"Or I can just cuddle with you." He snuggled in next to her. "You're softer than the bed railing."

"You know they're going to make you move the next time they come to check you."

"Shhhhh." He kissed her forehead. "Go back to sleep."

"Okay." She scooted over to give him more room. "Jeremy?"

"Mmm-hmm?"

"Just so you know, I am not going to ask you to stop climbing. I know this was a freak accident. I'm not going to lie that I won't worry, but—"

"If you wanted me to stop, I would." His voice was sleepy. "I love climbing, but I don't love it more than you."

She let out a long breath. She wasn't sure if he'd been drugged up the first time he said it, but he was more than lucid now.

"I love you." He said it again. "Just in case you didn't catch that. I wanted you to know, because I was walking off that hill, and about halfway down I had this moment where I realized that I really could have died. If I'd landed on my head or if my bone broke and cut an artery... it could have been bad. I could have died, and you wouldn't have known that I love you. And that pissed me off." He kissed her temple. "So I love you. Now you know."

She hugged his waist. "I love you too." She thought it would feel weird, but it didn't. Saying it felt like the most natural thing in the world.

"Are you saying that because I could have died?"

"No. I realized it the other day when I was acting really weird."

He froze. "That day you took the world's longest shower?"

"Yeah. It was kind of an existential crisis. I needed to conference with Daisy and Emmie for a while."

"You love me?"

"Really a lot." Tears came to her eyes. "I love you so much I would even go camping with you. As long as we go somewhere with toilets."

"Oh Tayla." His shoulders shook with laughter. "I can agree to toilets."

"Thanks."

"We'll work up to backpacking."

Give him an inch… "I came to a decision about that job."

"Please don't tell me you're not taking it because—"

"I'm going to try for it. I have a plan, and I really think that they're going to like it once I write up a counteroffer."

"It's your dream job, baby."

Tayla opened her mouth. Closed it.

"Was it the 'baby'?" Jeremy asked. "Is 'baby' weird? I've been thinking that in my head, but I didn't know if it was weird."

"I surprisingly don't hate it."

"Maybe just in private though?"

"Private works. Baby is nice in private when you use your low, sexy voice."

"Like this?" His voice dropped an octave. "You like this, baby?"

"I am forced to admit that you could say pretty much anything to me in that voice and it would work." She smiled. "You could call me dumpling and it would be okay."

His chest shook with quiet laughter. "I am never going to call you dumpling, even knowing I could get away with it."

"I appreciate that." She smiled against his chest. "I really love you, Jeremy Allen."

"I really love you, Tayla McKinnon."

"And I also realized something." She lifted her head to meet his eyes. "Working for a company like SOKA is my dream job. But it's not *really* my dream job if it forces me to leave people I love. I love living in Metlin. I love you. I love Emmie, and Ox, and Daisy, and Spider and Ethan. I love trivia night and book club and I even love hikes in the mountains."

His smile was slow and sexy. "Look at you."

"I know. My life has actually turned into a fucking Hallmark movie." She kissed him. "But this is my home. I'm gonna figure out a way to make it work."

CHAPTER TWENTY-FOUR

"WHAT I'M PROPOSING WOULD BE a departure for your company"—Tayla leaned forward—"but it completely fits with your model of employees finding their personal inspiration and drawing from that to contribute creative solutions. I am willing to compromise on this, and I really think this plan creates the most dynamic environment for my creative work."

She handed them one last chart. Kabisa, Azim, and Rudy were in on the meeting this time. Rudy had been called in when Tayla brought up telecommuting.

"As you can see, my overall input in social media went down when I moved to Metlin. But the quality and focus of my posts went up. My engagement went up. Interaction went way up. In short, my posts became fewer in number but better quality and more focused. And in the past month and a half—"

"Since you've incorporated more outdoor content?"

"Exactly. My network has grown considerably. Metlin's proximity to public lands and outdoor recreation activities has created an entirely new market that I think is full of SOKA's target buyers. Money to spare for outdoor recreation, globally minded, and environmentally conscious."

Rudy nodded. "And I want to second what Tayla was saying about midsized cities and ex-urban areas. If you look at demographic trends, more and more affluent retirees from major metropolitan areas and younger telecommuters are moving to midsized cities like Metlin. The cost of living is more affordable, and people surveyed say they prefer the pace of life in smaller cities."

"So my staying in Metlin would allow SOKA to keep their finger on the pulse not only of large cities but also smaller communities. We might even find craftspeople in those areas we want to work with. After all, SOKA consumers are everywhere. What is local to us is global to them."

"Good point." Azim tapped his chin. "Kabisa?"

She sighed. "I'm still struggling with the idea of Tayla only being in the office a quarter of the month. It's what we've consciously tried to steer away from. We want to provide that connection, that community. I still believe it's part of what makes us so strong as a company."

Azim nodded slowly. "We're going to have to think about this, Tayla."

"I completely understand, and I respect the culture you're trying to create. I still hope you'll consider my offer."

"We will." Kabisa stood and held her arms open. "Maybe I'm being selfish. I like you and I want you around all the time!"

Tayla gave her a hug. Hugs were coming easier and easier every day. "I appreciate that. But I can't ignore my family either. The people I love are in Metlin. And I just wouldn't be the person you need me to be if I left them."

Azim's eyes were warm. "We're a family business," he said. "And we respect that. Thanks, Tayla. We'll talk it over and let you know in a few days. Does that work for you?"

"Absolutely."

She left Azim and Kabisa in the garden while Rudy walked her to the door.

"So," she said. "What do you think my chances are?"

"The telecommuting?" He shrugged. "It's a hard sell for them, but they really like you. I give it fifty-fifty."

She nodded. "I'll take those odds."

Rudy opened the door, and Tayla saw Jeremy waiting for her at the curb, watching the traffic speed by.

"So is that your boyfriend?"

Tayla smiled. "Yep. That's Jeremy."

"What happened to the arm?"

"Rock climbing accident."

The young man looked impressed. "Sick."

"I know."

They shook hands, and Tayla walked to Jeremy. She slid her hand in his. "You ready?"

"Yeah." He lifted his arm. "You're going to have to call the car though. How'd the meeting go?"

"It was good." She got out her phone. "Now we wait and see."

———

TAYLA HAD TRIED TO CONVINCE GLORIA THAT JEREMY didn't need a formal dinner, but it was so rare that the McKinnon house hosted anyone outside the family she went a little crazy.

"Wow." Jeremy's eyes went wide. "Is this, like, regular for dinnertime?"

"No." Tayla glanced around the formal dining room where candles and silver were laid out. The long dining table was only set for four, all grouped around one end of the table, but there were fresh flowers in the middle of the table and soft music was playing in the background. "Gloria got a little excited to cook for someone new."

"Wow." He was still staring.

Tayla turned to him and clutched his hand. "I am sorry my family is so…"

"Rich?"

"Formal? But maybe rich too. I never had friends over when I was a kid because I didn't like the rich kids at Saint Fran's and I felt awkward around the normal kids."

He looked down at her. "Don't. It was normal for you. It's just different for me."

"It's different for ninety-nine point nine percent of the world." Tayla picked up a crystal goblet. "I mean, there's a reason I moved out of this house as soon as I was legally allowed."

"Gloria seems really nice though." He lowered his voice. "I don't want to offend her with the wrong fork."

"Please. You'll be fine. She's just happy to have someone who likes different food. My mom and dad have very bland palates. Since I moved out, she's been a little bored."

The dining room smelled amazing. Tayla pushed through the swinging doors that led into the butler's pantry where Mena's computer was and into the kitchen.

"When I was a kid, sometimes I acted out so my parents would send me into the kitchen to eat." Tayla glanced at the small square table where the household staff ate. She whispered, "It was relief, not punishment."

Gloria was in the kitchen, dressing individual salad plates with oil. "Dinner is only five minutes away, Miss Tayla."

"Thanks, Gloria. I was telling Jeremy how I used to eat in here if I misbehaved when I was little."

The older woman chuckled. "I think you were in here more than the dining room."

"I liked it," she whispered loudly. "You let me put hot sauce on my food."

"My mom made us eat at the breadboard if we didn't behave." Jeremy smiled. "See? Not so different."

"The breadboard?"

"Yeah." He walked to the counter and pulled out a board that she'd never noticed. "See? For cutting bread. Or isolating naughty kids."

"You learn something new every day." She walked around the large kitchen island. "Gloria, can we help with anything?"

"Don't be silly." She frowned. "Get out of my kitchen. Go tell your parents that dinner is ready."

Tayla and Jeremy walked to the sitting room where Bianca and Aaron were waiting in silence. The television was tuned to the gardening channel, and Tayla's father was reading his newspaper.

Still, they were in the same room instead of opposite ends of the house. She'd take progress where she could find it.

"Dad, Mom, Gloria says dinner is almost ready."

"Excellent." Aaron folded his paper and stood. "Jeremy, can I get you a scotch?"

It was a test. Aaron only drank scotch and considered it the only acceptable drink for grown men.

Tayla rolled her eyes. "Dad—"

"I like whiskey," Jeremy said. "Not too familiar with scotch though. My dad and granddad are bourbon men, so I mostly drink that."

Foiled. Tayla didn't try to hide her smile. Jeremy drank whiskey, but the non-snobby kind. Her father couldn't argue with that.

"Hmmm." Aaron walked over to the sideboard. "I have a bottle of Murray Hill Club that one of the junior partners gave me for Christmas. I'd never heard of it before."

"That's a nice bourbon," Jeremy said. "I think you'd enjoy it."

Aaron muttered, "I suppose I'll try it."

What was happening? Did Jeremy magic work on everyone? Tayla watched in wonder as her father poured two glasses of bourbon, added a large chunk of ice to each glass, and toasted her boyfriend.

They all walked to the dining room and sat at the end of the long table.

Bianca looked around as if just noticing where they were. "Aaron, we should have a dinner party soon. We haven't done that in ages."

Her father frowned. "If you'd like that."

"Maybe some of the junior partners would like to come over," Bianca said. "Especially with Tayla and Jeremy in the house now. It would be nice to have some young people around."

Tayla wasn't sure she'd have too much in common with the junior partners at her dad's firm, but it was a nice gesture. "That's a good idea."

Her father's eyes were narrowed. "It is. I'll speak to Mena about scheduling something."

Her mother sipped her wine and rang the crystal bell on the table to call Gloria. "Excellent."

Tayla turned to Jeremy and mouthed, *I have no idea.*

He only looked amused. When Gloria put a bowl of soup in front of him, he said thank you and started to eat with gusto.

Well, as much gusto as he could manage with his left hand.

"You never appreciate your right hand as much as you do when you've lost it." He looked up. "Temporarily, I mean. My mom says it'll be back to normal in about six months as long as I do physical therapy."

"Six months?" Bianca sipped her ever-present wine. "Do casts stay on that long?"

"Six months until I can climb again," Jeremy said. "I'll have to work up to anything serious though." He tried bending his fingers, but they were still immobile. "It's going to be a process."

"And you intend to return to rock climbing?"

"Absolutely." He glanced at Tayla. "I don't quit on things I love."

Aaron looked between Jeremy and Tayla "Admirable sentiment. Though possibly misguided."

"Dad, don't start," Tayla said. "It's really none of your business, and trust me, Jeremy's mom gives him enough grief about it."

"What does your mother do?"

Jeremy finished his soup. "She's a pediatrician."

"Interesting." Aaron nodded. "And your father was a public schoolteacher?"

"He was. And a football coach. I never played though. Too skinny."

"I imagine there was quite a lot of pressure to perform," Aaron said. "If your father was the coach."

"No, my sister played, but it just wasn't for me. I was pretty uncoordinated until my twenties."

Aaron leaned forward. "Your sister played what?"

"Football. On my dad's team."

Her father couldn't process it. He just kept blinking. Over and over.

This is marvelous. Tayla bit her lip to keep from laughing.

"Your sister played football? On the boys' team?"

"I guess it was a coed team once she was on it, right?" Jeremy puffed out his chest. "No one was surprised when she went out for the team. She's always been scary. Made a great running back but a terrifying big sister."

Bianca had her hand on her chest. "Your mother let her play football?"

"No one was really talking about the head-injury thing back then, but I'm sure she'd have reservations about Renée taking all those hits now." Jeremy turned to Tayla. "She doesn't seem loopy yet, but she's only thirty-five. We'll have to watch her."

"I love that your sister played football and it was no big deal in your family."

"Oh, it was a big deal. She and my dad fought for four straight years. But she's always been bossy, so no one was really surprised."

Tayla couldn't wait to meet Jeremy's sisters. Every person she met in his family was a new delight. They all made her laugh. They all embraced her with open arms. Physically and metaphorically.

It was so weird and completely wonderful.

The appetizer followed the soup, followed by the salad, and then a truly gorgeous roasted duck that made Tayla melt. Gloria had gone all out, and Jeremy appreciated every course. She didn't know where he put the food, but he ate every bite.

And the whole time he kept her parents talking—actually talking—about everything. He asked Bianca about growing up on a vineyard, he asked her father about financial news and trends on the West Coast, he peppered them both with questions about sailing and was properly excited when Bianca mentioned that they'd recently looked at buying a boat.

If she hadn't loved Jeremy Allen before, she fell head over heels for him when he made her mother and father laugh at the same joke.

It was settled. Her boyfriend was magic.

———

TAYLA STRADDLED HIS LAP, SLOWLY UNBUTTONING THE shirt he'd donned for dinner while he relaxed on the couch in her room.

"Magic," she whispered, kissing his neck.

"Pretty sure you're the magical one around here." He was running his left hand up and down her spine. "Tayla, we should move to the bed if you're going to— Oh." His breath caught when her hand landed on his cock. "Or you could just keep doing whatever you want."

"I have to confess, your being limited to one hand has forced me to be creative."

"In really wonderful ways." He breathed out. "Are you sure your parents don't mind me staying in here?"

She pulled back. "You're adorable."

"What does that mean?"

"It means my mother stated very clearly when I was sixteen that she didn't expect her daughter to do anything as vulgar as have sex in a car, so if I wanted to experiment with boys, I should just bring them home."

"Wow." Jeremy breathed out. "Your parents and my parents really do come from different planets."

She nodded. "Uh-huh. So no. They don't mind. They'd ask if something was wrong if you stayed in a guest room."

"How many guest rooms are there in this house?"

Tayla mentally counted as she continued unbuttoning Jeremy's shirt. "Five?"

"This isn't a house, this is a hotel."

She laughed wickedly. "I know. And isn't it always fun to do kinky things in a hotel?"

He took her mouth with his, capturing her lower lip between his teeth before he slowly let her go. "I left my ropes at home."

She looked around the room. "I think we can manage." She slid down between his legs. "Can you believe I'm still hungry after all that food?"

His eyes locked with hers when Tayla took him in her mouth. He never took his eyes off her when they made love. His attention —like his attention in everything—was focused. Intent. His lips were flushed and swollen from her kisses. His body was a mass of tension.

"I love you," she whispered against his skin. "Thank you for being you."

"Baby—"

"Generous." She lavished her attention, teasing every inch of him. "Kind. Funny."

He groaned. "You're trying to kill me."

"We may be different, Mr. Allen." She released him and sat on his lap again, straddling his hips as she lifted her dress and slid onto him. "But we're perfect for each other."

He smiled. "Perfectly different." He put his left hand on her hip and thrust into her, making her back arch. He leaned forward and kissed across her chest, running his tongue under the lace edge of her bra. "You know, when you don't have your hands, you can get so inventive with other parts of your body."

"Have you taught him to do tricks now?"

His laugh was wicked. "Let's see."

CHAPTER TWENTY-FIVE

Five months later...

"RUDY, we don't have time for that." Tayla tried not to lose her patience as the young man bounced in his seat on the other side of the video call. "Can you... Now you're just being ridiculous."

He'd pulled back and taken out his juggling balls. "You're asking me to design a unique portal for every SOKA user," he said. "It's a complicated problem and I need to juggle."

She leaned on her desk and waited for him to finish goofing around. "Anytime now."

"Are you at the bookshop?"

"Yes."

"Is Ox there? Can I say hi?"

Tayla's workspace had moved several times in the months since SOKA had agreed to her weird, hybrid telecommuting offer. She'd started out working from home but had gone stir-crazy within a month of spending most of the day by herself. Then she tried working in the office at INK, hoping that Emmie and Ox wandering in and out would prove sufficient stimulation.

Finally, after a particularly manic day, Tayla wildly threatened to knock down every wall in the office so she could see the sun, which led Ox to casually mention that they could open the office to the shop if she wanted because none of the office walls were load-bearing.

Within days, Ox and Jeremy had gleefully taken sledgehammers to Emmie's office walls, opening the back office to the rest of the shop.

Now Tayla's desk sat in the back of the bookshop, separated by low bookshelves but open to the hum of activity in the store and the buzz of the tattoo needle.

She couldn't have been happier.

Tayla turned her monitor around to point it toward the old barber's chair in INK where Ox was tattooing a client. "Ox, Rudy says hi."

Ox glanced up. "Hey, dude. How's it rolling?"

"I just came up for another idea for my back tattoo."

"Is it in binary again?"

"Yes."

Ox shook his head slightly. "Whatever you want, man. Just tell me what Saturday you want me to pencil you in."

"Awesome."

Tayla turned her monitor around. "There. Are you happy? Can you do the profile pages?"

"The app is not Facebook, Tayla."

"But it is a social network combined with an online store. Users want a place they can find items they've favorited, forums they're following, and also their profile info and posted pics."

Rudy threw his head back and groaned.

"Just do it," Tayla said. "This is directly related to what Kabisa was talking about at dinner last week. You can do it. I'll even donate your tattoo. Finish this by the end of the month and Ox will do it for free."

"Hey!" Ox said. "You can't just—"

"Shhhh." She waved at him and mouthed, *I'll pay you!* "What do you say, boy genius?"

Rudy stared at her through the computer, his eyes intent on the camera. "Fine." He spun around and picked up the juggling balls again. "Watch this— I just learned it from YouTube last night."

Tayla watched Rudy attempt to juggle the balls approximately half a dozen times before she made her excuses and shut down the video conference.

When working with Rudy and the other new hire at SOKA, Chevela, Tayla made a point of using video conference instead of texts or phone calls. It was more personal and allowed the office in San Francisco to feel like they were part of her office here in Metlin too.

When Azim and Kabisa had agreed to let her spend three weeks a month in Metlin, she'd been ecstatic. Tayla truly felt like she'd managed to "make the world her bitch" as Ginger so eloquently put it. She threw herself into proving she could be the model employee even from two hundred miles away.

Three months later, Azim had to sit her down and tell her she was stressing everyone out by trying to do too much.

Work and life balance was the key to happiness in any job, but when your office was in San Francisco, your home was in Metlin, and your market was the entire world, it could be difficult to create boundaries. The stress had gotten to her, and had even begun affecting her relationship with Jeremy, which was still finding its feet.

"You need to relax," Azim said, reassuring her. "We didn't hire you as a trial. We believed in your vision for your role at SOKA, and we believe it will work. Don't feel like you constantly have to prove yourself. Take a breath. You've done more work in three months than we expected out of you in six."

She'd taken charge of the social media accounts for the company and leveraged her network to create relationships everyone was really excited about. Two months after they'd launched the app, SOKA had a product go viral. A celebrity had shown up at a music festival, wearing a Kenyan dress she'd bought through SOKA. Fashion bloggers quickly found it, helped along by Tayla racing around the internet the day after the photo had been published, posting links everywhere.

Supplies had sold out almost immediately. The Nairobi office bought every version of the dress they could find. Kabisa had even been invited to a national morning show to talk about the dress phenomenon and the website. Of course the hosts were dazzled by her.

The vendor made more dresses, and they sold out just as fast. It was the trend of the summer. In another month, Tayla guessed Kardashians would be calling her.

In short, it had been a good five months.

Tayla stood. "I'm going to grab lunch for me and Jeremy."

Ox didn't look up. "See you."

"Is Emmie coming back with something for you?"

"Probably. But... she might forget."

Emmie and Ox were still living together in the apartment over INK. And Tayla technically was their roommate. But for the three weeks a month she was in Metlin, she lived an awful lot of it at Jeremy and Pop's house.

She zipped outside and unchained the brand-new mint-green cruiser she'd bought at the bike shop a few months ago. It was finally starting to cool down from the sweltering summer heat, and Tayla was enjoying her rides again. She called Tacos Marcianos on the way over, picked up a box of tacos from the take-out window, and put it in her bike basket before she rode back to the comic book shop.

When she walked inside, she heard a low whistle from the back racks.

"Jeremy?"

"Is that my girlfriend bringing me Martian tacos for lunch?"

"Yes." She set the food and her purse down on the counter. "Now with one hundred percent more Martians. Where are you and how are you seeing me?"

"I'm in the back corner by the manga."

She raised her eyebrows. "What kind of manga are you reading? Are tentacles involved?"

Tayla walked around the corner and saw Jeremy with a helmet that looked like something out of a comic book. The outside was painted bright aqua blue, and a long periscope shaped like a tentacle covered one eye and stretched up and over the bookcases. "Wow. Tentacles actually *are* involved. What is that?"

"Tarlec the Squid Man. Someone ordered a helmet and it just came in."

"And you needed to test the Tarkec—"

"Tarlec."

"Test the Tarlec the Squid Guy helmet out?" Tayla stepped closer.

"I mean…" Jeremy reluctantly removed the helmet. "If it was broken or something, he'd need to send it back." He held it out to Tayla. "You want to try it? It's pretty cool."

"Does the periscope actually work?"

"Yes."

She shrugged and reached for the helmet, but instead of handing it to Tayla, Jeremy carefully placed it on her head and then adjusted the eye piece.

"Oh cool." Tayla swung the periscope attachment toward the front windows. "Hey, you can see stuff!" She noticed Emmie walking out of Café Maya with no box in her hands. "Uh-oh. Ox is going to be hungry."

The helmet came off and Tayla turned to Jeremy. "Thank goodness we were here for quality control."

"It's cool, right?" He looked lovingly at the helmet. "I can't really justify spending that kind of money on something like this since I don't cosplay at cons or anything like that."

Oh, he was such an adorable geek. "But if you did cosplay at cons, it would be completely worth the money."

"Oh yeah." His eyes were wide. "This manufacturer works directly with illustrators to create genuine— You're messing with me, aren't you? You think this is stupid."

She broke into a smile. "Do you think hunting for hours for a vintage Louis Vuitton bag is stupid?"

"Uh…" He wrinkled his nose. "Honestly?"

"You don't have to answer, because I know you think it's stupid, especially since I already have one." She stood on her tiptoes to kiss him. "And that's okay. We all have our stupid things that aren't stupid to us."

"So you think I should order a Tarlec the Squid Man genuine helmet replica?"

"You can do whatever you want as long as you don't expect me to kiss you while you're wearing that thing." She nodded toward the front. "Come on. Tacos are getting cold."

She turned around, and Jeremy patted her ass as she walked away.

Tayla looked over her shoulder and smiled. "Just saying hello?"

"Quality control," he said. "I have to appreciate a fine ass when I see one."

"I hope your skinny ass is ready for tonight."

He wiggled his eyebrows. "I'm always ready."

———

"To your right," Cary yelled. "Your right. The other right!"

"You don't have to be so rude!" Tayla yelled down. She was three-quarters of the way up the tall wall. She'd made it farther than she had in two months. "This sports bra is cutting off circulation to my brain."

"You're doing great, Tayla!" Ashley and Jeremy were her constant encouragers. "You're almost there."

Dave was farther up and a little to Tayla's right. "Can you see the hold he's talking about?"

She tried to look. "Dude. My boob is genuinely blocking where I think he's pointing. I am not joking about this."

Dave couldn't stop laughing. "Okay, you're secure on your left foot and your right hand?"

"Yeah, I'm solid."

"Okay, it's no more than a crimp, but your feet are small. If you can get your toe on it, you should be able to boost yourself up to grab that jug with your left hand. Just remember to keep your weight in your legs."

"Okay." She felt for the hold Cary was yelling about. "I got it."

"You feel it?"

"Yeah." Glancing down at her harness, she checked the knot, just like she did every time she climbed this crazy wall. "You know, I told him I didn't want to do this."

"But you're having fun, right?"

"I am trying new things!" Tayla shifted her weight.

"Then you're home free."

Holding her weight with her upper-body strength was always an issue, but her foothold on the right was solid. She lifted her left knee and brought it up to the flat edge. Then her right arm went up. Her right foot found a nice wide jug.

"You're doing it!" Jeremy was going nuts. "You've got it, baby!"

Tayla ignored everyone. She could see the route in her mind now. She'd made it past the point she usually fell. She'd put her right foot there. Her left hand there. Up would go the left foot.

Within minutes, she was pulling herself up by her elbows and swinging her left knee over the top of the wall. She was panting. She was ecstatic.

"Holy shit!" She sat up and raised her hand, shouting down to Jeremy, Cary, and Ashley. "Big girls can fucking climb!"

"Whoo!" Jeremy was doing a dance. Ashley hugged him. Cary was holding her rope and nodding with a smile.

Dave was slapping her shoulder. "Fucking right they can. You killed it."

Everyone in the climbing gym was clapping. It was her first time all the way up the wall, and she'd garnered more than a few skeptical looks the first time she'd tried. She'd fallen so many times she'd lost count, swinging from her harness while she tried to ignore the looks and smirks of the more experienced climbers.

Jeremy had never let her get discouraged. He'd been working slowly, starting with bouldering while his arm healed, taking things easy.

"Just come with me. I'll only be doing easy stuff."

Ah yes, that's how she was lured in. Just the *easy* stuff.

Which led to slightly harder stuff.

Which led to Tayla being in a harness and weird ugly shoes, trying like hell not to make a fool of herself.

And finally she was up.

She stood and performed a graceful curtsy at the top of the wall. Then she turned around, checked with Cary, and carefully walked down the wall to the floor.

Where she was nearly tackled by Jeremy.

He grabbed her by the waist and spun her around before he kissed her. "I'm so proud of you," he said when he let her up for air. "I am so, so proud of you. Amazing."

She laughed. "I don't know how you did it, but you managed to make a mountain girl out of me."

"I love you like crazy."

Her heart felt like it was going to burst. It was probably from climbing the giant wall. "Okay, I will admit that I like this a little bit. But!"

He grinned. "What?"

"If you insist on me continuing this crazy hobby, I have one condition."

"Anything."

She looked down and grimaced. "You have got to find me some cuter shoes."

He burst out laughing.

"Because this"—she pointed to her feet—"this is ridiculous."

"Okay." Jeremy kissed her again. "Deal."

"Deal?"

He held out his hand. "Forever and all time, Miss McKinnon."

Tayla took his hand, stood on her tiptoes, and gave him a kiss. "I'm glad you see it my way."

———

Want more love stories in Metlin?
Continue reading with GRIT, the next Love Story on 7th and Main, featuring Cary and Melissa.

FIRST LOOK: GRIT

Cary didn't know how she was standing, but she was. Melissa Rhodes stood across from him, all five feet and a few inches of tough. In the past three years, she'd lost her grandfather, buried her husband, and taken over the family ranch. All the while, she'd continued to raise her five-year-old daughter and take care of her mother.

And now she was standing in front of Cary, doing the one thing he knew she hated more than anything—asking for help.

She stood with her shoulders back, hands in her pockets, staring intently at the ground. "I don't want to ask."

"You wouldn't ask if it wasn't important." Cary cleared the roughness from his throat. "What do you need?"

She blew out a hard breath and looked away. "Just advice, I guess. I have a degree. I know all this stuff on paper, but I have no margin for error. Calvin and I had been talking about this for a while. We have all the money together for the planting."

"You know you're not going to see a decent harvest for a few years, right? You need enough money to float the trees for around five seasons. Can the ranch carry that?"

She looked up, and he saw a flicker of the fire he'd thought she'd lost.

Her chin rose. "I can handle it."

"Okay." He leaned against his truck. "I'm not gonna sugarcoat it for you; it's a hard business and the drought has been brutal. The only reason our place has held up as well as it has is that we haven't had to carry debt."

Her blue eyes were steely. "What citrus variety will give me the best return the fastest?"

"You're planting your lower acreage? The Jordan Valley side?"

"Yeah."

Cary mulled it over. "If my dad were still living, he'd argue with me"—he stuck his hands in his pockets—"but I think you should plant mandarins."

"Not navel oranges?"

He shook his head. "I can point you to some hardy varieties of small mandarins, and I think the market is turning hot for them. Plus you'll get a full harvest a year sooner. How many acres?"

"Fifty for now."

He nodded. It was a decent start for a new grower, especially one who already had a ranch. "I can give you advice, but are you sure you have time for this? The ranch—"

"I can handle the herd," she said. "Don't worry about that. I have seasonal workers, and Ox said he can help out more too."

Depending on family was tricky, but Cary knew Ox, Melissa's brother, was solid. "Okay."

The Oxford and Nakamura families had been neighbors for Cary's and Melissa's entire lives. The Nakamuras grew citrus. The Oxfords raised cattle.

Melissa Oxford was twelve years younger than Cary, and as kids, they'd never been friends. They knew each other in passing at best. Nothing had prepared Cary for the gut-punch of full-grown attraction he'd experienced the first time Melissa had come back from college in Texas.

She'd left California a leggy teenager obsessed with horses and returned a strong, stunning woman with sandy-brown hair, legs for days, and a defiant smile.

She was also engaged.

It was just as well. Falling for the neighbor girl promised a few too many complications. But Cary was happy to become friends with Melissa and Calvin when they moved back to the ranch in Oakville. Cary and Calvin got close, and the latent attraction he felt for Melissa was solidly locked away.

When Calvin's truck had been hit by an eighteen-wheeler ten months ago, Cary and his mom had been devastated. Calvin, Melissa, and their little girl, Abby, were family. Cary's mother, Rumiko, and Melissa's mother, Joan, mourned together. Cary had dealt with his grief by offering to help, but there was only so much he could do. Melissa was the cattlewoman; Cary grew trees.

And now she was taking fifty acres of their prime grazing land and planting citrus.

"You're sure about this?" he asked.

She nodded. "Yeah. Mandarins sound good. It's always been the plan to diversify."

"Okay. I'm here if you need advice. I don't know shit about cows, but I can help with the trees." He debated asking the question, mostly because it was a sore subject for both of them. "How you doing?"

Her daughter Abby's birthday was coming up.

She shrugged. "I'm fine. Busy. Ready for Abby to start school, that's for sure."

Abby was going into kindergarten, the first of many milestones Calvin wouldn't see. It hurt. And it made him angry. "Seriously, Missy—"

"Don't." She blinked hard. "I'm fine, Cary. I don't want to talk about it."

"Do you talk to anyone?" She didn't have many friends. He

didn't know if she preferred it that way or if she was too consumed with the ranch.

She opened her truck door and hopped in. "I'm talking to you, aren't I?"

He frowned. "I'm not sure that counts."

She slammed the truck door shut. "Sure it does."

"Melissa, don't—"

"I gotta go."

She started the truck, and the engine drowned out his words.

Stop hiding, he wanted to say.

Let yourself grieve.

Let yourself miss him.

I do.

———

He looked at her, her body worn out by hours of labor, rocking back and forth on her mother's porch with a bottle of beer propped between her knees. Her skin was pink from the sun. She'd stripped off her long-sleeved shirt and was finally relaxing in a tank top and jeans, her feet kicked up and resting on the porch rail.

She was sweaty and dirty. It did nothing to detract from her beauty. Her skin glowed and her eyes were dancing. She was exhausted, but she was smiling. He hadn't seen her look so alive in months.

He wanted to kiss her.

He didn't. Of course he didn't. It was just a spontaneous reaction to seeing her so happy for the first time in what seemed like forever. That was all.

Keep telling yourself that, idiot.

"We got a lot done," Melissa said.

"We did."

"Tomorrow, you think?"

"Yeah." He rolled his sleeves up and pushed the rocking chair back and forth with his toe. "I think by tomorrow they'll be done. You'll have some that won't take. You know that, right?"

She nodded. "Second season."

"Maybe a few in the third. By the fourth, you should have a solid grove of pretty little mandarins." He reached his beer bottle across and clinked the neck with hers. "Congratulations, Melissa Rhodes. You're officially a citrus grower."

Her smile lit up the night. "Thanks, Cary. For everything."

———

Two years later…

The rain was pouring down, and she could barely see him through the sheets of water. Cary had never been very graceful on a horse, but he was a competent enough rider that he could make it over the hills.

"How'd you find me?" she yelled.

"Ox said you'd be out here." He slid off her mother's gelding, PJ. "I followed the fence."

"Do you have a—" She saw the posthole digger strapped to the side of the horse. "Oh, thank God. I thought I was going to have to ride back."

He waded through the mud to get to her. "You can't use the old hole?"

"The water washed too much of it away. I'll never be able to secure a new post in this storm, and the herd has already tried to break through and go down the hill."

He squinted through the rain. "And we're not letting them because…?"

"More flooding in the lower pastures, and I don't want them crossing the creek. Too many calves. Believe it or not, this is the driest place on the ranch; they've got tree cover here."

265

The cattle were huddled under the low oaks that spread across the hills of the upper pasture in Christy Meadow. Unfortunately, the storm had already damaged one of the posts securing the fence that kept them away from a muddy road that crossed a rushing creek.

Melissa had thought she was going to have to repair it herself when Ox told her he was stuck in town with a client. She had no idea he'd called Cary.

"Tell me what to do," he said. "I've never done this, but I'm good at following directions."

If there was one thing she loved about Cary, it was his lack of ego. The man was incredibly competent in many, many things, but he had no problem admitting when he didn't know something and he didn't get his ego bent out of shape.

As she shouted directions at him, they managed to repair the fence well enough to last through the storm.

"That's good." She rolled a rock over to prop the new post up. "Can you...?" She pointed to another large rock on the other side.

"Got it." He bent over, his shirt plastered to his torso, and rolled the basketball-sized granite stone over to brace the new post.

As his shoulders flexed, Melissa felt a stirring in her belly.

What?

She hadn't felt that in... a while. Years.

"Just this one?" Cary grunted as he rolled the rock.

"Yeah, one should be enough."

His hair was coming loose from the low ponytail where he'd secured it. Wet strands stuck to the defined line of his jaw and brushed the strong cord of muscle in his neck.

Melissa swallowed the lump in her throat and forced her eyes from his arms as he rose. He must have caught her stare, because he frowned.

"What?"

Oh God, how embarrassing. "Nothing. Thanks—I'm surprised we got that done so quickly."

Cary smiled. "We're a good team."

His smile was a little crooked. Had it always been that way? He turned and reached for the posthole digger, then tied it to PJ's saddle. Her eyes fell to his ass, which was framed by a pair of wet Wranglers.

Melissa forced her eyes away. What was wrong with her? She wasn't a fifteen-year-old girl anymore. This was Cary. Her neighbor. Her friend.

Stop checking out his ass, Melissa!

Once she'd noticed it, she couldn't stop looking. Had he always had that sexy line from his shoulders to his hips? She'd always thought of him as stocky, but he wasn't. His shoulders were just really broad.

"...after we get the horses put up."

She blinked. "What?"

"You feeling okay?" He frowned. "We should get you back to the ranch."

"I'm fine!" She took the roll of barbed wire and walked across the road to the run-down wagon that served as a storage spot. She carefully placed the wire under the old green tarp covering the wagon and walked back to the horses.

Cary was waiting for her, his eyes narrowed.

"What?" she asked. "Do you want to leave the posthole digger here?"

"Do you need it back at the ranch?"

She shrugged, trying to be casual and not look at his jaw. Or his hair, the thick black-and-silver falling across his cheek. Why the fuck was she suddenly noticing all the attractive things about Cary? "We might need it. I can carry it."

"No big deal. It's already on my saddle."

"Okay."

"Okay."

Was it her imagination, or did he look her up and down? Was that a *look* look? Or was he wondering if there was something wrong with her?

Oh God, this is not okay.

Melissa mounted her mare, Moxie, and nudged her down the muddy road.

She wasn't in high school anymore. She wasn't even in college anymore. She was a thirty-one-year-old widow and mother of a seven-year-old who still believed in dragons and had a goat obsession. The kid did. Not Melissa. She had a ranch she could barely handle and a new grove of mandarin trees that was eating up all her savings.

She did not have time to notice that Cary Nakamura was sexy as hell.

Not now. Not ever.

———

Three years later…

"Missy?"

She was at the hospital. She hated the hospital. Disinfectant stung her nose, reminding her of death. Calvin's death. Her grandfather's death. Her own traumatic miscarriage. Melissa's eyes scanned the room and she saw him.

He was standing. He wasn't on a gurney.

Thank you, God.

Her knees nearly gave out with relief. Wait, there was blood all over his shirt. Why was there blood?

"Cary?" Her pulse was pounding; adrenaline coursed through her. "Why are you covered in blood? What happened? Why didn't you call me?"

"Jeremy is the one who got hurt. He has a compound fracture in his right arm—that's why there's blood."

The rest of his words washed over her.

Jeremy. His rock climbing partner had been hurt, not him. "You're fine? The blood…?"

"Not mine."

Not his.

He was fine. He was whole and healthy. She saw his golden-brown arms held out to her, swirling ink covering his skin. Drying blood stained his shirt, but his arms were the same.

Strong arms.

Steady shoulders.

Strong hands.

She couldn't stop the tears. She covered her face. "Oh my God."

Not his blood. It wasn't his blood.

"Missy?"

No, don't call me that. Don't make me soft. If I give you an inch, I'll fall apart.

She couldn't face him. She turned and shot out the door.

Once she was in the fresh air, she lifted her chin, took a deep breath, and tried to stop the tears.

Get it together, Melissa.

What was Cary going to think of her? He probably thought she was an emotional wreck. Or insane. Maybe insane. And maybe hung up on him.

She didn't have time to be hung up on anyone.

Melissa's legs ate up the sidewalk, heading to the parking garage across from the hospital in Metlin.

"Melissa!"

Shit!

He was taller than her by at least six inches. His legs were longer. And he was strong. So damn strong. He'd be able to catch up unless she ran, and she was not going to run.

She stopped and turned, wiping the back of her hand across her eyes. "What?"

He nearly ran into her. "You thought I was hurt?"

"Ox didn't give me details on the phone. He just called and said that you and Jeremy were in a climbing accident. I jumped in the truck and..."

"I'm sorry."

"Not your fault." She cleared her throat. "Is Jeremy going to be okay?"

"Yeah, he'll be okay. Just banged up, and he has to have surgery to sort his arm out." Cary edged closer and his eyes narrowed. "You thought I was hurt."

"Don't..." Her heart started to race again, this time for other reasons. "Climbing accidents can be bad and—"

"You thought I was hurt"—his dark eyes burned into her —"and you drove straight into town."

"Yes." *Turn and walk away. Just turn and walk—*

"You drove thirty miles into town and straight to the hospital because you thought I was hurt."

"Don't do this." She clenched her jaw. "Cary—"

"No, I'm going to do this because that is not the reaction of a woman who told me... What was it? 'We're friends, Cary. Don't let yourself get confused.' Is that what this is?" He reached for her arm. "You feeling a little confused, Missy?"

She could smell him now, past the scent of hospital disinfectant. The warm, sweet scent of orange blossoms he carried on his skin, mixed with pine from the mountains. His strong fingers encircled her wrist. He stepped closer and hooked a finger through her belt loop.

His chest was broad, his shoulders solid muscle. She had to fight the urge to lay her head over his heart. She wanted to hear it beat. Wanted the simple reassurance of his body pressed to hers.

His breath tickled the hair at her temple. "Talk to me."

She shook her head.

"Then tell me to leave you alone."

I can't. Her mind was a jumble of relief and gratitude and need. But she didn't want him to let go.

"Missy, look at me."

"Don't—" She looked up, but his lips stopped any retort she might have mustered.

Oh, fuck it. Reaching up, she grabbed the thick hair that fell to his shoulders and gave in to years of temptation. She reached behind his neck and gripped. She slid her knee between his and pressed her body into his.

He tasted so good. His hand moved from her wrist to grab the small of her back. His fingers curled and dug in. His grip was so tight it would probably leave marks.

So good.

Damn, Cary was an excellent kisser. Way better than she'd ever imagined. It had been six years since she'd kissed anyone, and she didn't even think about fumbling. His mouth was too demanding. His lips were too sure.

For a few sweet seconds, all Melissa thought about was the taste of Cary Nakamura's mouth, the warmth of his hands, and how his chest was just as solid as she'd dreamed.

Oh shit, I'm standing on a sidewalk in Metlin.

Melissa broke the kiss and stepped back. "We can't do this."

"Fuck that," he growled. "We already are."

She shook her head.

"Stop lying to yourself," he said. "What are you so damn afraid of?"

"Afraid?" A bitter laugh burst from her. "Oh… you have no idea." She turned and started walking back to her car.

"Fine!" He yelled. "Walk away, but don't pretend like this is finished, because it's not."

You idiot. This never even had a chance to start.

"I know what you're thinking, Melissa Rhodes. And you're wrong."

She didn't have time to argue with him.

Melissa kept walking.

She didn't have time to kiss a man on the sidewalk.

She didn't have time to dream about a sweeter life.

She didn't have time for Cary.

———

GRIT is now available to buy
in ebook and paperback!

"This is everything that made me fall in love with romance."

THE SASSY NERD BOOK BLOG

ACKNOWLEDGMENTS

A lot goes into me being able to write full time, so I'd like to take a moment and thank some of the people who help my homelife function in a semi-normal fashion so I can focus on writing books, which is kind of a consuming process. Since Metlin is based on my hometown and these are people who live and work there, it feels appropriate.

To my sister, Gen, who makes life happen and reminds me to sign books, pay bills, and leave my office occasionally. The Book Which Shall Not Be Named is going to happen. Eventually. And there will be so many doctor jokes.

To my house cleaners, Veronica and Veronica. You are both amazing professionals, and I just want to say I'm so sorry again for the smell that won't seem to leave my son's room. He's fourteen. That's the only explanation I have.

To Javier and all the guys on your crew, thank you. I know we keep changing things in the garden and the construction went on way longer than we told you. You're very flexible and it is so appreciated. Also, thanks for keeping the leaf blower noise to the minimum. You're rock stars of gardening.

To Mike, who is literally the best pool guy on the planet. I hope you can retire some day because you totally deserve it, but know that you are the pool professional all others will be measured against. Also, the dogs might love you more than they love us. What kind of treats are those?

———

Moving on to the publishing professionals...

I'd like to thank Jenn Beach, my marketing PA, graphic designer, and also my friend. You are a treasure and I am so thankful every day for you. Thank you for always going above and beyond. Sorry for all the middle of the night messages.

To Emily, who has to listen to me being neurotic almost as much as Jenn does. You're a rock star and I am so grateful for you and all the staff at Social Butterfly PR.

To Jane Dystel and Lauren Abramo, my many thanks for all your years of work, and I'm sorry I'm still so bad at mailing things back to you.

To Anne and Linda at Victory editing, I'd apologize for all the extra commas, but at this point, you know I'm not going to improve, so maybe just try to think of them as job security? You know I will always, *always* need you.

———

Thanks to my family, the whole crazy bunch of you. Thanks to all the Imago crew. Thank you to my amazing reader group on Facebook and all the wonderful readers over so many years who have bought, shared, reviewed, and supported my books. I can never thank you enough.

ABOUT THE AUTHOR

ELIZABETH HUNTER is a *USA Today* and international best-selling author of romance, contemporary fantasy, and paranormal mystery. Based in Central California, she travels extensively to write fantasy fiction that explores world mythologies, history, and the universal bonds of love, friendship, and family. She has published over thirty works of fiction and sold over a million books worldwide. She is the author of Love Stories on 7th and Main, the Elemental Legacy series, the Irin Chronicles, the Cambio Springs Mysteries, and other works of fiction.

ALSO BY ELIZABETH HUNTER

Building From Ashes

Waterlocked

Blood and Sand

The Bronze Blade

The Scarlet Deep

A Very Proper Monster

A Stone-Kissed Sea

Valley of the Shadow

The Elemental Legacy

Shadows and Gold

Imitation and Alchemy

Omens and Artifacts

Obsidian's Edge (anthology)

Midnight Labyrinth

Blood Apprentice

The Devil and the Dancer

Night's Reckoning

Dawn Caravan

The Bone Scroll

The Elemental Covenant

Saint's Passage

Martyr's Promise

Paladin's Kiss

(Spring/Summer 2022)

The Irin Chronicles

The Scribe

The Singer

The Secret

The Staff and the Blade

The Silent

The Storm

The Seeker

The Cambio Springs Series

Long Ride Home

Shifting Dreams

Five Mornings

Desert Bound

Waking Hearts

Linx & Bogie Mysteries

A Ghost in the Glamour

A Bogie in the Boat